THE COMPLETE CASES
OF THE DEAN, VOLUME I

THE COMPLETE CASES OF
THE
DEAN

™

VOLUME 1

MERLE CONSTINER

ILLUSTRATIONS BY

JOHN FLEMING GOULD

ALTUS
PRESS

BOSTON • 2016

EDITED AND DESIGNED BY
Matthew Moring

PUBLISHING HISTORY

"Strangler's Kill" originally appeared in the August, 1940 issue of *Dime Detective* magazine. Copyright 1940 by Popular Publications, Inc. Copyright renewed 1967 and assigned to Steeger Properties, LLC. All rights reserved.

"You're in My Way" originally appeared in the December, 1940 issue of *Dime Detective* magazine. Copyright 1940 by Popular Publications, Inc. Copyright renewed 1967 and assigned to Steeger Properties, LLC. All rights reserved.

"One Corpse Too Many" originally appeared in the March, 1941 issue of *Dime Detective* magazine. Copyright 1941 by Popular Publications, Inc. Copyright renewed 1968 and assigned to Steeger Properties, LLC. All rights reserved.

"The Puzzle of the Terrified Dummy" originally appeared in the August, 1941 issue of *Dime Detective* magazine. Copyright 1941 by Popular Publications, Inc. Copyright renewed 1968 and assigned to Steeger Properties, LLC. All rights reserved.

THANKS TO
Chad Calkins & Cathy Clark

TABLE OF CONTENTS

STRANGLER'S KILL

INTRODUCING THE DEAN—SPECIAL CONSULTANT IN LIBANOMANCY, CATOPTROMANCY, THABDOMANCY, ALEUROMANCY—AND IF THAT DOESN'T MEAN ANYTHING TO YOU, A MIGHTY GUY WITH EITHER BRAIN OR BLUE-STEEL—FEES NEGLIGIBLE.

CHAPTER ONE
WITH THE SOLES
OF YOUR FEET

AT THE age when most kids are pushing cast-iron trains across the floor, I was taking down and assembling my old man's pistol and diagnosing the entrails of the mortise locks around the house. The older I got, the more I fiddled with guns and tumblers until finally I worked myself up to a sort of technical trouble-shooter for a small safe company. Then overproduction and a new efficiency system sneaked into the factory and canned me. After six weeks of walking the streets and sleeping in alleys, I met the Dean. I hate to think of what I might be doing right now if it hadn't been for him. He said: "You got dangerous talent, son. Dangerous to society. You join up with me and stay on the right side of the law."

Everybody you talked to, the grocery boy, the neighbors, the clerk at the corner drug store, thought the Dean was a screwball and a crank. He was so friendly and pleasant to strangers that if they ever found out he always carried a shoulder gun about the size and weight of a plowshare, they would have laughed it off and insisted he used it to crack nuts with.

Your impression when you met him was that he was about the most useless man in the world. The police and newspapers knew different.

We lived in an old brick rooming-house in the slums and had three grimy rooms on the ground floor where the Dean practiced fortune telling with the indirect sanction of the police commissioner. A tin sign tacked on the front door read—

PEDOMANCY

Fortunes Divined from the Soles of Your Feet
Learn the Secrets of Love, Hate, Riches
SPECIAL CONSULTATIONS IN: LIBANOMANCY
CATOPTROMANCY RHABDOMANCY ALEUROMANCY

FEE NEGLIGIBLE

Believe it or not, there is a branch of fortune telling called pedomancy. The fee was not only negligible but elastic. Sometimes, if the Dean got miffed with a customer, he sky-rocketed it ridiculously high. Usually though, the charge was small. Frequently there was none at all.

The whole set-up was merely a front. I don't mean that the Dean didn't tell his fortunes conscientiously and accurately—he could read half a dozen Eastern languages and owned a collection of sheepskin and papyri that would have struck a museum curator blind. When he told a fortune he did it as carefully as he'd play a game of chess. He'd make a little speech telling the customer that it was all hokum and then get to work. His manner was so frank that the toughest customer would usually break down and confide in him. And let me tell you that all that stuff the Dean heard stayed buried in his skull. No confidence ever slipped through his lips.

I FINISHED dusting the reception-room—a morning chore which I despised, for the Dean was worse than an old maid with wiping his finger under the mantel or across

the table-top looking for dust—and went back for breakfast.

The Dean was seated at the table, an empty plate before
him. My plate was empty, too. And so were the coffee
cups, and the bowls and platters which customarily held
cereals and bacon and eggs.

I grinned as I came through the door. He'd pulled this
gag before and I knew what it meant. The first time I had
been surprised. He'd explained to me how back in the
eighteenth century there was a poet named Blake and how
when Blake loafed too long and the family bank account
got too low, Mrs. Blake set out the empty dishes and her
old man got the idea and went to work again.

"It's about time," I said.

"Sit down, Ben." The Dean nodded to a chair. "I want
to talk to you." He wouldn't be hurried. "I want to talk to
you about arson and murder. And it's a hard thing to
believe, Ben, but the arson is worse than the murder." He
pawed through his pockets and located the snipe of the
thin Cuban cigar which he always produced when he had
a bit of heavy conversation to get off. The average man,
keyed up, looks tense. The Dean looked tired, his shoulders
drooped, the corners of his mouth relaxed.

"Arson?" I asked. "The firebug?"

"This is no firebug, Ben." He had a trick of speaking
with his eyelids closed. "This town is being terrorized by
a series of fires that are caused by no half-witted boy with
a handful of oily waste and a craving to watch the engines
go by. These burnings are sane and vicious."

I knew what he meant. Every few weeks, for almost six
months now, some building had collapsed in smoke and
flames. Most of them had been groceries, delicatessens or
small tradesmen's shops.

There had been a death, too. Frederick Ortman, local manager of Solidarity Insurance, had been lured from his home and murdered. The police learned the details from his wife. The Ortmans had been asleep in their bedroom when, about four o'clock in the morning, they were awakened by the ringing of the bedside phone. Ortman, his wife recounted, spoke but two words—"Yes" and "Thanks." He then dressed in a frenzy of excitement. As her husband left the house, still wearing his bedroom slippers and leaving his lower plate on the shelf in the bathroom, he said: "It's all over now. I'll be back in an hour. We've got this thing whipped."

That morning at dawn the Acme Photographers went up in fire. Ortman's charred body was identified in the wreckage. There was

The Dean cut loose with his Magnum and the clerk crashed into a showcase of orchids.

a loop of scorched picture wire about the corpse's neck and the coroner's opinion was "murder by strangulation."

"This is no firebug," the Dean repeated. "This is just good old-fashioned crime of a very virulent and contagious type. It seems to be spreading. I feel the time has come, Ben, for us to dynamite these babies loose."

THE SOLIDARITY INSURANCE COMPANY was locally owned, organized and financed. Fred Ortman had promoted the business on a shoe-string. The idea had taken hold and the town had gone for it strong. Business clubs agreed that the Solidarity had a big future. Then came the down-swing—first the fires then Fred Ortman's murder. The fires continued, increased, and at present were riding a new high. Solidarity was in a bad way.

The manager's offices took up the entire third floor of the new black-glass-and-metal building. Lettered in gold across the double plate-glass door panel, the company's slogan said—*He Liveth Best Who Serveth Best All Things Both Great And Small—SOLIDARITY'S YOUR FRIEND.* Inside, we could see a fleet of golden-oak desks, with their typewriters and wire baskets, manned by a none too busy crew of office workers.

We had a little difficulty in attaining the private sanctum of Hilliston Keith, Solidarity's new head-man. I'd heard around town about Hilliston Keith. He'd been imported from Chicago to take over a dying business where Ortman had left it. Mr. Keith styled himself a "business doctor" and he was considered very high-pressure.

The Dean and I took in a load of the pseudo-manorial office furnishings. Stagy was the word for it. I saw the Dean wince. The room had been completely redecorated for Mr. Keith. The dark walnut wainscoting, the huge desk and the peach-bloom rug, had been imported along with Mr. Keith, from Chicago. So had the strawberries-and-cream blonde who sat so demurely on a silken hassock by Mr. Keith's ankle.

You know Hilliston Keith's type. The perpetual college man. He was fifty and had the mannerisms of an eighteen-year-old. His expensive tweed vest was studded with college emblems. I could make out, among others, two diamond-set fraternity pins and a little gold football. He ignored us as we entered. You would have thought we were just a couple of window-cleaners who had got lost in the building. He lighted a cigarette, whipped out the match and tossed it in the waste-basket.

The Dean bowed from the waist to acknowledge introductions which weren't forthcoming and said pleasantly: "Don't drop matches in the wastebasket. It's an unintelligent habit and very hazardous. You'd make a precarious assured, Mr. Keith." The blonde smiled. And she had a nice smile.

Little red veins stood out in Keith's face. He turned china-blue eyes on us and took out a memorandum from the desk drawer.

"The Dean," he read. His loose lips pursed with scorn. He turned to the girl and raised his eyebrows. "Dean of what and when?" he asked her in a theatrical voice. "No one seems to know. Livelihood, fortune telling." The blonde perked up. "Hobby, amateur detective. Reference, the police commissioner himself." Keith wrinkled his nose. "Something smells. Whatever he's selling, we don't want any—do we Bitsey?"

"I do," the blonde said brightly. "This little girl does. She wants some."

"I came here to offer you a proposition, Mr. Keith," the Dean said amiably. "I intended to charge you ten thousand dollars to break up this arson ring that is wrecking your company. My proposition was satisfaction in six days or no pay. I've changed my mind. I don't like you and I don't like your insolvent company. Good-day, sir."

Hilliston Keith lost his composure. "Get out of here!" he shouted. His voice creaked. "Get out of here, you meddling fourflushing charlatan!"

The blonde scrambled from the hassock and intercepted us at the door. She touched my elbow. "How do you tell these fortunes?" she asked. "I mean how. I mean cards or stars or crystal ball or what?"

I grinned. She was as hard as manganese but you couldn't help liking her. "You'd be surprised," I answered. "He can do it with rods and incense and flour and roosters. But our big play is reading the soles of your feet. Yes, I said reading the soles of your feet."

I knew it would floor her. And it did.

Out in the street, the Dean said: "A very profitable interview."

I gave him a cut with my right eye to see if he was kidding. He wasn't.

"We really have him softened up," the Dean chuckled. "We've got him plastic, boy, plastic. He's headed for twenty thousand and he doesn't suspect it. It's a great business. You'll learn to love it."

This was a sample of the Dean's own particular brand of guerrilla skirmishing. I couldn't for the life of me tell what he was talking about but one thing I knew, from past experience, was that when he started to forage he always brought in big game at top prices.

He popped a *non sequitur* at me before I could comment. "How about your gun, Ben? Have you got it with you?"

"Of course."

"Well, keep it handy. You may be needing it."

CHAPTER TWO
THE FEEBLEWIT
HAD BEEN AROUND

THERE WAS no way of knowing just how many people in our town called the Dean friend but the total would have been astounding. He developed his most casual acquaintances into deep friendships. He would do a favor whenever he could and save the return until he needed it. He had a hundred and one interests. He could milk a rattlesnake, fashion jewelry from Mexican coins, or load a pair of dice like an expert. Take his homemade camera, for instance, and you'll know what I mean. The Dean was sitting in a dentist's anteroom one afternoon waiting for his appointment and leafing through some boys' magazine when he came across directions how to make your own camera for forty-seven cents. At home that night, he put one together. It was a good one, too. He took a picture of Mrs. Duffy, our landlady, setting out the milk bottles and won fifteen bucks in a big photo contest.

Nobody, not even me, knew what he did when he was away from the house. I found out by accident once that he was a professional piano-tuner. When I mentioned it to him, he said it got you into exclusive places like brokers' homes and backroom dancehalls.

We grabbed lunch at a cafeteria. The Dean bought a fresh copy of the *Journal*, turned to the editorial page and indicated a paragraph. He seemed to be expecting it.

"Just off the press," he said. "Wait until Keith sees this."

It was a single paragraph winding up a long bitter editorial.

... should leave no stone unturned in our effort to curb this wave of incendiarism. Citizens in responsible positions appear to show little or no interest. It has come to us reliably, for instance, that only this morning, Dean Wardlow Rock, well known local investigator, and his assistant, Benton Matthews, driven by civic motives, offered their cooperation in point to a certain heavily involved insurance company and were emphatically discouraged.

I did a little mental arithmetic. It was impossible. The linotype operator must have had the copy at least an hour before our interview with Solidarity's new manager.

"That's right," the Dean remarked as I opened my mouth to inquire. "The newspaper had the information before our visit. As a matter of fact, I phoned it in to Hank Edwards, the city editor, before breakfast—while you were going over the reception-room with your maidenly cheesecloth. I once helped Hank in a little libel fiasco."

I shook my head and frowned.

"You don't like it, eh? Hold on tight because unless I'm wrong it's due to get worse and worse."

How true.

We separated in front of the restaurant. I headed for the apartment. The Dean had mumbled something vague about getting a little air. Actually, he wasn't fooling me—and he knew it. When a case was in the making, he would disappear for a few hours and shoot a high-velocity charge of personality through his network of friends and admirers. He had dished out favors—now he was on the receiving end. He was about to put out the word to his informers.

I knew results would be immediate, for when the Dean stirred up action he didn't fool.

MRS. DUFFY, our landlady, was sitting in her bay window, shining her silver plate and keeping an eye cocked for me through her ribboned and rosetted curtains. As I entered the hall she opened her door a crack and beckoned. The customary gust of hundred-proof lilac perfume enfolded me.

"Mr. Matthews," she whispered in a stage voice, "there's two strangers"—anyone who didn't live in our house were strangers—"in your reception-room. Sitting there saying they want their fortunes told. I don't like their looks. If you should ast me I should say beware." The door closed as she withdrew.

Well, of course, I should have taken her advice. Her husband, Pat, had been a policeman for twenty years before he died, so Mrs. Duffy knew a thug when she saw one. It was the Mrs. Duffy atmosphere, the lilac perfume and the whispering and the cerise fingernails, that made me careless. If she were to tell you that arsenic was poisonous you'd discount it as Duffy whimsey.

I'm here to tell you I should have bewared. These two boys were poisonous. I could see, as soon as I stepped into the room, that the future was very dark and I didn't need the Dean with his thaumaturgics and grimoire to spell it out for me. One of the lads, short and chunky, and dressed in what sometimes is known as a symphony of browns, was stretched out on the Dean's priceless antebellum love-seat, sound asleep. He blinked and sat up as I entered.

The second man stood leaning against the fireplace. He was long and lank and his clothes were ill-fitting and wrinkled. He had a little bony vicious face set in jaundiced skin. His right ear was trimmed off close to his skull.

The gaunt man's elbow was resting on the mantel shelf and he was whiling away the time and tedium by drawing imaginary beads on various articles of furniture with a .45 Colt automatic. He swung the gun in a short efficient arc to cover the pit of my stomach and said: "Shut the door. There's a draft."

The chunky man in brown got to his feet, yawned, came over to me and snapped a sudden backhand blow at my chin which knocked me to my knees.

"That's for waking me up."

"Get his gun, Herb," the gaunt man said. "And shut up."

I allowed him to take it. There was nothing else to do.

"My, my," Herb said clicking his tongue. "A bad man's gun—a bulldog. And it comes out so easy. Ain't this the guy, Dorf, that's supposed to be a wizard with one of these things?"

"I know a butcher shop when I see one," I said.

"Hold it, Loose Lip," the gaunt man said coldly to Herb. "I'll take care of this." He held a copy of the *Journal*, folded to the Dean's editorial, before my eyes. "This make sense to you?"

"Yes," I said. "It's true. We tried to get an in but they wouldn't have us. They gave us the bum's rush."

Dorf studied me with his deadly eyes. "I believe you," he said finally. "I believe you're telling the honest truth. That alters cases. You don't know nothing or they'd have bought it." Back of his bleak eyes, he was turning the thing over in his mind.

"What do we do?" the chunky man asked.

"We give this bimbo the beating of his life. Here and now. We send him to the hospital. We don't knock him off. We just learn him and his boss to stay in their own back yard."

Herb slipped a pair of brass knuckles on his hand and tiptoed to my side, like a dancer.

There was a boisterous thumping on the door and Mrs. Duffy's voice called: "I'm coming in, Mr. Matthews." Herb stuck his hand in his pocket and the gaunt man hung his hat over his gun-fist.

"Be good," Dorf said.

Mrs. Duffy minced into the room. She carried a tea tray covered with a piece of her fanciest linen. "And here's your bit of tay, Mr. Matthews," she said. I couldn't get the Irish dialect—her name before she married was Blugenheim. "I brought you some of them nice licorice muffins you're so crazy about." Licorice in any form gags me. "I just threw a scrap of rag over them to keep them warm," she added.

She placed the tray on a table by my hand and smiled. "They's enough to go round. Help yourself and pass them to your fascinating friends."

"Scram," Herb said. "You're intrudin'. We're getting our fortunes told." She flounced out.

"Would you like a cup of tea and a licorice muffin," Dorf inquired with heavy sarcasm, "or shall we get on with our business?"

I said: "You've asked me. I've told you I don't know anything. You're way out of bounds. I don't like it and the Dean'll like it less. Anybody can make a mistake once so button up your coats and highball out of here before you get hurt."

Herb slapped splay-fingered at my cheek and I caught his thumb and snapped it for him. Dorf stepped in and they gave me my beating. It was a regular routine five-dollar beating that is the stock-in-trade of any poolroom thug. They started it off with a blackjack behind my ear to get me groggy and then went to work.

THE DEAN was pouring brandy down my throat and Mrs. Duffy was washing a cut in my scalp. "Where are they?" I asked weakly.

"Gone," the Dean said. "But not forgotten."

Mrs. Duffy fluttered. "Why didn't you use the pistol?"

I sat up. "What pistol?"

She lifted the cloth from the tray. Beneath, glinting blue steel, lay a Police Positive—Pat Duffy's old service gun. My vision blurred.

Mrs. Duffy's voice came to me. "You're just too tender-hearted. You knew it was there all the time, Mr. Matthews, you can't fool me. You'll have to learn to assert yourself a little, that's what's wrong with you. There are some very unpleasant people in this world. There are some very nice ones, too, of course, take for instance—My, I almost forgot!"

It was then she told us about our other visitor—the old lady.

An old lady, very quaint, had called on us early that morning. She wore a lot of old-fashioned lace and artificial flowers and things and was very sociable and Mrs. Duffy took to her right away. She left us a message but it was so mixed up a person couldn't remember it. Mrs. Duffy made a valiant effort. It didn't make sense, she insisted. Something about five diamonds in the north and five diamonds in the south.

We were to find out later that this cryptic information was really very simple and very important. We struggled with it a little while and gave it up. Had we spiked it then for what it so transparently was, we could have put a stop that very night to the wave of fire and murder that was flooding our town.

The phone call from Huey, the pawnbroker, came through that night after supper. I was still a little fuzzy from my mauling. The pawnbroker rang to pass along a hot tip. He had a customer in his shop, he said, whom the Dean would like to talk to. Something to do with the Ortman kill. Come right away. This customer was a nut. Huey would try to hold him until we arrived.

"This lad Huey," the Dean said eight minutes later as we piled into a cab and headed for the waterfront, "is a real friend. He has a brain as big as a watermelon. If he says he'll hold him, he will. But maybe we'd better hurry." He leaned forward. "How about a little more speed, driver?"

I'VE SEEN tenderloins and tenderloins—in fact I was raised in one—but Huey's neighborhood was tough enough even for me. There was the smell of brackish sea-water and the musty ammoniac odor of decaying fruit from the warehouses. The streets were bright with the lights of poolrooms and taverns and the alleys were as dark as the mouth of Hades. Huey's pawnshop was a narrow one-story frame matchbox wedged between a cement-block bowling-alley and a crumbling brick flophouse. The windows were curtained tight with sleazy black chintz. Huey's was temporarily closed.

The pawnbroker let us in. He was little and quick and bright in his movements like an English sparrow, the bird that can make a plump living in any gutter in the country. He nodded silently and waggled his thumb toward the interior of the store.

A grimy, unshaven man in a tattered olive-drab overcoat stood draped against the glass showcase, an old-fashioned stereoscope glued to his face.

"O.K.," he said suddenly. "Change her."

Huey picked up the top card from a stack of photographic slides on the counter and made the change. "This here is Niagara Falls froze over in winter."

"What in the world is this?" the Dean asked.

The pawnbroker smiled mirthlessly. "You tell me. This guy's a hobo and a feeblewit. I been showing him scenes to keep him on ice for you." Huey talked before the man in the tattered overcoat as though he were a child. "He's got Fred Ortman's wallet and driving license. He showed it to me. He came in to hock it but he won't let loose of it—he keeps switching the price."

"O.K.," the bum commanded. "Change her."

Huey slipped in a new slide. "This here is called *The Doctor's Vigil*.... Well, that's how it stands. Maybe you can do something with him."

The Dean touched the man on the shoulder. He blinked at us with bleary red-rimmed eyes. Without a word, he took the leather from his pocket and held it guardedly for our inspection. It was the wallet, all right—the one that police testimony reported burned. It was thick, with gold corners. The smooth ostrich hide was probably loaded with thumbprints.

"How much?" the Dean asked curtly.

The bum showed brown-streaked gums. "No dice. I'm keeping it. I've changed my mind. I ain't letting loose of it."

Huey grunted. I said: "The gentleman does not desire to hypothecate."

"Put it this way," the Dean said. "Let Huey keep it tonight. Here in the shop. He's got a burglar-proof set-up and a good strong safe. How does that sound? Tomorrow, we'll do business."

The man grimaced angrily. "You fellows quit picking on me. Here's what I say—let Huey keep it tonight, he's got a yegg-proof set-up and a good safe. Tomorrow we'll do business. How does that sound?"

I think we all blinked. It was that easy.

"May I ask," the Dean inquired, "how you happened to get it?"

"Between the eyes."

Huey cut in: "He keeps saying that."

"Tell me about it," the Dean said soothingly. "Tell me how come."

"Oh. You wanna know how come. I was traveling into town on a string of gondolas and when we pass under Cherry Street some guy leans out over the bridge and lets it go. It sails down and socks me between the eyes."

"Did you see this man?"

"Oh sure. They's a light on the bridge—"

"Can you describe him?"

"No boss. I can't even describe nobody."

"Listen," the Dean pleaded. "Think. Was he tall? Short? Thin? Heavy? Was he light-complected or dark?"

The bum smiled helplessly. "That there stuff's too much for me. I can't describe him but I can tell you who he was—if that'll be any help. He was Sprigsey O'Hare."

"Sprigsey O'Hare! Are you sure?"

The hobo's stubbled, repellent face set in coarse malicious lines. "Sure I'm sure. I know them all. Big and little, in and out. I'm Daddy Melton and I been around. Yessir, you're talking to Daddy Melton, gents. Now if you'll so kindly open that door I'll be going."

We took the wallet back under Huey's jeweler's light and dusted it. Believe it or not, there wasn't a fingerprint on it. Not one. The leather had been rubbed down and cleaned with what smelled like tan shoe polish. And our hobo had been deft enough to get it out of his pocket and lay it on the counter without leaving so much as a smudge. Daddy Melton might have been a feeblewit but it looked like he was telling the truth when he said he had been around.

"Lock it up, Huey," the Dean said. "We're through with it. Tomorrow, notify the police but leave out the O'Hare angle. Daddy Melton won't be back—it looks as though you scared him when you called us in."

CHAPTER THREE

MURDER IN FOUR SUITS

THREE POLICE cars and an ambulance were parked at the curb before our rooming-house. Gawkers congested the entranceway, stretched over the iron-pipe banister in their effort to peer into our windows. Something was causing a lot of excitement in our apartment.

A harness cop passed us into our living-quarters. A circle of detectives stood in the center of the reception-room, gazing at the floor. At their feet, surrounded by a ring of polished shoes, lay a pathetic huddle of wine silk and faded lace. I knew, and the Dean knew, that our visitor had returned. The old lady had come back and now she lay contorted in violent death.

"It'll get worse,"... the Dean had warned me. I looked away, a little sick.

There was a lot of bustle going on. The Dean was taking casual invoice of those present. Some of the police force were friendly to us—and some were pretty much the opposite. I suppose that's the position all private investigators are in. The Dean's drag with the commissioner both helped and hurt us.

Captain Kunkle was in charge and Kunkle was sociable enough if it didn't cost him pennies in prestige. Malloy wasn't in sight.

The M.E. said loudly: "Well, brethren, it's death by strangulation—or so it appears without autopsy. A loop of picture wire about her throat. Knotted in the back with the same twist that we found in that Ortman business."

Mrs. Duffy, seeing a light beneath our door and getting no response to her knock, had entered and discovered the body. She had called the police and retired to the seclusion of her boudoir.

Captain Kunkle, pressed and starched and powdered and heavily lotioned prowled the room. He would take a step and stop, frown, wink, and shake his head. He was celebrating for the benefit of his subordinates. Suddenly he wheeled and came to a caisson halt before the Dean.

"Spent the evening out, eh, Rock?"

"That's right." The Dean got his little Cuban cigar going.

"Doing what, may I ask?"

"Pricing a second-hand billfold."

There was a laugh. The captain flinched. "Jokes later, Rock. Please. We're in the presence of death. All we want is your help. You must know something helpful. Who is this party?"

"Never saw her before, Captain. No identification in her pocketbook?"

"No pocketbook, Rock. Strange thing."

The Dean said: "She's a complete stranger to me. I don't know a thing, but if you're interested I can tell you what

I think. It's my conviction that this, in some way that is completely obscure to me, ties directly with this arson wave. Of course, I may be entirely wrong. She may have come here for a reading and walked in on a cat—but I doubt it. The missing pocketbook suggests that she was robbed. If it wasn't robbery and murder, your guess as to why it was done here in my living-room is as good as mine."

The exultant voice of Lieutenant Malloy rasped from the bedroom: "Come here a minute, Captain."

I thought the Dean was going juramentado when we got a look at our bedroom. Clothes were thrown from the dresser and closet and lay strewn about the floor. The Dean's expensive, specially built mattress was slit from end to end.

"Who did this?" the Dean asked coldly. "You, Lieutenant?"

THEY SAY there never was a man who hadn't at least one mortal enemy. Malloy was the Dean's. Which was too bad, in a way, because in my estimation Malloy was the best man on the force. I think the Dean resented Malloy because he was so efficient and had the added advantage of the police system to aid him in getting results. And Malloy—everything the Dean said or did brushed him the wrong way. He knew the Dean had a much better brain and knew the commissioner realized it.

"Everything was this way when we got here," Malloy sneered. "Maybe you keep it this way. Maybe the old lady tore it up."

We waited. There was a crafty and satisfied look in Malloy's eyes. "Me, I've been browsing in your private, and I mean private, library. Get me, Rock?"

The Dean said woodenly: "No, I don't. And I wish I did."

The captain puffed out his breath and glared. "What's all this horseplay, Lieutenant?"

Malloy drew down the corners of his mouth. "We got him where we want him, Captain. Salted and peppered and ready to serve." With a flourish, he laid three leather-bound books on the dresser. "I found these in that tin steamer trunk under the bed. Take a look at them."

One by one, Captain Kunkle picked up the volumes and inspected them. The first was entitled *Spanish Garrote, The Art of Instant Suffocation*, the second was called *The Bola*. The third book, no bigger than a sweet-girl-graduate's diary, was the deadliest of the three. Kunkle glanced down the yellowed table of contents. "*Mm.* Why this is terrible. It's horrible. This is a kind of handbook for stranglers. Just listen to this. *The Science of Throttling, London, 1821. Thuggee—The Brotherhood of Kali—The Silken Scarf—The Bowstring—*" He closed the book with distaste and snapped the covers with his thumbnail. "I never saw the like. There should be a law. Rock, are these your books?"

The Dean said: "No. But I wish to heaven they were. The last one, by the way, Malloy, is worth a hatful of dollars. I imagine if you'll call the City Museum you'll learn that all three were stolen from their rare-book collection." Malloy reached for the phone. "They were left here in a not too subtle attempt to frame me for this promiscuous choking."

Malloy finished his conversation and slammed down the receiver. "He's right. They were stolen and not reported to us. There's a reward."

HALF AN hour later, after the tumult and the shouting had died and we were alone again, Mrs. Duffy paid us a short, snappy visit. She had the old lady's pocketbook, a big shiny patent-leather one, under her arm.

She told us about it. "I seen the streak of light and opened the door and there she lay, poor thing, as pretty as a bride in her nice silk dress. Well, I stood and looked and all at once it come over me that she had been slew. I said, 'Seraphina, that nice old lady's been foul kilt right here under your own rooftree.' So I called the officers."

The Dean started to ask a question but she waved him to silence. "First I picked up the pocketbook. Pat always claimed that officers brought strangers in the house—reporters and such. So I picked it up and took it to my room. Did I do right?"

The Dean patted her reassuringly on the shoulder. "You certainly did, Seraphina—if I may call you by what has hitherto been a concealed delight. Now go to bed and get a good sleep."

The pocketbook contained thirty-seven cents, a big brass door key, a tatting shuttle, and a newspaper clipping.

"Nothing here," I said. "We'd better turn this stuff back where it belongs."

The Dean said: "She was bringing us something. I've been sure of that all along. Was it this brass key, Ben?"

"I hardly think so."

"I agree. Then it must have been this news item." We held the clipping between us and examined it. It was torn from a column in the *Journal* and carried the masthead *Bridge Puzzlers*.

The clipping read—

'Populor' sends us this problem. What is the correct bidding for hands North and South? Solutions should be in the office of the Editor of this column not later than midnight, Thursday. Address communications, this department, care of the *Journal*.

So get out your thinking-caps, fans, and see what you can do. Here it is. This week's Puzzler:

NORTH
S—K9385Q
H—(None)
D—KA45
C—287

WEST
S—J1064
H—QJ109
D—(None)
C—K10934

EAST
S—(None)
H-843
D—Q10
C—57AJQ867

SOUTH
S—2A7
H—K25A67
D—253J
C—(None)

"I don't like it," the Dean said. "I don't like it a bit." He clipped a pair of spectacles on the bridge of his nose and settled back in his favorite broken-down Morris. I opened a couple of bottles of ale and brought out a platter of cold crackling bread.

"It's a cipher and a very simple one," the Dean observed. "You can almost read it by sight. It was evidently chosen for persons who weren't particularly bright—like our friends Herb and Dorf—who would have difficulty in remembering a complicated key. Before we tackle it, let's do some reconstructing."

He closed his eyes. "I think our elderly visitor was a bridge addict who followed this column in the paper. I imagine she has encountered these messages before this—for I am sure they have appeared in the past. The first few times she was no doubt astounded and confused at the unorthodox presentation—it is likely that the hands presented no problem at all. In any event, it is certain that no bridge problem was ever set up in such a manner—note how the suit sequences are jumbled numerically. This is so symptomatic as to preclude the possibility of mere typographer's error."

I had noticed this myself. The proper arrangement for Spades in North's hand should have been KQ9853—from the highest to the lowest—instead of K9385Q.

"To get back to our old lady," the Dean continued. "At first she was bewildered. Then she must have begun to wonder. Maybe she was a bit of a cryptographer herself—many recluses are. In any event, it is evident she was disturbed to find a five of diamonds in the hands of both North and South, two club sevens in East's hand as well as other duplications. I think we can take it for granted that she broke this message down and smelled a rat. Why she came to see us, we can only conjecture. Possibly because of our previous newspaper publicity. We can say that she solved the message and that her murderers, finding it out, trailed her here and killed her."

Subsequent events proved the Dean correct in his logic. The old lady had made a disastrous blunder.

"A deck of playing cards," the Dean explained, "offers many methods of communication. This particular system is all right if the entire deck is used helter-skelter. It seems to me to be a little limited to selection used in suit sequence." He touched his ale to his tongue. "However and however."

He was way over my head. My jaw dropped when he said placidly: "I'm going to let you solve this for us, Ben."

"Listen," I said. "This is no time for monkey business. Me solve a cipher? I can hardly figure out the directions on a box of aspirin."

"You've been to school, haven't you?"

"Through the sixth grade."

"Quite sufficient. A first-grader could break it down—if he could count to fifty-two."

"Nuts," I said. "You're taking me for a ride!"

"Take a pencil and paper," the Dean advised. I did. "Now, Ben, how many letters in the alphabet?"

"Twenty-six."

"So far so good. Two times twenty-six are—?"

"Fifty-two." I grinned. I was beginning to see light. "Then a deck of cards equals a double alphabet?"

"That's right. Two suits equal one complete alphabet—the four suits equal two. The next thing is the suit order. I imagine we can take the customary bridge rating as given here—spades and hearts will be the first group, diamonds and clubs the second."

He developed the probability. "We'd better check into that. The ace of diamonds would be the first letter in the second alphabet, or "a." The five of diamonds would then be "e." And that's the card that bothered the old lady because of its duplication. Check. The overuse of "e" is characteristic of the novice cryptographer. All right. Get to work. You take over from here."

WELL, IT'S hard to believe but I broke it down in seventeen minutes. First, I made a list like this. I put the two suits, spades and hearts together, to form one alphabet, running from the ace of spades to the king of hearts. Then I ran off the diamonds and clubs to match.

Spades—

A	2	3	4	5	6	7	8	9	10	J	Q	K
A	B	C	D	E	F	G	H	I	J	K	L	M

Hearts—

A	2	3	4	5	6	7	8	9	10	J	Q	K
N	O	P	Q	R	S	T	U	V	W	X	Y	Z

Diamonds—

A	2	3	4	5	6	7	8	9	10	J	Q	K
A	B	C	D	E	F	G	H	I	J	K	L	M

Clubs—

A	2	3	4	5	6	7	8	9	10	J	Q	K
N	O	P	Q	R	S	T	U	V	W	X	Y	Z

And then I substituted in the original problem and managed to get this—

MICHEL

MADE

OUT

(Blank)		(Blank)
KJFD	BAG	UQP
YXWV	ZORN ST	LJHFG
ZWVPQ	BECK	RSAXY

The Dean inspected it. "There you are," he said. "East and West are blank—catch-alls for unused letters. The message is 'Michel made out. Bag Mr. Beck on Zorn Street.' This paper clipping was our visitor's death warrant."

"What does it mean?" I asked.

"It means more devilishness. Probably more fire."

I started for my coat. "Zorn Street, eh?" He stayed me with his hand. "We're too late, Ben. I'm sure of that. They've got the wind up. It was this clipping that was the object of so strenuous a search here in our bedroom. Yes, Mr. Beck's delicatessen—or grocery—or whatever it is, has gone up in flames some time ago. These people are desperate. They know we're hot after them. Just relax a bit before we do anything."

For a few minutes, he was silent. "What irritates me," he said abruptly, "is the nature of the whole affair. It's essentially transparent but I can't seem to unveil it. Believe me, Ben, we're dealing with one mind—a criminal mind which has put a new twist to an old racket. Let's see what we know about our quarry. We know, first of all, that his financial returns are so great as to cause him to kill to protect them. To kill at the slightest excuse whenever, and as often, as he feels his profits are in jeopardy. Secondly, in choosing his cipher he gravitated to the bridge column in the newspaper. Not the want ads, for instance, but the bridge column. Dorf and Herb would gravitate to spit-in-the-ocean and red-dog. Thirdly, and most important, I think our criminal mind has had legitimate business training. I can't explain it to you but the imprint is there, a pattern of routine and systematic attention to detail. Yes, Ben, when we spear him our fish will turn out to be a man of ledgers and accounts."

"What about this Michel?" I asked. "Who is he? And what do we do about it?"

"Building on the theory of an arson ring, we can suppose Michel to be the fixer—the go-between who makes the arrangements. Who he is, I can't tell you at this moment. Forget him, Ben. His days are numbered." The Dean smiled.

"You forget him. I won't. In fact, he's number one boy on my list."

THE PHONE buzzed and I answered. "Your offer is accepted!" a voice shouted into my ear. "You're hired. Get on the case. Now!"

I cupped my hand over the mouthpiece. "Our offer is accepted," I told the Dean. "It's Hilliston Keith. He says we're hired."

"Tell him it's twenty thousand now," the Dean said.

"We've made new terms," I relayed. "Twenty thousand or no soap." I could clearly hear Keith's breathing, a sort of fluttery sputter. Finally he said: "Accepted. Call Mr. Rock."

I nodded and the Dean shared the receiver with me. "I'm rather busy," the Dean explained. "So you had better let me do the talking, Mr. Keith. Has the Solidarity in its employ an ex-convict by the name of Sprigsey O'Hare. Or don't you know? He might be using another name, you understand."

"I know the man you mean," Keith said slowly. "Or rather I know of him. He worked for Ortman until Ortman canned him—about three days before Ortman's murder. The police have been all over that field without result. O'Hare has vanished. Information indicates he is an itinerant somewhere in the Middle West following the sugar-beet crop. I really don't see—"

The Dean closed his eyes in admiration. "There's genius behind this. A blocker in the beet fields. Who would ever think of that! That's about all. By the way, how much was Beck insured for?"

"Fifty thousand, building and stock. That's what I called you about." Keith gasped. "Wait a minute. Where did you hear about it? It just happened."

The Dean chuckled. "I read it in this morning's paper. Don't tell me you passed it up? One thing more. Is Miss Bitsey about?"

Keith coughed. "Why, yes she is. By a remarkable accident, by a strange—"

The blonde's tiny voice chirruped: "It's me. It's this little girl. Mr. Rock, I wanted to ask you this morning—do precious stones vibrate in harmony with their zodiacal signs? I mean, is the amethyst under the power of Sagittarius and can it make you go to sleep or get rid of a hangover, like a man I met on the train said?"

"So the ancient lapidists affirmed," the Dean said gravely. "Now, my dear, you can help me if you will. I am casting Mr. Keith's horoscope for him—without his knowledge, as a sort of surprise. Can you tell me if he has a middle name?"

"Why, yes," she said. "He does have. Now how shall I say it? You know about the two Irishmen?"

The Dean waggled his head. "The girl's good," he whispered to me, and into the phone, "Patrick?"

"No. The other."

"Michael?"

"That's right."

The blonde was rattling away, talking a mile a minute about astral spheres and planetary influences as the Dean eased the receiver down on the bracket. "I like that whelp," he mused. "I don't know why, but I do.... Tell me, Ben, what do you know about the name Michael?"

"Only that it's as Irish as the shamrock," I retorted.

"Wrong on all counts. A common fallacy. No, it's not Irish but Latin. It is from the Hebrew *Mikael* which, I believe, means: Who is like God. It is a very popular name and found in many languages. In Italian it is Michele, in Spanish it is Miguel. In French it is Michel."

THE BRICK building had been gutted from basement to eaves. Its front wall had collapsed into the cobblestone street, throwing hot bricks and fragments of plaster as far as the mailbox half a block away. By the time we arrived, the department had checked it as safe. Workers had cleared the debris from the car tracks. Though it was after midnight, a handful of owlish slum children stood about, staring at the wreckage. The wet ashes gave off a strong, sickening smell. In the gutter lay a shattered wooden sign: *JOHN BECK—FURS.*

The Dean tapped the sign with his toe. "Furs. The racket is expanding. It'll have to be scotched and soon."

A mangy cat stepped daintily around the puddles and sniffed at the burnt timbers.

"She smells her nieces and her sisters and her cousins and her aunts," I said. "Many a cat pelt went up in that blaze."

One of the children, a little undernourished kid with tufts of cornsilk hair at his ragged collar, turned a pale, wrinkled face in our direction. He couldn't have been over nine but he spoke with the hostility of a tired, old man.

"Get wise to yourself," he slurred. "Beck's skins were all Grade-A. You uptown mugs get in my hair." I grinned. I knew how he felt. I had been a slum kid myself.

The Dean edged into the conversation. He showed a friendly, toothy grin and waved a big paw. He was putting on the harmless-crackpot act. "I hesitate to interrupt—but isn't that a kitchen range I see there in the wreckage?"

The boy watched him warily.

The Dean went on: "B'Jove, it is! So Mr. Beck lived in his store. Now he is homeless!"

"He'll get by," the kid burst out. "We get by down here. We got a good friend."

The Dean raised his eyebrows. "And who might Mr. Beck's friend be?"

A tiny five-year-old came to life. "Johnny Carter, he's our friend. He helps poor people. He gives kids candy at his drug store."

The older boy cuffed the youngster. "Button your lip," he said.

The Dean passed out seven quarters to seven unresponsive palms—and we withdrew.

We returned to our apartment and hit the hay. For a long time, I lay in the dark, thinking. I was stiff and aching and frustrated. It had been a big day and as far as I could see nothing had been accomplished. A couple of red-hots had worked me over, a bum had taken us for a ride, an old lady had been murdered on our broadloom and a man named Beck had burned down his store because a man named Michel had told him to. I tried to disabuse my mind of the confusion by concentrating on the twenty thousand.

The Dean's rumbling baritone came to me from the bed in his corner of the room. "A guardsman's uniform, Ben. Red pants, silver-plated sword and a bearskin shako." He sighed. "That would do the trick."

"Listen," I said. "I can stand just so much."

He paid no attention. "Oh well, I guess we'll have to fall back on my old reliable—the country-garden nosegay."

I heard him roll over and a second later came the soft, controlled breathing that told me he was asleep.

CHAPTER FOUR
POOR MAN'S BLACKMAIL

I STARTED off the next morning bull-mad. We had a long talk at breakfast and the Dean explained to me the nature of the crime we were tackling. I remembered that yesterday he had said, "…arson and murder—and the arson is worse than the murder." Now I knew what he meant, and agreed with him.

Shopkeepers were falling into the clutches of a new racket. Or rather a new combination of two old rackets—an arson-blackmail ring. From various sources, for some time, little bits of information had come to the Dean suggesting the existence of such a syndicate. Now he was convinced.

"Indescribably vicious, Ben," he said. "It's hard to believe. The usurer's racket—from which this borrows its method, I might add—is naive by comparison." His eyes smoldered beneath their shaggy brows. "Today we wind this case up."

I stared at him. "You know the strangler?"

"The strangler! Yes, I know the strangler. I could leave this room, find him and shoot him down in thirty minutes flat." Worry creased his brow. "But that wouldn't stop the burning and killing. It's the brain behind this ugly business we must smash. We'll have to depend on my country-garden nosegay."

I let that one pass.

He went on: "Their *modus operandi* is cruel and direct. Their prey is the small merchant, none too thriving, timid, without influence. A mark is selected and approached by the contact man—Michel, we can say—who implants the idea of insurance fraud, offers the services of arsonists to do the job, and guarantees immunity from suspicion. If the shopkeeper is interested, his goose is cooked. If his character and honesty outweigh his cupidity, the syndicate follows up with strong-arm intimidation. The merchant is bound to lose. He can't even level. His store is burned. The insurance is collected in its entirety by the syndicate."

The Dean talked on. He was a little white around the corners of the mouth.

"This is just a beginning," he said. "The victim, guilty of crime, is ensnared in a net of blackmail. From then on, though his family go hungry, he must pay to keep himself from jail. I have heard, in a roundabout way, of an Italian family living down by the river whose four boys turn over their weekly paychecks to save their father from imprisonment and disgrace."

I said: "Poor man's blackmail!"

"Yes," the Dean agreed. "And it's pretty beastly."

A city directory revealed to us that John Charles Carter ran a drug store at the corner of Elm and Water Streets. Mrs. Sprigsey O'Hare was a little more difficult to locate. A call to the commissioner, himself, informed us, after a lot of fuss and feathers, that she was living under the name of Celadine La Varre at the Hotel Lord Ashton on West Third.

"The *Journal* first," the Dean said. "I've had a growing premonition."

In the cab on the way downtown, he clammed up. "We know," I observed, "that the editor of the bridge column is intentionally or accidentally involved. He was involved in that cipher. You can't get around it."

The Dean grunted. "We'll see."

"Take it this way," I insisted. "Those notices were messages. They had to appear on certain days—definite days. That presupposes connivance. You can't get around that. This bridge editor is in deep."

"Deep," the Dean rumbled. I didn't like the way he said it.

We were always welcome at the *Journal's* office. Dean Wardlow Rock was news anytime. Today he was red-hot. The boys at the *Journal* respected him, and let me tell you they were a hard bunch of lads to fool.

Edwards greeted us with a scoff. "Murder in detective's parlor. Man bites dog—that's news."

The Dean shook hands. "No, Hank," he corrected. "Man bites dog—that's Kynanthropy, as you no doubt were about to remark, is a form of ensorcellment closely related to lycanthropy, or wolf-madness. The lycanthrope, or kynanthrope, is variously known as the werewolf or loup-garou."

Edwards laughed. "You should be working for the Britannica."

"I have," the Dean said amiably. "A little monograph on the hippogryph.... Tell me, Hank, is the bridge editor in?"

The city editor looked disturbed. "It isn't a he—it's a she." He paused, considered a moment, and came to a decision. "You're a friend, Dean. I'm going to blow my top to you. We have a funny situation here. Things have been happening that I don't understand and don't like. Our bridge editor is an aristocratic dame down on her luck—by the name of Arabella Trimble. We forward her mail and she sends in her copy. I've only seen her once in my life, yesterday, when she came in to get a confession off her chest. It seems that every three weeks or so, she'd receive a 'problem' in a plain envelope, containing instructions to publish on such-and-such a day. With each of these requests there was enclosed a twenty-dollar bill. She figured at first that it was some crank that like to see his stuff in print—and boy there are plenty—so—"

"So she succumbed," the Dean finished. "Is that all?"

"No. She was all steamed up. Acting mysterious. Wanted a confidential detective."

"And you suggested me?"

"I might have. Come to think of it—"

"That," said the Dean to me, "was her death warrant." And to Edwards, "Did she leave any of these notes with you?"

"No, she didn't, Rock. She said they must have come from a woman because they were saturated with lavender sachet." He shrugged. "Maybe she made herself a little unethical dough but she caught herself in time. No harm done."

"No harm done!" The Dean glared. "Strangled on my carpet and he says no harm done. Call up the city morgue, Hank. You'll find your Arabella Trimble. Twelve hours murdered and still unidentified!"

THE SUNSHINE PALETTE FLOWER SHOPPE was the answer to our search for a florist. For a moment, we stood on the sidewalk and marveled. Along the curb were set a row of bright scarlet potted plants. The little store, with about eight feet of window space, was all dressed up like it was going to a children's party. A green-and-yellow awning about the size of a cigarette paper shaded the passerby. We stepped through the narrow doorway, around a gilded milk bucket crammed with jonquils, and pushed our way inside.

A male clerk, built along the lines of Peter Pan, was sprucing up a display of snaps by picking off the dead blossoms. He hesitated, as though he were caught in some guilty act, and trotted up to wait on us.

"And today it is what?" He v'd the muscles in his cheeks and showed us a couple of dimples.

"And today it is an old-fashioned bouquet," the Dean grunted. The clerk was off like a butterfly. "Hold on," the Dean ordered. "Now wait." The clerk was all arrested motion and attention. "This is a special kind of bouquet," the Dean explained. "A country-garden nosegay, you might say. It must have a touch of modesty—calendulas, possibly. And a rustic cabin-in-the-woods atmosphere. American heather ought to fix that up. There must be, too, a suggestion of sentimental sweet sixteen, maybe you can figure that one out yourself. Put them all together so that they spell innocent schoolgirl."

"Oh. They're for a schoolgirl?" The clerk was interested. "Then may I advise—"

"No, you may not. And they're for no schoolgirl. If this girl went to any school at all it was the correction home. Now shuffle them up. We're in a rush."

When they came in or how they came in, I couldn't tell you. All at once they were there. Standing a little to one side and behind us like a couple of wax dummies from a back-street sideshow. Dorf and Herb—a man without an ear and a man in a brown suit.

Their hands were in their pockets and their faces were tense. They were all ready to click. It gave me a jolt that frosted the back of my neck.

"I thought we told you not to pry," Dorf said hoarsely. He was trembling with suppressed fury, his sallow face livid to his ear stump. "See that old sedan out front? Get going."

The Dean seemed mildly interested. "Followed us from the newspaper office, eh? Just like you did the old lady."

Dorf's chunky companion blurted out: "That—that wasn't us."

"Reef it, Loose Lip," Dorf warned. And to us, "O.K. Single-foot it out of here."

The Dean shook his head regretfully. "Sorry, we must decline. You boys toddle back to your sandpile."

Bedlam broke loose. I went into a half-crouch. Dorf's heavy gun lifted a wisp of tweed from the shoulder of my coat and slammed the elfin clerk into a showcase of orchids. The retracting carriage of his automatic jammed. He cursed. Out of the corner of my eye I saw the Dean going into action with his Magnum, saw Herb's brown ensemble jerk and collapse.

The gaunt man pivoted and ran, behind the counter to the rear. I dashed after him. We sprinted through a back room littered with green waxpaper, tinfoil, unfolded cardboard boxes, around a work table, over a floral piece depicting two clasped hands, and out the back door. He was in the open all the way, I could have snapped him off like a clay pipe—but he was unarmed. He was home-free and he knew it. When he hit the alley nothing short of a cordon could have caught him.

I chased him three blocks for the principle of the thing and then he slipped me.

Whistles were skirling and sirens were screaming toward the Sunshine Palette Flower Shoppe. The cops arrived at the shambles. The Dean had left. He was lining up his double play. I caught a cab to West Third and told the driver to wait.

IF THE Hotel Lord Ashton had ever been clean, sanitary and respectable, its era of gentility must have faded out about the time of Custer's last stand. Despite dim corridors, fly-specked light-bulbs and musty carpet, it still attracted its modicum of guests. In a manner of speaking, it was a family hotel—but what a family. Of the four characters sitting around in the lobby as I passed through, I spotted two on parole and one dodging his fourth sentence. The other was probably wanted.

The day-clerk, a small time grifter named Saracetti, was sprawled behind the desk trimming his fingernails. He was using a stag handled shiv with an illegally long, sheepsfoot blade. We'd met here and there around the spots and didn't like each other.

"Your chief's in Three-thirty-three." Saracetti tried to be pleasant but he just couldn't put it over. He showed an edging of squirrel teeth between his lips. "What's little Celadine been getting into?"

Little Celadine. See what I mean? Family hotel.

"Forget it," I snapped.

I stopped on the second floor, took my hat and coat off, hung them out of sight in a broom closet, and knocked on the first door I came to. A nautical-looking bimbo with a tattooed forearm opened up, glanced at my shirt-sleeves.

"Hate to trouble you," I apologized. "I'm next door. Ran out of writing paper. Could you spare me a sheet of hotel stationery? Getting it at the desk is like pulling teeth. The way they dole it out you'd think it was black bread and we was in the Russian army."

He broke into a guffaw and brought me a mittful.

I took the paper with its printed letterhead and returned to my coat. Getting plenty of old time arm-movement into my Spencerian, I wrote—*Better scram for the day. Take*

*the service stairs. There's a cop called Malloy prowling the lobby
asking about you. Told him you were out. Did I do right?*

I signed the day-clerk's name—Saracetti—and tacked
on the T.N.T.—*P.S.:-He keeps asking do you know a hobo
named Melton?* I walked to the elevator and pushed the
bell. When the creaking cage lifted, I said to the boy:
"Here's a buck. Deliver this to Three-thirty-three in exactly
ten minutes."

It was like shooting fish. The Dean had said do it. Mine
not to reason why. I put on my hat and coat and went up
to Three-thirty-three.

Celadine La Varre, more intimately known as Mrs.
Sprigsey O'Hare, peeped an inch of soft cheek around the
corner of the jamb and let me in. I took a long, hard look.
This was what Sprigsey had deserted for fields full of beets.

She was a little brunette, slim and tapered. From the
dainty crown of her lacquer-black hair to the high instep
of her continental pumps, she was as trim a bit of domestic porcelain as you'll find outside the New Jersey potter-
ies. The frock she stood in had cost eight C's if it had cost
a penny. Her violet eyes, pollen-soft, were warm and inviting.

She reminded me of another waif I once knew who
robbed the mission collection to get a pistol to shoot her
sister.

My eyes popped a little when I noticed that she was
wearing a bouquet of old-fashioned flowers. There was the
American heather and there were the calendulas.

The Dean was sitting on a red-and-gold chair, grinning
wolfishly. He introduced me. "Very pretty flowers, Miss
La Varre," I commented.

"Aren't they too lovely!" She really meant it. "Mr. Rock
brought them. He says it's a country-garden nosegay.

They're supposed to express my character. The calendulas are for modesty and the heather is for innocence, I believe."

"Very tastefully selected," I affirmed.

"Thank you, Ben," the Dean put in complacently. "As a matter of fact, I picked them out of the showcase and arranged them myself. I did it a little hurriedly—"

Celadine caressed them. "They're beautiful. And that nice thing you said about my being—what was it?—an unsophisticated country-garden girl."

This kind of stuff embarrasses me. I was irritated to see that the Dean was enjoying himself immensely. "I get no credit for that observation," he remarked. "Everybody says so. It's all up and down the avenue." He coughed. "Now just a question or two more. You haven't heard from Sprigsey since Ortman's death?"

"Yes. But the police have been all over—"

"I know. But I want to find your husband for you. You want him back, don't you?"

Her eyes warmed wistfully. "We were happy as doves."

There was a knock on the door. The shabby uniformed arm of my elevator boy thrust in the letter. She slit the envelope and ran down the paper in a single sweeping glance. Her eyes flickered. There was fear in her face now. Unmistakable terror. The Dean leaned back in his chair and hummed military snatches from the *1812 Overture*.

Miss La Varre came over and kissed him on the forehead. "You boys had better leave now."

She unleashed about a million dollars' worth of smile.

ON THE main floor, we dog-legged around the desk, out through the coffee shop, and piled into our waiting cab. "Watch the servants' entrance," the Dean said. "She'll be bursting out like a ball of fire. That letter really rang the chime!"

"Did I carry it off?" I asked.

"Perfectly." The Dean became somber. "Ben, Miss La Varre has supplied the key." He lowered his voice. "That girl's a dominicide."

"And what's a dominicide?" I asked.

"You don't understand? Why that half solves the case." He sighed. "Oh, well. To tell the truth, I half suspected it. It seemed strange that— There she comes!"

Celadine La Varre came out of the servants' door carrying a patent-leather traveling bag. She came like she was being chased by bats and snakes. Her little heels flying, she ran across the sidewalk, leaped into a gray coupe parked at the curb, and ground the starter. She was off in a screech of gears, around the corner and out of sight.

"Let's move," I said to the cabbie. "Don't lose her and there's money in it for you."

The gray coupe went down Highland to Adams. At Adams she set her brakes, twisted suddenly to the left, cut under the viaduct and out Canal. We stayed on her tail in and out of the Italian neighborhood, in and out of the riverfront district, and headed for the wharves beyond the city limits.

So suddenly we almost bumped into it, the little car pulled up before a rambling three-story building. From where we stopped, a block away, the big sign read: *WAREHOUSE 29*. An indefinable emanation from the Dean told me he was highly satisfied.

The cab driver said sententiously: "The end of the rainbow. And is that a screwy dame! She checks out of a hotel, bag and baggage, and checks into a warehouse. What do I do now?"

"You turn around, drive downtown and collect a well-earned bonus."

"Where next?" I asked.

"The Solidarity Insurance Company," the Dean decided. "It's about time we talked with our employer."

MY FIRST impression was that the scene hadn't changed. Hilliston Keith, still at his desk, fiddled with his fraternity pins. The blonde was still demurely on her hassock at his ankle. Then, with a shock, I noticed that Keith had aged ten years since we had seen him. The "business doctor" was showing strain.

"Rock," he said, "I'm glad you dropped in. I've been trying to get you on the phone. It looks as though our break has come. This affair is clearing up."

"It's been perfectly clear to me right along," the Dean remarked quietly.

"Here," said Keith, ignoring him, "is something that will interest you." He laid a square of brown paper on the desk before him. It was the usual criminal's handicraft—printed letters, cut and pasted. It said—

DID JOHN BECK'S FURS BURN? GARAGE OF COTTAGE BACK OF FERRY STREET PIG YARD TEN TONIGHT—BRING ROCK & MATTHEWS.

"Slipped under my door this morning," Keith supplied. "What do you make of it?"

"This case has been solved for two hours," the Dean commented. "However"—he studied the message— "academically interesting. Letters cut, not from a newspaper as is customary, but from an old mail-order catalog." He touched the paper to his nose. "Faint smell of lavender sachet."

That touched the blonde off. "The lavender sachet is me. It's me that smells that way, Mr. Rock. I always use lavender sachet."

"And a very charming scent it is," the Dean endorsed gallantly.

"It's my lucky perfume. Shall I tell you about it? A gypsy out in Tulsa explained a dream I had and said I should always—"

Keith broke in. "This business ought to be investigated." He seemed at a loss for words. "Unfortunately I have an engagement this evening—so you'll have to go it alone. You and Matthews."

"An engagement?" the blonde asked. "With whom?"

"Why, with you, my dear." Keith smiled. "You remember now, don't you?"

"That's a lot of Creole gumbo," she retorted. "Since when did you start having unbreakable engagements with me?"

The Dean said suavely: "I get the idea, Mr. Keith. And that's what we're paid for." He added casually: "Ortman. What's his widow doing now? Ortman left her well fixed, I presume?"

Keith looked embarrassed. "No, he didn't. As a matter of fact, she had a pretty tough time getting by. So we took her on. She holds down a desk here. Sort of pasturage. We figured we owed it to her."

The Dean was actually startled. I knew that somewhere his calculations had sprung a leak.

"Are you telling me," he said slowly, "that Fred Ortman left no life insurance?"

Keith's discomfiture reached its climax. "It's terrible isn't it—the head of Solidarity and he wasn't insured himself.

Don't let it go any farther. Please. He probably did it from spite. He and his wife weren't so pally."

The Dean sighed with relief. "Man, you really had me twisted. So that's it. That's all I want to know. That explains the tan shoe polish."

CHAPTER FIVE
SEVEN STICKS
OF DYNAMITE

THE FRECKLED, whistling clerk behind the cigar counter of John Charles Carter's drug store was a gunsel if I ever saw one. He had a boyish shock of straw-colored hair, cut in a teddy-bear pompadour, and a happy-go-lucky lilt to his tenor voice but his eyes were as inhumanly bleak as a chicken hawk's. He was coked to the ears—and working in a drug store. Already, as soon as I took a look at him, I began to get ideas about Johnny Carter, the benevolent druggist, the poor man's friend.

The Dean unsnapped the old-fashioned clip-purse he carried and selected a calling card from his assortment. He laid it with a flourish on the green felt dice board and bowed. "Mr. Carter?"

The boy was flabbergasted. "I'm not the boss," he blurted. "I just work here." He was sure enough flattered. The Dean had a manner about him. The card said, *Athelstane Berrymeadow—Fur Broker.*

"Wait a minute," the kid said. He disappeared through a curtain at the rear. A second later, he was back. "O.K. The boss'll see you."

Now, I'm no authority on prescription-rooms, but I'm here to tell you that the set-up in the back of Carter's drug store was the weirdest sight I'd beheld in many a day.

Every inch of the walls that wasn't shelved with rows of bottles and jars, was plastered with expensive anatomical charts, foreign importations, they looked like, and across the face of these charts were scribbled notes in pencil. The floor was littered with bright bits of yarn and scraps of dainty cloth.

John Charles Carter sat in the midst of this disorder—sewing. The druggist was a little fat man with down on his cheeks. You got the impression that he didn't have to shave. His eyes were frog-lidded and had long, curling lashes.

He took the gold thimble off his finger, dropped it into the sewing bag which hung from the arm of his chair, patted the tiny pink baby dress on his knee. Yes. Baby dress.

"The third I've finished this week," he said proudly. "It's my hobby, gentlemen. Making baby clothes—dresses, vesties, little flannel gowns—for underprivileged infants."

The Dean was hearty in his approval. "Now that's a real charity, isn't it?" He picked up a needle and a piece of thread, made several cumbersome attempts at threading the needle and gave it up.

John Charles Carter watched him with sudden interest. "The thread's a little large" he said. "So you must twist it into the needle's eye."

The Dean tried again.

"No," the druggist explained pettishly. "You're twisting against the lay. You must twist with the lay."

"The lay?" The Dean raised his eyebrows. "That's a new one on me."

"The lay of a rope or cable or thread is the direction in which the strands are twisted—also, the degrees of tightness or division between strands."

"My," the Dean observed. "I didn't realize there was so much to sewing. I wonder if my grandmother knew that."

"Probably not," the druggist said silkily. "But sailors know it—and hangmen."

"So I was thinking," the Dean said.

The room became deathly silent. Suddenly, for no understandable reason, the gruesome charts upon the walls gave me a sensation of freshly opened graves. There was something evil here, too evil to comprehend. The scraps of cloth upon the floor seemed like snippings from shrouds, the little toadlike man became a pall-maker.

"You wanted to see me about what?" the druggist asked. "About Beck's furs?" He spoke with open contempt. "They burned, you know, Mr. Rock."

"So you know me?"

"I know you both. I know you are too intelligent to be threatened. But I will say this—get out of town."

The Dean turned to me. "I brought you here for a reason, Ben," he said calmly. "This man is our strangler. He kills for profit and he kills for love. The time will come soon when you must shoot him down. Shoot him like a dog, with a clear conscience. You have heard the admission from his own lips."

We left John Charles Carter, strangler, rigid in his chair, the little pink baby dress across his plump knee. Outside, I burst into a torrent of invectives.

The Dean hushed me. "Please, Ben. I feel the same way. This method is best. We want that killer, and we'll get him, but more even than Carter we must have the man behind him. I've just had a hunch. Let's drop around to headquarters."

LIEUTENANT MALLOY was standing by the battered Victorian fountain in the tiled rotunda of City Hall, watching the sluggish carp poke among the peanut shells. He pretended to observe us by accident but something in his breathing suggested that he had seen us coming and had taken a quick run to head us off. He looked up as we approached and gave a blink of surprise.

"Gaze, Ben," the Dean declaimed, "at our ichtholatrous friend. Now we know from what pastime comes that piscine look in his eye."

Malloy snorted. "Save it. It's being wasted here." He studied the Dean's rugged, intelligent face. "Last night, down at your place, you told us you didn't know the old lady." He smiled wickedly. "You remember—the one murdered in your living-room? This morning you drop into the *Journal* office and tell them it's a crank that works for them."

The Dean nodded. "Substantially correct."

"You wouldn't be suppressing evidence, would you?"

The Dean started to wisecrack and thought better of it. "No." The urge conquered and he said: "Not much."

Malloy flushed. "I ought to shove you in the can. The both of you. You"—he fumbled for expression—"you fray my patience."

"I know we do," the Dean said seriously. "You have the same effect on me. We're too good for each other." He was being perfectly honest and I knew it. The next breath he was off again, lying like a sea-lawyer.

"I have a client that's up against a queer proposition. It's too involved to go into. That's why I'm here. I want to talk to you. I want to ask you a question. Do you know of a Frenchman, a gambler, first name Michel, who might be mixed up in an oil deal?"

Malloy thought it over. He was only half fooled but he was smart enough to take a chance. The Dean had come to the right man. Malloy had the well-earned rep of never having forgotten the face or photo of a wanted man.

He said: "At the convention out West eight years ago, I looked through some pictures. There was a guy wanted by Denver, named Michel André Cartier. He wasn't a gambler and he wasn't a con man. He was a druggist. An escaped murderer. He had nutty hobbies—knotting fishnets, making lace, and hanging around the fancywork booths at county fairs."

It was just like looking in the back of the book for the answers. John Charles Carter was Michel André Cartier—Michel, the fixer for the syndicate. That lets Keith out, I thought.

The Dean appeared discouraged. "I don't think I'll be able to use it," he said. "It hardly seems possible. This man, the man I want, followed a carnival pulling spikes with his teeth. Thanks just the same."

"Think of that!" Malloy retorted harshly. "Well, there's two thousand reward outstanding. Dead or alive. There's police widows and their children that could use a slice of two thousand."

The Dean nodded absently. He hardly seemed to hear.

I had observed a big deal negotiated—and barely realized it. Those boys really understood each other.

WE POLISHED off a double supper apiece in Gino's Kitchen, the first food we'd had since breakfast, and the Dean slept in his bent-wire chair for two hours. At nine o'clock he raised his eyelids and said: "Let's stroll down to the waterfront."

I'd been thinking about Hilliston Michael Keith and his anonymous tip. There was plenty about it I didn't like. Keith didn't like it either, or he wouldn't have crawfished.

I got to my feet. "As you say, Cagliostro. And against my better judgment."

River fog shrouded Ferry Street, hung about the sparse lights in clouds of steamy mist, condensed on our wrists and foreheads. It was a neighborhood of junkyards, wrecked-car lots, coal and lumber yards. Rusty machinery and abandoned squatters' shacks loomed in the haze like crippled monsters from some prehistoric slime. In seven blocks we passed no one.

The Dean halted, hands deep in his coat pockets and pointed, African fashion, with his chin. "Here's our pig yard—pig iron," he said. He glanced over his shoulder. "There should be—and is—our cottage, facing us."

Why such a dwelling had been built in such a location, we wondered. A little four-room Cape Cod. When the painters and carpenters had finished it, it must have looked, in its poisonous surroundings like an apple-cheeked country lad fresh come to town. Now the city had claimed it. It was vacant, its windows were boarded, its plumbing, no doubt, long since looted, sold for brass, lead and iron. At the rear we could make out the silhouette of a squat, one-car garage.

We crossed the street, took a cinder path around the deserted house and hesitated before the garage door. We were twenty minutes early.

"Looks more like a shop than a garage," the Dean observed. "If it's a garage, where the deuce is the drive?" He flashed his pencil-light over the cinders. Over the sandy lawn, straight up from the curb, were deep wheel ruts. "There's been a car, though, Ben. Just one and recently."

He made no attempt at concealment, nor at lowering his voice. I figured he knew what he was doing, that there was no danger.

THE DOUBLE doors were hasped with a dime-store padlock. I grinned. "This is very elementary, Mr. Rock," I said. "A child could spring it. You have been to school, haven't you? How many letters in the alphabet? I am going to let you solve this for us."

The Dean was irritated. "Don't clown around. Open it up. Let's get in."

I put my handkerchief over it while I unlocked it. The performance bugged his eyes. He could have opened it himself with a bent nail but you could never have convinced him.

"Ben," he said in awed tones, "that's sheer witchcraft. You just put your hand under that handkerchief and it opens."

"That's right," I said modestly. "I'm pretty good."

I didn't mention the fact that I unlocked it with a key. I always carry three standards—a cheap padlock key, an oldtime trunk key, and an ordinary desk key. They're great time-savers if they happen to be the proper size.

We swung out the door and stepped into the dark.

I reached for the light-switch on the wall and a great weight struck my wrist, almost breaking it.

"Leave that alone!" the Dean whispered. "Don't move." He took three plumber's candles from his pocket and lighted them, moving with the greatest caution. "This place is a charnal house," he said. "I can smell it."

Celadine La Varre's gray coupe bulked before us in the flickering candlelight. Slumped in the seat, her head on the steering wheel, was the girl from the Hotel Lord

Ashton. Was this, I wondered, what my note had sent her to? She had been dead for some hours. Knifed—not strangled.

The Dean was unmoved and unsurprised. "She's come to the end of her crooked mile," he said softly. "She has been given what she gave her husband and now she is with him in those mythical beet fields."

"Sprigsey dead?" I gaped.

"For weeks."

"And you knew it?"

"And so did you, Ben. I myself told you that Celadine had slain her lord and master. That, of course, was the solution to the whole case. That exposes the identity of the man behind this ugly business."

"You know that, too?"

"Of course. And so should you. Anyway, you'll meet him face to face within the hour."

My wrist ached from the blow he had given me. "Hurt you a little, eh? Look here." The Dean pointed over his head.

Where the ceiling overhead light should have been there was plug—with a wire running to a workbench in the corner. The wire disappeared behind a small, shiny radio. We broke the connection and took a look.

The walnut veneer cabinet was cleaned out. Inside, were stacked seven sticks of dynamite, waiting for a contact spark. Very simple. You flick the light-switch and it's all over.

The Dean examined the bench. He rubbed his finger on a brownish stain and touched it to the tip of his tongue. "This was their shop, Ben," he said. "All the tools and materials have been moved. It is here their chemist designed his fires."

The fog had lifted. We caught a stray cab by luck, and relaxed. "Listen, Dean," I said. "Did you ever hear of the old device known as the spring-gun alibi?"

"Oh, come now, Ben." He looked at me with amusement.

"It's a fact. A guy sets a guntrap, kills his victim, and all the time he's making a speech at a charity banquet. No evidence against him and a perfect alibi."

"Are you pointing a finger of suspicion towards Mr. Hilliston Keith?"

I let him figure it out for himself.

"Listen," I said at length, "tell me this. Did you know we were heading for that dynamite tonight?"

"There's no danger in dynamite, Ben," the Dean said smugly. "It can't possibly explode unless you detonate it."

"You're nuttier than a keg of peanut brittle," I flared. "I don't know why I left the security of my alleys and garbage cans to work for you."

CHAPTER SIX

THE HOUSE ON THE ROOF

WAREHOUSE 29 was dark and menacing. We obscured ourselves in the shadows of the wharves and gave the building the once over. There was no glimmer of light from its shuttered windows, no indication of a watchman at his rounds. After a few minutes survey, we circled the rambling structure and approached from the rear.

A little prowling and we located the loading platforms. The Dean started up the steps toward the heavy corrugated shipping doors but I stopped him.

"Lesson two in breaking and entering," I whispered. "Expensive locks on doors, childish gadgets on windows." I flashed my light under the platform. It illumined the frame of a ventilator window.

Three seconds later, it was open. "Simple, isn't it?" I asked. I prayed it wasn't rigged up with an alarm.

"It's a squeeze," the Dean said. "But maybe I can make it." We wormed through and dropped to the floor.

We were in a huge basement storeroom. The cement floor was piled high to the ceiling with packing cases, barrels and crates. Narrow aisles, canyon-like, cut through the stacked merchandise in a rabbit warren of cross paths. We took a quick survey… canned goods, hardware, bolts of cloth, photographers supplies, china ware.

For the most part, the cases were nailed and banded and ready for shipping. Black lettering on the white pine showed us that they were headed for Central America.

The Dean nodded. "Well, Ben," he said softly, "here we have earned our fee from Solidarity. In this room is half a ship load of evidence—evidence of fraud. If this stuff can be identified—and there should be little difficulty—the merchandise, itself, will revert to the insurance company and outstanding unpaid claims will be voided."

"You mean these goods were looted from the insured stores before the fires?"

"Certainly. The racket appears to be worked on the European industrial plan of utilizing all by-products. Merely a sideline. They've Central America as a safe market."

A heavy ply-wood box blocked the path. It was about the size of an electric refrigerator and was tilted against an I-beam upright. The painted address on it was still wet. The address said: *Harley P. Reams, Beartrack, Wyoming.*

The Dean gazed at the box in fascinated silence. "It has to be," he said at last. "Think of that! Well, this is a surprise. An unlooked-for development." He turned to me and tapped the wooden case with a stubby forefinger. "Very valuable shipment, Ben. But incorrectly addressed." Wolfish wrinkles creased his eyes. "Want to take a look?" The cover was as yet unnailed. He lifted it.

I sensed something pretty shocking was coming but I wasn't braced for what I got. Inside the box, arms stiffly at his sides lay the fat little body of Michel André Cartier. He was packed neatly and firmly in a bed of excelsior. He had been knifed, as had been Celadine La Varre, in the throat. With his round cheeks and long lashes and cruel, simpering mouth he looked like some diabolical doll on a toyshop shelf.

Without a word, the Dean replaced the lid. He took a half-inch of blue crayon from his vest pocket and crossed out Mr. Reams of Beartrack. In swift strokes, he printed: *Lt. Bill Malloy, Police Headquarters, City Hall, City.* Down in one corner in bold heavy letters, he wrote, *PERISHABLE.*

"That's tampering with evidence," I exclaimed.

He grinned. "No didactics now, please, Ben. Let's go upstairs."

THE GROUND floor and the second floor were the same. More boxes, numbered but unaddressed. The top floor was empty. And when I say empty, I mean clean. Not a cobweb or a granule of dust.

"A clean floor leaves no footprints," the Dean remarked. "We'll explore a little."

An iron stairway, bolted to the back wall, led us to the roof. In the center of the roof, hidden from the street below by the brick facing which extended from the walls six feet above the roofline, was a small, one-room cabin. It lay in the moonlight like the superstructure on the deck of a boat. Yellow light flowed from the unshaded window. From where we stood, we could see gay wall paper and cretonne curtains, an army cot, a small safe and a desk.

At the desk sat Dorf, the gaunt man, checking down a ledger's page with a grimy thumb. By his elbow was a pile of currency that would have choked a horse.

The pebbled tar roofing made noisy walking, but we made the door without flushing him. Even after we had stepped into the room, our guns in our hands, it took him a split second to shake himself loose from his pipe dream.

He was speechless from surprise and anger. I slipped a cylinder gun—he had evidently finished with automatics—from his belt at the small of his back.

The Dean gazed at him pityingly. "You're an old-timer— a Westerner—you carry your gun for a backhand draw. Old-timers have a sense of loyalty. It's going to be hard to do business with you."

I put in: "This is the hooligan that gun-whipped me."

"Quiet, Ben," the Dean ordered gently. "Listen, old-timer. See that door? Get out. We're through with you. Good-bye."

The gaunt man stood motionless. Terror grew in his eyes and little flecks of foam gathered in the corners of his mouth.

"Go now," the Dean said kindly. "Good-bye."

"It's the old escaping-arrest gag," Dorf whispered hoarsely. "I been in Mexico—I know how it works. I won't reach that door."

I watched the Dean. He was perfectly capable of a one-man execution and I knew it. He had depths that couldn't be plumbed.

"I'll do business," Dorf said huskily. "Why not? I was a sucker to mix with you in the first place. I didn't want any part of you but they told me you could be handled. What do you want to know?"

The Dean took a little voile doll off the telephone and called police headquarters, asked for Malloy. He gave directions and hung up.

"I want to know what you were doing in this room. I know you don't live here. I know who does."

A harried, cornered look pinched the gaunt man's face. "I said I'd do business and I will. Here's the lay-out. There's the big boss, the guy that lives in this dump. Carter works for him. Me and Herb worked for Carter. The racket's smashed. I just dropped in—"

"To do a little farewell looting?" the Dean suggested. "I see. Figured on going into the blackmail business for yourself."

He couldn't deny it. A briefcase on the cot was crammed with letters. The top one said—

> I am doing this against my will. Now I am in it, I can see no way of getting out. Have your truck in the alley at ten tonight and the furs will be ready to move.
>
> John Beck

There was more of the same beastly stuff. Payments had been posted in the ledger.

I looked around.

In a waste basket under the table was an old mail-order catalog. Its pages had been sliced with a razor blade. "That's it," the Dean said. "He's really snared."

"Now, Dorf," he remarked, "you are in this up to your neck—but no murder. Right?"

"No killing, chief," Dorf said earnestly.

"You and Herb worked through Carter, the druggist. You took care of the strong-arm intimidation. You set the fires. You made the collections. But no knifing or strangling. Right?"

"As I breathe—"

There were crunching footsteps on the pebbled roof outside and Lieutenant Malloy sauntered through the door. Behind him came Hilliston Keith and his esoteric blonde.

HILLISTON KEITH'S flabby jowls were flushed with excitement. He elbowed the girl to one side and pushed his way to the forefront. "What's this all about, Rock? I demand to know. What do you mean, calling in the police without consulting me? Fortunately, I have some influence and was informed—"

"He tagged along," Malloy said dryly.

The Dean picked up the mutilated mail-order catalog. "Here," he said to Keith, "is the source of your anonymous tip."

The manager seemed taken by a sudden seizure of spasmic goodfellowship. "That's earning the fee, old boy!" He patted the Dean's back, attempted to put a chummy arm around his shoulders.

"Don't fondle me," the Dean snapped. "And don't get the impression that I'm being retained by you. We're working for Solidarity. I don't like you, never did, and never will. In my opinion you're just another untrapped skunk—if you grasp my meaning."

The blonde put in pertly: "I can grasp your meaning, Mr. Rock. This little girl can. She's getting to feel the same way."

"Break it up," Malloy barked. "What is this anyway? What's it all about? Who's this earless guy?"

"Permit me to inform you," the Dean said with relish. "This man is Dorf. He's a touch-off man for the arson syndicate. The ring is run by one man—but more about the higher-up later. Under this higher-up was his killer-chemist, Michel André Cartier, the Colorado druggist."

The Dean went on. "Michel André Cartier, alias John Charles Carter, was the man you were after in the Ortman killing. He killed Arabella Trimble, trailed her on her second visit to my apartment and strangled her on my living-room rug. For a newspaper clipping. It was Cartier who tore up my room—to attract the attention of the police to those books he stole from the rare-book department of the City Museum which he left in my steamer trunk to frame me. This is a guess, of course, but I am certain the curator of the museum will recognize Cartier when he identifies him at the morgue."

"So Cartier is dead," Malloy said.

The Dean nodded. "Yes, Lieutenant, there are two murders not yet brought to the attention of the police. It is the manipulator of the racket, the big-shot himself, who is responsible for these. These are personal killings. Cartier has been knifed. Also a girl known as La Varre."

"Keep talking," Malloy said.

A gay, boyish tenor from the door behind our backs called out: "Hello there, Mr. Berrymeadow!"

It was the freckled, drug-store gunsel. At his shoulder, light licking along the fifteen-inch barrel of a sawed-off shotgun, was our old friend, Daddy Melton, the feeblewit hobo. It took an effort to recognize him. Professional-looking rimless glasses were clipped to his nose and his cheeks were rosy from barber-shop massage. He was wearing as good tweed as ever crossed the Western Ocean. He was right out of Dunn and Bradstreet.

The Dean got out his Magnum and caught Melton in the arm as he tightened on the trigger. Melton meant to kill us all. You could tell by the cold glint behind those rimless glasses. Dorf chose this moment to make a break for the door—and blocked the full blast from the exploding shotgun with his chest. Lieutenant Malloy, standing erect and prim in model range-stance, pumped three rhythmic slugs into Melton's heart that could be covered with a dollar watch.

It seemed like I had poured myself a cold cup of tea. The freckled gunsel refused to annoy. From the first, he had stood with his hands in the air. "No trouble," he kept saying. "If Michel is finished, deal me out."

ABRUPTLY IT was all over and there was a vacuum. The blonde said: "There's a fortune teller on Front Street, Mr. Rock. A gentleman called Yogi Shakun-something. He uses little lumps of dirt and a cloth marked in squares like a checkerboard."

"He's not a Yogi," the Dean explained calmly. "He must be an Arabian *fakir*. I know what you mean. He tosses the dirt over his shoulder and looks to see what square it falls on. Then he refers to a certain table and does his calculating. It's a very old form of divination. It's a form of geomancy. I've never seen a geomancer," he mused. "They're very rare."

Malloy picked up the phone and called in. He walked over to Daddy Melton. "So that's the answer," he said coldly.

"Yes," the Dean said. "It's Fred Ortman."

"Ortman?" Keith gasped. "It's impossible!"

"Tell us, Rock," Malloy said.

The Dean glanced at his watch. "I'll have to cut this short. I feel that I'm going to have an engagement. Well, it's not too cheerful. Ortman didn't like married life and Solidarity's salary. He met and became infatuated with the attractive Mrs. Sprigsey O'Hare. Her husband was an ex-convict. Together they worked out a scheme of arson-blackmail that Ben can explain to you later. Ortman gave Sprigsey a job at the company, gained his friendship. The new racket was so successful that Ortman decided to withdraw from his old environment and expand. Sprigsey was lured to the Acme Photographers and strangled by Cartier. This was, of course, the charred substitute body found in the fire. Sprigsey's murder cut down the split and got Sprigsey out of the way." The Dean paused.

"Ben and I entered the case and things began to get warm. They worked Ben over, killed the old lady. Ortman took his wallet to Huey to throw suspicion on the missing Sprigsey. He knew Huey was a friend of mine, figured he would call me in. He put on a good act. He fooled me.

"Ortman got the wind up when Celadine lammed to him from the hotel—and killed her. He and Michel had already sent Keith the note and planted the dynamite in the shop. They drove the body there in the gray coupe. Anything else?"

"Yes," Malloy said acidly. "There are still two bodies missing."

"Oh! Miss La Varre." He gave the Ferry Street location. "Now, about Cartier. He was killed because he was weakening. Somehow he had picked up a big scare and was hysterical." The Dean hesitated. "Dead or alive, he's worth money Lieutenant. I'll make a trade. This is blackmail case. Publicity—the wrong kind of publicity—can hurt a lot of innocent people." Malloy's eyes were blank. The Dean, however, seemed satisfied. "The body's in the basement." He told them about the illicit merchandise addressed to Central America.

"Pardon me if I get in on this," I said "You've been saying all along you knew who was behind this. When did you find out?"

"Ben," the Dean said paternally, "I knew it was Ortman but I didn't know where he hid out. I knew it was Ortman ten minutes after he had left Huey's pawnshop. As soon as we had examined the wallet."

Malloy blinked.

I said: "But there were no fingerprints on the wallet. It had been rubbed with shoe polish."

"Now, look, Ben," the Dean explained. "Ortman's prints should have been on that leather plus Melton's. Two different sets. Ortman-Melton realized this and eliminated *all* prints. He gave himself away by being too careful. What about Sprigsey's prints, if Melton's story was true? Melton was Ortman, there was little doubt about that. Then whose body was found in the fire? Who was missing? Sprigsey."

"The lavender sachet?" I asked.

"An attempt to embroil Keith and his charming lady."

Hilliston Keith beamed. "When I clean up a job, I do it right. I'm a business doctor. Solidarity can never repay me—"

The Dean eyed him balefully. He bowed to the room at large and offered his arm to the blonde. She smiled that nice smile of hers and took it.

"You'll excuse us," the Dean said. "Ben can clear up the tag ends. We have to see a geomancer about some lumps of dirt."

YOU'RE IN MY WAY

TAKE AN UNDERTAKER'S SCRAPBOOK, A BUTCHER BIRD, FOUR LIPSTICKS, A DECK OF PLAYING CARDS, A LOOP OF STRING AND A LUMP OF PUTTY—THROW THEM ALL TOGETHER IN A HEAP, THEN FIND A MULE WHO DANCES ON HIS HIND LEGS TO CAVORT IN A GRISLY RIGADOON AROUND THE PILE. THAT'S WHAT THE DEAN DID—AND CLEANED UP A TANK TOWN THAT HAD GOTTEN TOO TOUGH IN THE PROCESS, TO SAY NOTHING OF SOLVING THE RIDDLE OF THE EMBALMER WHO EMBALMED THE EMBALMER

CHAPTER ONE
CURB SERVICE

ABOUT THE grisliest thing I've ever seen was this small-town undertaker's scrapbook. There was something goofy about it that made my skin crawl. I'm tenderloin born and raised and have pretty definite opinions. Something told me to lay off.

But the Dean claimed it was money in the bank—and the Dean's my boss.

Wardlow Rock is a private investigator who knows how to make money. We run a play that really brings in results. The boss tells fortunes as a front and has an under-the-rose connection with the police commissioner. The Dean's a simple-acting duffer and strangers write him down as strictly foggy. There are those, however, that have a different view of the matter. You should see him with a burr under his saddle. He carries a shoulder-gun in a holster as big as a carbine boot—and likes to use it. The strangest thing about him is his hobbies. He has a hundred accomplishments from paper-making to fletching. Me, I just know two things—guns and locks.

I was down and out and getting the wrong kind of notions, when the Dean picked me up and gave me a job. He said: "Ben, we'll make a good team. You're too dangerous to be running loose. Hop over on the right side of the law before you cause some damage." We've been together ever since.

I WAS stretched on the bed with a glass of ale and a saucer of parched corn when the little man in race-track checks fluttered through the reception-room doorway. The Dean was at his work-table in the corner, pointing a camel's hair brush on his lower lip and fighting a flake of gold leaf he was laying on an illuminated manuscript. Neither of us wanted to be disturbed.

The little man's eyes bugged and blinked. "Am I in the right place?" he asked.

"There's a limit to prophecy. Who knows?" The Dean put down his brush. He looked the visitor over with care. "Yes," he amended. "I think you are. I think I smell embalmer's fluid."

We've had some queer people in our reception-room. A fortune teller at-

The momentum of her twisting body threw her into Creegan as she fell.

tracts them all. We've had old ladies with omens that wanted to become picture stars. And butchers with dreams that wanted tips on the market. And swanky wenches with time on their hands that wanted to be told how fascinating they were. They dropped in at all hours of the night and day. And they all got the same thing—a little introductory speech from the Dean informing them that divination was the bunk, and then a scholarly job of forecasting according to the formulae. If the Dean liked them, the fee was negligible. If they displeased him, it was outrageously high.

Our caller stood with his shoulder hunched and his arm clamped across his stomach. My first impression was that he had been shot but then I saw that he was carrying something underneath his coat. His chin was cocked to one side and his whole stance was strained in an attitude of listening. It's hard to tell you what I mean but the tilt of his head gave the picture of a man, say, in the swamps who has outsmarted the dogs.

"Which one of you gentlemen is Mr. Wardlow Rock?" he asked.

The Dean wagged his hand. From then on, I was completely ignored. "I understand, Mr. Rock," he said, "that you tell fortunes." He was being foxy.

The Dean studied him intently. "That's right."

"That you are an adept in the occult sciences?"

"No," the Dean corrected pleasantly. "You've been misinformed. I've never been able to encounter any occult science. I have, it is true, occupied myself in a small way with various branches of ancient divination—but solely as crafts and sleights. Between you and me, it's hooey."

The little man went into a spasm of facial motions. He pulled down a tremulous eyebrow and inflated his cheeks. "Caution! Caution!" he admonished. "There are things beyond the comprehension of the mortal mind. Things demoniacal!"

The Dean led him on. "Pshaw!" he exclaimed affably. "Malevolent demons! I know about them all. Their signs, their sabbats, their theurigic hymns. All of them—from Prince Thenth to Prince Meresin." The tone of his voice got confidential. "The whole covey of them together couldn't trip a ten-cent mousetrap." He produced the snipe of a thin, black Cuban cigar, tucked it in the corner of his mouth and got it going. "Have they been bothering you?"

The story came out. Our visitor was named Mervin J. Kutchin. He was plenty bothered—but not by evil demons. He was worrying about the death of his brother Arnold.

It seemed, as near as we could piece it together, that Mervin and Arnold were small-town undertakers from the nearby county seat of Palmersville. Arnold had died suddenly, two weeks ago—he had been swiped by a hit-and-run. His skull had been fractured. Until the demise, the brothers had been in business together—partners.

Kutchin placed a fifty-dollar bill on the marble-topped table. "I want you to contact Arnold's spirit. I want to ask him a question. One question."

The Dean's risorial muscles twitched. He was getting ready for a backtrack. "It'll be difficult," he meditated. "Voyance isn't my strongest specialty—but I believe we can do it. What's the question?"

Kutchin was disturbed. "If you don't have the faith— The circle must be complete, you know."

"I know. Now what's the question?"

The little undertaker faltered. "Ask him why he locked that lump of putty in the safe."

"A lump of putty!" the Dean roared. "You're wasting my time."

The Dean was right. I used to be trouble-shooter for a safe company. You find strange things in safes. Take baby shoes, for instance. Many a safe has a pair of baby shoes in it. The Dean bore down on him. "Anything else—no trivia, please."

Kutchin hesitated, decided to take the plunge. "This book." He unbuttoned his coat and slid out a large, flat folio. It was an ordinary scrapbook, the sort that can be picked up on the counters of any variety store. The Dean's face flushed. It was what he had been working for.

Hardly was it out in the open than he had it grasped in his big blunt fingers.

"What does it mean?" Kutchin asked. "Turn to the back."

The Dean took it swiftly and systematically. In the center of the title page was enscribed in spidery copperplate the single word: *Alstetter.*

"This was my brother's work," Kutchin explained. "He was a bit eccentric."

THE BOOK was a collection of clippings. Death notices cut from newspapers. Page after page of obituaries, arranged in columns and pasted neatly by their corners. Dozens of them. Farmers, tradesmen, women, children. All ages and classes. And the causes of death were as varied as the subjects themselves—tetanus, old age, electric wires, horse-kick, ptomaine.

"From our county paper," the undertaker remarked. "Turn to the last page."

There were but two clippings on the final page. The first item was a flowery eulogy—

> A pall of grief sombered the hearts of the citizens of Palm-ersville last night when it was learned that Mrs. Lucinda Frost, one of the city's most active socialites, died at her home before she could be removed to the hospital, following an accident.
>
> Mrs. Frost, née Markham, daughter of the late Paulus Monroe

Markham, civic benefactor and philanthropist, had but recently returned to Palmersville after an absence spent in New
Orleans. Her return was an unexpected pleasure and her sudden
passing a shocking tragedy to the entire county.

Mrs. Frost was most active in guiding the town's social and
cultural aspirations, acting as President of The Golden Moment
Chamber Music Group, the Garden Society, the Mane and
Fetlock, the Young Girls' Vocational Institute and the Chim-
neycorner Book Circle.

She is survived by her husband Manfred Frost.

The Dean tapped the page. "How did this one go?"

Mervin Kutchin showed a row of little doll's teeth in a
cornsilk-cigarette-behind-the-barn leer. "It isn't generally known. But I have it from a confidential and reliable
source that the cortex of her brain was unnaturally flushed,
that the neuronic synapses were extended, inhibiting the
nervous impulse from axon to dendrite in such a fashion
as to make her muscular articulation erratic."

The Dean took this patiently. "She was drunk, eh?"

The undertaker flicked his eye at me to make sure that
I was in on the scandal. "So they say."

The Dean pursued the point. "What was the accident?
Not hit-and-run like brother Arnold, was it?"

Kutchin went soggy. Like one of his own cut-rate jobs
of embalming. It was a sickening thing to watch. The Dean
had really driven a wedge. The self-righteous smirk dropped
from his mouth. You could see it dawn on him. The fear
that he had been trying to submerge came out of the
caverns of his mind and took possession of him. He'd been
living with terror for a long time and now it had him.
"Yes," he acknowledged, "it was." He tried to pass it off
with a gesture. "Just a coincidence, of course. She stepped

from the curb in front of her home and was struck. She was dazed. Arnold was hit in the alley behind the morgue."

He got himself under control. "This scrapbook, Mr. Rock—it's an enigma. Arnold kept it for years. All of a sudden, a few weeks ago, he became terribly excited over it. He said it contained the power to make us wealthy. He wouldn't say how. Does it mean anything?"

The last clipping in the book said—

Visits in Birdland

No. 12

This week, in our pilgrimage through the kingdom of our feathered friends, we meet Butcher Bird, the body-snatcher.

The Butcher Bird, or Northern Shrike, or, to give him his proper Latin appellation, *Lanius borealis,* is a true ghoul and gets his name from his custom of impaling the corpses of his prey upon thorns. The observant nature-lover strolling along rustic lanes frequently encounters the bodies of field mice or small birds hanging spiked from thorny bushes or barbwire fencing. Here is gruesome evidence that Butcher Bird hunts in these haunts.

This was the step-off. It was this little idyl, so neatly scissored and tabbed, that scared me. And I don't scare much easier than the next man. Coming as it did, at the end of a long list of death notices, it was so meaningless and yet so hideous that it was like the slap of a wet towel.

"What's that doing in there?" I exclaimed. "That's no obituary!"

"You're wrong, Ben," the Dean said queerly. "It is, I fear, the obituary of Arnold Kutchin." He turned to our visitor. "Can you give me any reason, any reason at all, why your brother might sanely collect death notices? Are these, by any chance, records of bodies embalmed by your establishment?"

The little man looked sly. "Arnold was tricky," he bragged. "Not one of those bodies was prepared by us. For three years there has been a competitor in town. Whenever we missed a cadaver and our rival got it, Arnold clipped out the information from the paper. Get the idea? We could keep a check on our competitor's turnover. We could estimate gross income and annual profit. The last item, about the bird, I don't understand."

The Dean drew back his lips in a mirthless, lupine grin. "So this book registers 'no sale.' These are the ones that got away!" Quick as a flash he whisked the fifty from the table and thrust it in his pocket. "I'll answer your question for you—not as a medium but as an investigator. Your brother was murdered, an amateur blackmailer nipped in his bud. More information will cost you more money."

The Dean paused. A wistful look came into his bleak eyes. "You wouldn't be interested in paying fifteen thousand dollars to have the whole thing cleared up, would you?" He sighed. "I was afraid not. Well, take your blackmailing brother's prying book and get out. I'm through with you. Pull your freight. Now!"

Ten seconds later I observed: "That was the bum's-rush if I ever saw one—and I've seen some beauties."

"Ben"—the Dean was excited—"there's money in this waiting to be collected. Big money." He hesitated, looked foolish, and added: "But I'm not just sure whom to collect it from. Or why."

"You'd better turn in and get some rest," I said. "You're suffering from habromania. Which name means delusions of an agreeable nature. And if you don't want me to read your books and broaden my vocabulary—don't leave them laying around."

I'M JUST toweling off my bedtime shower when Lieutenant Malloy called. Captain Kunkle was chiseling in at his elbow. Malloy was as good a cop as you'll find in any city and maybe a little better than you'll find in most—but he didn't like free-lance operators. Our tie-in with the commissioner was gall to him. Added to this, the Dean's record of bringing in quick, clean results made him seethe. Malloy's outstanding ability, on the other hand, kept us fighting for the rail. He was a source of constant irritation to the Dean. They made a formidable pair and were as jealous as a couple of prima donnas. Captain Kunkle was small-caliber, in fact buckshot, compared to his lieutenant.

The Dean sat up in bed, his old-fashioned nightshirt askew, and fumed.

Captain Kunkle, prim and foppish, drew himself erect. He spread his hands according to position seven in the old school of elocution and zoomed into a torrent of Third Ward oratory. "Like a Vestal lamp, burning always in devotion to civic security, you have repeatedly proven to this progressive community your interest in its better-ment—"

The Dean turned icily to me. "Can you explain all this, Ben?"

"Well," I suggested, "here's one explanation. A circus train has been derailed. The animals are loose."

"I'll answer that when I'm off duty," Malloy retorted. "Put on your pants. We're going down to the station."

The Dean blew up. "Not me. If you've anything to say get it over with."

Captain Kunkle fought his way back into the spotlight. "There was a guy, a gentleman, socked at your curb by an unidentified driver an hour or so ago. Just died at the hospital. Made a little statement and we're checking on it. That's all—just checking. Gentleman insisted he was murdered, so to speak. Said it was intentional. Nonsense. Mumbled your name. Help us please, Rock."

The Dean seemed mildly sad. "Think of that! Mervin Kutchin—undertaker—Palmersville. Didn't know him personally. He'd just borrowed a scrapbook of mine. Did he have it with him? Good. Ship him back to Palmersville and let his rival fancy him up. The embalmer embalms the embalmer."

Malloy wasn't diverted. "About this book—"

"Just leave it at the commissioner's office, if it's not too much trouble. I'll pick it up later."

CHAPTER TWO

THE CALL OF THE BUTCHER BIRD

NEXT MORNING, half through breakfast, the Dean laid down his knife and fork.

"We're leaving, Ben," he said. "This minute—for Palmersville." On the way to the garage to rent a car, he went into detail. "This is a case that can't be solved unless we are on the spot. It's a confusing case and I'll tell you why. There have been, to our knowledge, three murders and each victim, an ordinary, average, normal person, has been slain by professional killers—doubtless for professional reasons."

"Professionals?" I exclaimed. The whole affair seemed definitely amateur to me. It had the appearance of one of those crazy expanding kill-sequences that bunglers get into. One of those chains that run havoc because of the very ineptitude of the killer. And that indicates the non-professional.

"So I believe. This is an example, pure and simple of the functioning of organized crime. By that I mean just what I say. The victim is eliminated because he jeopardizes some criminal corporation. Now here's a thought for you, to complicate matters further. It is my conviction that of the three victims, not one of them at the moment of their murder could have told you who killed them or why!"

"That makes it tough!"

"On the contrary, it makes it much easier. When you touch the fringe of such a corporation you touch its heart. These three victims have been worked upon by the skilled craftsman and they bear the toolmarks of his trade."

PALMERSVILLE AND our town are almost twin cities. Our town is over a hundred thousand, of course, and Palmersville is about three thousand. It is the county seat of the adjoining county and its city line almost touches ours. A part of the town, the vice district, projects like a scrofulous finger right up to our back door. Many a torpedo raids us from Palmersville. The set-up is ideal from a commuter's standpoint.

It wasn't hard to tell when you were there. The stretch of good highway ended and you were driving over a crooked job of contracting. The road was as cracked and rough as the icing on a bride's cake. The berm ended in scummy ditches and was flanked by swamps and trash dumps. There was about a quarter-mile of this and then we hit a cluster of weathered buildings and passed the gambling joints and honky-tonks. When you've peddled papers as a kid around the spots you get so you can size up a neighborhood pretty quick. I can read a poolroom through its window about like the Dean can go down a column of Mandarin character.

Something told me that the underworld here was clicking. That means a lot of things. First of all it means monopoly—no price wars, no competition. It means that one outfit is handling the entire production. This means plenty of strong-arm. You can't handle this sort of business with lump sugar and a pat on the head. The town was tough.

"What do you think?" the Dean asked.

"I hate to tell you. It's a good place to go armed."

"Are you, by the way?"

I grinned. The Dean seemed satisfied. He carried, I knew, his .357 with its half-pound trigger pull. He was never without it.

"The first thing," the Dean remarked, "is to locate a fifteen-thousand-dollar client. I have a feeling the surviving husband can be of assistance here."

Events proved him wrong.

Manfred Frost, according to the city directory at a neighborhood drug store, resided at the corner of Adams and Maple Streets. The location was easy to find. One of those anachronisms you run across in small towns—a mansion, complete with iron stag and lilac hedges, smack in the center of the business district. It was one of old Paulus Monroe Markham's philanthropies to himself, built in the early nineteen hundreds, a pile of brick turrets and limestone verandas. It sat back fifty yards or so, in a weedy unkempt lawn. At the rear of the house you could see the gable of its bright red stable and back of that, across the alley, rose the grated windows of the county jail.

Paulus Monroe Markham had bequeathed it to his daughter Lucinda. Lucinda had died and passed it on to Manfred. Manfred had sold it down the river.

We parked the car, got out and stared. In the middle of the lawn, shiny with new paint, stood a huge wooden sign which read—ALSTETTER FUNERAL HOME

"My!" The Dean was startled. Suddenly he seemed immensely pleased. "So that's the Alstetter—the rival undertaker who inspired Arnold Kutchin's scrapbook. Let's go in. This'll be an experience."

The Dean's a hard man to understand. Last night he was all in smoke over the book, lying to officers of the law about it. This morning at breakfast when I mentioned it, he showed no interest at all. "Let it lie at the commissioner's office," he remarked. "I can work on it better from a distance." That, I might add, turned out to be the truth.

Now it was cropping up again.

We took a glazed brick walk to the porch, crossed flagstone and entered a bare, gilded foyer. Graceful cherry stairs with a ram's-horn newel ascended at our right and made a U-turn to the second story. The place was desolate. It had been stripped, the furnishings sold. Screw holes in the wall-facing told of the removal of a pier glass. The floors were carpetless.

Through a half-open door, Italian carved in deep floral relief, we wandered into what had been the library. It was now the office of Alstetter, Mortician.

A man sat at the desk. He was dressed in the conservative gray suiting of the semi-successful businessman. A pince nez dangled from one of those old time spring-and-chain gadgets on his vest. He was amusing himself in a curious way. He had a piece of string which he would cast in snarls upon the desk-top in such a manner that it fell in loops, the ends being retained in his hand. Again and again, he gathered the string in and tossed it out.

He dropped it as we entered, whipped down his glasses and pinched them on the bridge of his pudgy nose. He glared at us in baleful silence.

The Dean diagnosed him with obvious distaste. "You Alstetter?" he barked.

The man gave his head a single curt negative shake.

"Well, produce him. I want to talk to him."

The man gritted ill-made dentures into effective speaking position and said: "Out."

"When will he be in?"

The man ignored us. He stood up, lifted his hat from the mantel, took a card from the desk drawer and hung it on the doorknob. The card said—*Gone To Lunch.*

He did not go out to lunch, however. He went up the circular staircase to the second story.

Rarely have I seen the Dean so infuriated.

A LITTLE directional gossiping on the drag uncovered the information that Frost, broken up by his wife's death, had put her homestead on the block, lock, stock and barrel, and had moved to Lockbridge Court.

Lockbridge Court, out on the edge of town, was the best thing—in fact the only thing—the town had to offer in the way of apartments. It was so new that the walnut stain on the pine finishing still smelled of alcohol. Jerry-built. White stucco with a red off-plumb roof and a crack under the front door big enough to roll a .38. To one side of the entrance, about chest-high, a little plate sticking out on a strip of curlicued metal said—*Superintendent.*

We went down six steps below sidewalk level and pushed a doorbell.

The duck that opened the door was glad to see us. He was holding a pretzel and a bottle of strawberry pop. His clothes whispered hard times. His trousers bagged and the rims of his cuffs were positively furry. He dragged out a bunch of keys, waved them in our face and said, "Can I show you something," before we had a chance to open our mouths.

The Dean exposed a five-dollar bill, pleated it into a bow-tie, twisted it into a corkscrew, and returned it to a vest pocket. "I'm a hard man to please."

The superintendent set himself for a sales talk. "We like them that way. That means they're elite. So was Mr. Manfred Frost when he came—you know who he is, of course. He had a terrible blow. His wife died. Came straight to me and said, 'Harmer'—that's me—'Harmer, I want to put up in genteel rest and quiet because my old home is now ashes in my mouth—'"

"I'm a hard man to please," the Dean interrupted. "We don't want to engage one of your charming suites—not just now. Quite possibly later. At the present we want but one thing. Five minutes conversation with the very gentleman you're mentioning."

Harmer looked alarmed. "Mr. Frost is difficult of access."

"So I presumed. That's why we came to you." The Dean laid the five on his broad palm and added a ten. The superintendent was embarrassed. He purpled. "It's impossible. He's not here. He went away on a short business trip."

The Dean seemed troubled. "Is that so? My! Too bad. We've come to do him a mighty important favor. I suppose there's no chance of getting into his quarters for a few minutes?"

Harmer went over the falls in a barrel. "Do him a favor, eh?"

The Dean winked. "Don't let's go into it. It's a little personal. Such is life!"

The tiny, two-room apartment was on the third floor, stuck way back in the cul-de-sac of a T-shaped corridor. Harmer waited nervously outside while the Dean and I gave it a quick frisk. To turn a room off properly requires experience and it was a pleasure to watch the Dean work. He quartered like a ginger setter.

We found some interesting things—and it didn't take a Kentucky bird dog to point them. Two pairs of chiffon hose hung from the inside doorknob. Three sizes of frocks hung in the closet of the bedroom-living-room. A Spanish comb lay on the dressing-table and photos of five different gals were stuck in the mirror. Four lipsticks, each a different shade, were lined up on the sill of the kitchen window. The Dean crackled with anger. "The lipsticks, Ben. Note the lipsticks."

"Manfred Frost—just a broken-hearted hermit," I said.

There was a time-table in the waste basket, checked in blue pencil—*Palmersville to New Orleans*. Beneath the time table were fragments of a torn letter. Assembled, it read—

Darling Widower—
Sell out and come South. The magnolias are in bloom. We
have been separated too long.
                    Love,
                        H.

The Dean's jaw went rigid. "We've been chiseled," he grated. "We've been rooked out of our fifteen-thousand-dollar fee."

The superintendent rapped on the door. "Time's up!" he called.

"Floor nurse says go home. Visiting hours over." The Dean grinned. "We've mislaid a client but I think we're on the spoor of our criminal. Let's go."

WE HAD to sleep somewhere and the Farmers and Commercial House was the only hostelry in town. It was on a side street, back out of heavy traffic. The neighborhood smelled of horses and decay. Across the street a tin-fronted building had been converted into a dime-a-drink recreation hall. There was no lobby to the Farmers. Just a door set between two dingy shops. A half-dozen broken-down kitchen chairs were set out on the sidewalk for the hotel's guests. It looked pretty bad to me but the Dean was charmed.

"This is our home, Ben," he exclaimed. "Here we stay."

I parked the car at the curb and waited at the wheel while he ran in to give it a casing. I knew just how he was working. He'd put on his crackpot expression and in three minutes he'd learn from the clerk a complete action plan of the establishment—fire-escape, basement, roof and kitchen.

I was sitting there in the sunlight, slumped on the cushions, thinking how I hadn't liked the case from the beginning, when this sailor in a peajacket comes out of the recreation hall across the street.

At first, I hardly noticed him. He was staggering drunk and his kisser was frozen in a smile a yard wide. He stumbled off the pavement, caracoled to the center of the narrow street, pulled up about two feet from my radiator. Still grinning, he produced the smallest harmonica I ever saw. About an inch long. He put on an act. He tossed the harp in his mouth and pretended to swallow it. All at once he was playing sweet music. *La Paloma.*

It was a neat trick. I waved. He waved back, as pleasant as you please—and then surprised me. He walked up the avenue as sober as a judge.

A vicious snarl said at my back: "Concert's finished. Don't move!" The machinery was smooth in Palmersville.

I eased my head around. A gunsel with skin like wet paper was resting a .45 on my car door. The lad was really carrying pressure. He was stoked up until the needle bent and crying for a chance to go to town. His eyes played over me from shoe strings to hat brim and I'll swear he couldn't focus on a thing. He was dusted to the ear lobes. "Be good," he ordered. "We're on our way." He piled in the back and leaned forward on the seat. I could smell violet breath perfumers. "Start your engine!"

"Scrabble, bum!" I said.

"I here tell you carry a bulldog and handle it passably well," he baited. "You wouldn't want to take a chance in a raffle would you? It comes in my contract." He was begging me to get myself slaughtered.

I tried to catch the Dean in the rear-view. No luck. He probably had some menial cornered and was unloading a lecture on the conjuring books of Great and Little Albert. We drove away unmolested.

Three blocks and he stopped me—behind a shoe factory.

I took a flier at detecting. "You wouldn't be the Butcher Bird, would you?"

"Nuts!" he said. "You'll think so, if you don't cut the chatter and leave me do the talking." He got organized. "Now here's the way it is. There's a party in this town that understands you and Rock are here trying to make murder out of the Kutchin kill. Now that's disagreeable to this party. This party don't want nothing stirred up." An envelope slid over my shoulder and dropped in my lap. "There's ten grand. It's the top and only price. Take it back to your boss and the two of you leave the county."

"Listen, hophead," I said, "money never did and never will buy the Dean off a case. Make him the proposition personally and he'll break your jaw."

A flicker of shadow on the windshield told me it was coming. I tried to turn and meet it but I was too late. I got a whiff of violet breath tablets. The thug leaned forward, one grimy hand grabbed up the envelope—and about twelve pounds of gun-sight caromed off my skull behind my ear.

The next thing I knew I was sitting in our room at the Farmers and Commercial House, trimming a hangnail on my thumb. I discovered later that I drove back, parked the car in a lot nearby, chatted with the clerk, and wobbled into our quarters as white as a sheet.

"So he took the money. And then what?" the Dean asked.

"Who?" I inquired.

"The man."

"What man?"

The Dean had been ghost writing a banquet address for the police commissioner. He screwed up his fountain pen. "Don't bother. I presumed you had reached the end of your narrative. Ours is a lively profession, Ben. Lively." He drew down his shaggy brows in concentration. "We'll have to step warily. I've made the mistake of underrating our opposition. These babies are big-time."

That was like the Dean. To take the blame on his own shoulders. For a moment I forgot that I'd been played for a sucker.

THEY BROUGHT us supper in our room—a special and extraordinary service for such a rustic inn. To our astonishment it was top-notch. Steak about the size of a bath mat, a sheaf of spring onions, and a bowl of peas and new potatoes. I stood at the window and looked out over the city roofs. If you want to understand a small town, look down upon its business section—the gingerbread false fronts and the cheap crenelated facades.

"I've been brooding," the Dean remarked, "about that misanthrope at the Alstetter funeral home. The man with the string and the grab-bag false teeth. I tell you Ben, that's one reason I don't like to operate in small towns. You can't tell what sort of person you'll run into. Now take this megalomaniacal businessman—"

I cut him off with a horse laugh. "You're a swell detective. That boy wasn't a businessman—and he isn't small-town." I gave it a minute to sink in. "Now I'll tell *you* something. Rackets, real rackets, are as old as the hills. Kidnaping, bank robbery, dope running—and the like—are not, strictly speaking, real rackets. The meaning of the word got switched, I believe, around about the prohibition era. Real rackets are flimflams or juggling tricks and are the livelihood of small-time grifters. You've seen the pitchman on the sidewalk, selling his wares with what looked like a butcherknife stuck through his arm? You know how that's done, of course. You should. You've got a diagram of the gimmick in a book in your library. It was written and published in England before the Pilgrims landed at Plymouth Rock. The book was written as an exposé but the play is still going strong."*

The Dean pretended amusement.

---

* Reginald Scot, *The Discoveries of Witchcraft*, London, 1584.

"Don't give me that," I said. "It's information to you and you know it is. I'll name three rackets coining money today and I'll bet you a burnt-leather pillow-top that you have never heard of any of them. First, the pencil? No? Well, it's an ordinary-looking octagonal pencil, each side a different color. A guy loafing in a pool room idly rolls it on a pool table and the red side comes up. He rolls it again. Again red. Bets eager bystanders it'll repeat. They figure they are getting eight-to-one odds and cover him. It's gaffed, of course. If he rolls it overhand it comes up red—underhand the other seven colors.... Another racket is working the chive. I'll explain this one to you some other time. It is foolproof too."

"And the third?" the Dean asked casually. He was hooked.

"The third is the string. A bimbo throws it out in loops. You bet him, put your finger in a loop, and he pulls. If you've picked a loop that catches, you win. The trick is that he can throw it in what looks like a tangle but is so arranged that no loop will catch. It sounds simple but it takes a lot of practice. You don't stand a chance."

"You are getting around to what?"

"To the simple fact that the geezer at Alstetter's has at one time lived by his wits. He can't break his old habit of keeping sharp with his string. If you ask me, he's probably got a record. He's eaten off many an iron table, as the boys say."

"Gad! You're right! You're right!" The Dean grabbed his hat. "Of course! It all fits in. It's the Markham house again for us. This time we'll try the rear."

WE TURNED into the alley at a Greek shoe-shine stand. Half a block and we were back of the jail. Across the cobblestones was the bright red Markham stable, enclosed on either side by a seven-foot board fence. The Dean thrust his hand through a hole cut in the gate, unfastened a halter-latch. We stepped around the corner of the carriage house and found ourselves in the backyard.

The old mansion was pretentious from the front but it had patches on the seat of its pants. We were standing in a junk heap of bottles, tin cans and rusty bed-springs. The only thing that saved the picture was the girl that was sitting on the porch steps.

She wore some sort of medical smock and held a cigarette, long-shoreman's style, cupped in the palm of her hand. She was having a quiet little smoke alone and didn't care much to be disturbed.

When I looked at her skin in the sunlight I thought of how the Dean once told me that the ancients possessed the secret of molding ivory.

I saw the Dean's eyes glint—he appreciated beauty when he saw it. I figured that he'd open with his Southern Gentleman act but he skipped the routine. He studied her for a moment and then said somberly: "Where's Alstetter?"

She raised long curling lashes and looked at him. "I'm Alstetter."

"I knew it," the Dean said. "I knew it as soon as I saw you. You're no ordinary person. It had to be you."

"A woman undertaker!" I exclaimed. "Who—"

"Quiet, Ben." He produced a card—and wonder of wonders—it was his own. "I'm Wardlow Rock and this is my assistant, Ben Matthews." He laid the card upon her knee. The card was the Dean's idea of a business card. It was wholly filled, on both sides, with advertising matter in small type. It listed a dozen or so forms of primary and secondary divination interspersed with the Dean's own comments and evaluations.

She read it through. Every word. "It says here that you are a student of Onomancy—"

"Name?" the Dean asked brusquely.

"Jane."

"Is that so? Too bad." The Dean shook his bearish head. "Onomancy, not to be confused with nomatechny, or prognostication from names, hasn't much to say in favor of Jane. The occultists don't like that name. It's too mixed. Tender at times. At other times it marks excess, sensuality and general viciousness. It's the feminine phase of John, which comes from the Hebrew Yehokhanan and which carries the signature of self-control, honesty and lofty ideals. Jane is a bad name. John is a good one. It's regrettable that your parents didn't name you John."

He was trying to throw her off her poise but it was no dice. She was amused. "If you'll pardon my changing the subject," the Dean added, "we understand that Mr. Frost once lived here."

"He did," she answered casually. "Until his wife died. Then he sold to me and moved to Lockbridge Court. The place here had unhappy associations for him. Mr. Frost, I understand, is a very sentimental person."

"Then you don't know him?"

"Only through business deals."

"Ah!" The Dean beamed. "And speaking of business relationships, who is the gentleman inside holding the desk, the man with the warped dentures?"

She smiled and got to her feet. "Now you'll have to excuse me. I'm in the middle of a job."

The Dean remarked: "That wouldn't be Mervin Kutchin, would it? He was murdered on my doorstep last night. How's he coming out?"

"Beautifully." She paused. "What do you mean murdered. It was an accident?"

The Dean slacked out and came in on a tack. "The hounds are loose, Jane Alstetter. You'd better come in on our side. There's yet time."

She turned to me. "He talks like a valedictorian of a dramatic school. Is he crazy?"

"Yes, he is," I agreed. "Like a fox."

She gave me a slow goodnatured wink, shook her head in mock concern, and swung voluptuously from our sight through the latticed doorway into the kitchen.

Back in our car, I said: "Wasted time. She doesn't know a thing."

The Dean snorted. "Her knuckles, Ben. They were as bloodless as ice. She was paralyzed with terror. We've quite possibly saved a life."

THE REST of the evening, until we turned in, we sat in our stuffy bedroom and waited. Waiting for local buyers. Like a couple of traveling salesmen displaying their wares.

No one showed up.

This was a good example of the chaotic way the Dean did business. Undertakers were embalming each other's corpses, loogans were clipping me on the head with gun barrels, a murder syndicate was measuring us for our pelts—and we sat placidly on our fundaments hoping that strangers in a strange town would come rushing in with a tip that would explain everything.

"I don't know why they don't come," the Dean said petulantly. "They know we're here."

"They certainly do." I tried to be pleasant. It was hard. My head was splitting. "Who are we expecting? Or is it a secret?"

"I have half expected the murderer— the head man—to drop in. But I guess he won't. Oh well, tomorrow is another day."

"Take this murderer," I philosophized. "You want to see him. Check. But"—I put a lot of stress in it—"does he want you to see him? There are two sides to everything, remember."

The Dean yawned. "That's right. Always platitudes." Suddenly he went rigid. "Ben, my boy, you've just about solved this case for us. Do you realize what you said?"

"I said you wanted to see him but does he want to be gazed upon?"

"Not that. The other thing." He clicked out the light and crawled between the sheets. "It isn't the identity of the murderer that concerns me. It's the Butcher Bird business. And thanks to you we'll have that settled before long."

CHAPTER THREE
TWO SIDES TO EVERYTHING

THE NEXT day sawed it off. We got up about nine. I'd been awake for an hour, trying to make sense of it, before the Dean showed signs of life. Abruptly, he rolled to his feet, he batted his eyes, dragged his Magnum from beneath his pillow and inspected it. Then he got dressed and the way he did it gave me goose flesh. He shaved and primped until you'd think he was headed for matrimony. After that, he pawed through his luggage, located a little chamois bag and got out his precious diamond cuff links. That was the touch-off as far as I was concerned. Those cuff links were his outstanding vanity. It reminded me of when I was a kid and how my aunt always put on a clean petticoat when she went to town—so if she was taken dead she'd look her best.

"Are we attending a fiesta?" I inquired.

The Dean was humming a gay tune. He stopped. "We're giving one. And it'll be quite a jubilee, I suspect."

He watched me while I slid the idea under the microscope and approved it. I grinned. Action is something that I can appreciate. "It's about time."

The clerk behind the desk wanted to gossip. "Now wait a minute," the Dean declaimed. He slid our key across the register. "Everything in its proper time and place. You want to converse—I want to listen. But first I desire to send a telegram. Have you facilities?" The clerk produced a pad of blanks. The Dean wrote our landlady's address. He considered a second and added: *Seraphina—Please go office commissioner of police and demand scrapbook of obituaries stop Don't take any back talk stop Am sending cab driver for it will pay him this end stop Hope new arches giving feet relief stop Respectfully yours—*

The clerk was busy reading it upside down. "How does it sit?" the Dean asked politely.

"It's your telegram," the clerk suggested, "but you could say 'Go commissioner demand scrapbook send here.' That's six words. Then, maybe, 'Much love to all.' That would make a nice message and only ten words."

"Very ingenious," the Dean complimented. "But we'd better send my version. Can you secure a taxi for the mission? Good. Now what were you about to say before I interrupted you?"

"I was going to mention the gentleman that wanted to see you last night."

The Dean composed his face. "I'm afraid you're traveling a little fast for me. I don't know what you're talking about. What gentleman?"

"This man that came in last night and asked for you. He stood right where you're standing and said he wanted to see Mr. Rock. Well, I thought it over and decided that you'd probably had a hard day and needed a little undisturbed rest. So I told him you weren't in."

"So the Farmers House offers clinic service. That's something I hadn't exactly calculated on." The Dean gave me the sign to keep silent. "Who was this caller?"

"Now that I couldn't tell you. I'm new in town."

"How did he look?"

"Now that I couldn't tell you. Take a man in a Vandyke and no one knows how he looks. It disguises him. It hides scars and tattoos."

"It certainly does," the Dean agreed heartily. "How big was he?"

"He wasn't big. Not any taller than I am. He just seemed big because he was so enormously fat."

We were half a block away, headed for breakfast, when our new helper rushed up behind us pounding the sidewalk with his heels. "Excuse! Excuse!" he called. We stopped. "Silly old me." He grimaced, rolling his eyes and tapping his temple. "I almost forgot. The gentleman left an epistle."

The note, in a sealed envelope, was unsigned. It said: *If you are interested in earning a liberal fee easily and honestly see me at number 14½ Orchard Alley.*

ORCHARD ALLEY was in the bottleneck section of town, the district that stuck out towards the county line, the tough section. It was the neighborhood we had driven through yesterday when we arrived. Early forenoon and the pool halls and beer joints were doing a boom-town trade. "It must be payday," the Dean observed.

"Every day is payday here," I answered. "This neighborhood is geared. It's a gold mine."

Number 14½ turned out to be a shabby storeroom—and a vacant one at that. It's front door, propped open with a paving brick said come in, but the general atmosphere said be careful. The building, at first glance, looked like an old derelict, poor but respectable, its blistered paint peeling, its windows screened with chicken wire. Your eye hardly caught the strip of metal set close to the window sash. The burglar alarm was new—and expensive. I pointed it out to the Dean. "I don't like this drum," I said.

"Let's go in," he answered.

We went in. An ape with a bucket and a washrag came out of the gloom at the rear and started sponging down the rows of empty shelves. The lump in his hip pocket wasn't a book-end.

"Would you inform me—" the Dean began.

The ape bared green-filmed teeth and took a greasy card out of his hat. The card proclaimed in cheap printing: *I AM DEAF AND DUMB. I CAN NEITHER READ NOR WRITE.*

Piggish eyes watched our reaction.

The Dean said quietly: "I'm Wardlow Rock. I have an appointment here. Now listen, son. You're a good boy"—he was at least the Dean's age—"if a bit overgrown. But you're bringing on a lethal situation. I don't like a run-around."

When the Dean used that tone the birds went south. The ape led us around a partition in the back. He pointed up a flight of stairs. "He's up there. Watch them steps," he said helpfully. "They're steep."

The entire second story had been torn out to make a single room—a big, bare office. Against one wall was a huge old-time safe painted with landscapes. Under a skylight that looked suspiciously like bullet-proof glass was an old-fashioned ball-claw table. The orderly stack of correspondence on the table was paper-weighted by a small blue automatic. The gun had a specially built, extended magazine. It was a pigmy machine gun. The octogenarian sitting behind the table was not fat and was not wearing a Vandyke.

He was garbed in black broadcloth and wore a stiff winged collar. The whole outfit, including the man, was eighty years old if it was a day. His hands were thin and wiry and hairy to the fingernails. He appraised us through slotted, red-rimmed eyes. "You'll do," he said.

"What goes on here?" The Dean was burning. "Who's that oaf downstairs?"

"He's my bodyguard."

"Who are you? Where's the fat man with the Vandyke? Who am I supposed to see?"

"The fat man is Mr. Christopher, my confidential secretary. It is I whom you wish to see." The old man had a patronizing way of sneering out his words. "I'm Judge Lucullus Brant. Independent candidate for mayor. I'm the man who is going to clean up Palmersville." He glanced about for applause. The Dean was stony. "I did it when I was judge in '97. I can do it again. You're helping me."

"So we're already retained," the Dean said gently. "We're working for you."

"Of course. You'll receive what I consider a fair fee when I decide you have earned it. Your job is to clean up this town." He didn't want to talk money. He wanted to talk about his campaign. "Palmersville is in a bad way but there are better days ahead."

The Dean said: "I'm going to clean up this town anyway and I might as well get paid for it. I'll take it."

"Surely, you'll take it." Judge Brant jeered. "You'd sell the shirt right off your back. I know private detectives. When I was judge in 1897—"

The Dean halted him with an outstretched hand. "Later. Why can't I have a little luck once in a while? Why can't I—just once—get a client that doesn't disgust me?" And with a lightning change of manner, "The whole thing hinges on that lump of putty. What do you know about it?"

The old man quivered and slavered. "What lump of putty? Is this an example of your much-touted investigative ability?"

"It is. But I don't expect you to realize it. Did you know Lucinda Frost, née Markham?"

The judge's watery eyes were baleful. "Certainly I knew her. She stole my tulips at the age of six. She stole other girls' beaux at the age of fifteen. She left town for New Orleans—goodness knows how she put in her time down there. Finally she came back with a husband. Her second, I hear."

"What did she steal when she came back?"

"Publicity and social position."

"Social position. But she was wealthy, as I got it."

"Wealthy?" the judge rapped out. "Her old man left her a starved farm and that liability, the so-called Markham 'mansion.' They built an apartment house on their farm but couldn't make a go of it. It's a failure from the basement up."

The Dean's eyes glowed. "Now let's take this item by item. You're telling me that there is an apartment? That this apartment is Lockbridge Court? That it is owned by Mr. Manfred Frost under his wife's will?"

"There was no will. Her husband inherited under the laws of the state." The old man took out a cumbersome silver watch. *"Tempus fugit,"* he said. "Start earning your money."

ON THE street, the Dean chuckled. "We'll lift that splay-back right out of his 1897 braces. We're topside in this business now." He drew a grave breath. "Ben—do you know whom we're after?"

"The Butcher Bird?" I hazarded.

The Dean flinched. "You depress me when you talk like that. You, yourself have solved the Butcher Bird angle. For once and for all—there isn't any Butcher Bird. You remember what you said? You said, 'there are two sides to everything.' That's the answer. Arnold Kutchin cut a clipping and tabbed it in his book—"

"Turned over!" I exclaimed. "To hide it!"

"Precisely. What we want to know is on the other side. And we'll find out before long."

Mother Gill's Restaurant—Home Cooking—carried a public phone plaque on the window. We took a chance on a decent meal and lost. "Home cooking!" the Dean snarled. "Orphans' Home. I don't know why I'm so gullible. Mention 'country food' or 'home-cooked meals' and I'll stick my neck out. The terms themselves are contradictions. Cooking requires experts—not amateurs. You wouldn't advertise 'home-cut emeralds' or 'home-made false teeth.'" The Dean pushed back his chair. "Which reminds me, we must call Lieutenant Malloy. You want to get in on this. It'll be explosive."

It took a few minutes to get the call through. All at once Malloy's voice vibrated the cigar counter. The Dean shared the receiver with me. The town had an independent line and the service gave the officer's voice a metallic, almost angelic quality. "Lieutenant," the Dean said, "this is Rock. I'm prepared to offer you a trade."

"Louder," Malloy said. "I can't make you."

The Dean raised his voice. "It's Rock. Wardlow Rock. I'll offer you a trade. I'm in Palmersville. How would you people back there in headquarters like to have Palmersville cleaned up?" I nudged the Dean. The restaurant was deathly silent. "Let them listen," the Dean whipped out. "I mean it." To Malloy, "I've about got the dope that will wind things up. This community is crime-ridden—but that's about in the bag. I need some information—" He paused. "Do you know a man answering this description: loose dentures, pince nez and a habit of throwing loops with a piece of string?"

There was an interval. Malloy had a freak memory. He never forgot a face, a name, or a photo. "Yep," Malloy answered slowly, "I place him. My wife's cousin's old man is plainclothes, retired, in New Orleans. Two summers ago he visited us on a trailer trip. I think he mentioned this lug. The name is Little Money Creegan. Trails races. Small-time."

"He's a big-time now," the Dean said. "Was he ever up for homicide?"

"I'd say off-hand—no. It wouldn't be in his nature. He's a grifter. What's up?"

"Watch the papers. Good-bye."

"Wait a minute," Malloy yelled. "What did you say?"

"I said good-bye."

Malloy laughed sardonically. The Dean looked alarmed. "Good-bye is right. I've been trying to contact you for an hour. Now get this and get it all. You're wanted for man-slaughter, possibly homicide. Not by us—by those cowboys there in Palmersville. A guy named Christopher, a fat guy with a beard, was discovered dead last night in the alley behind your hotel. Hit-and-run. Anonymous telephone tip this morning to the police from somebody claiming to be a witness tied it up with you. Christopher was holding part of your paint job on his broken teeth. They just found scratches on your fender to confirm it." Our car had been standing in the parking lot since last night. It had been there all morning, too.

"When did the accident occur?" the Dean asked.

"Coroner says around midnight. And now—good-bye!"

THE RAILROAD station was five blocks away. We picked back streets and kept a weather eye out for the local law. We stopped twice. At one store the Dean purchased a standard two-cell flashlight—at another, he acquired a new deck of playing cards.

I asked questions.

"This is going to save our necks," he grinned. "It's going to make us a lot of money, too."

He stepped into an alley, slipped a random card from the case, trimmed it with his penknife into a circle and punched a tiny pinhole in its center. He then unscrewed the bull's-eye of the flashlight and refitted it, placing the cardboard disc as a shield over the lens. The scraps and trimmings of the card he slipped carefully back into the box with the remainder of the deck.

I was shocked. "Where did you learn to make one of those?" I demanded. He had rigged up a burglar's light. Getting caught with one of them on you was a sure trip up the river. Slip the switch in the dark and it would throw out an almost imperceptible thread of light. No honest man had an excuse to be carrying one.

The Dean stowed the deck of cards lovingly next to his wallet, thrust the flashlight in his belt. "No time for homiletics, Ben. We're on our way."

Important railroad traffic passed through Palmersville but you wouldn't have guessed it to look at the station. It was rotting on its foundation. Cedar shingles, moss-thatched and curled, cracked windows patched with strips of adhesive tape. Jimson weed and wild carrot grew to the landing stage. The town's two taxis were pulled up by the platform waiting for the one-eighteen. The two drivers and the station-master were dangling their legs from a stack of ties in the shade. They were discussing the duplicity of womankind.

The Dean gave a stiff ambassadorial bow. "Unless I'm mistaken," he said sedately, "one of you gentlemen took a little trip this morning and brought back a book...?" He left the sentence up in the air. There was no response. The station-master looked frankly as though he thought we should be netted. One of the cab drivers twisted a match and picked his teeth. The other, a jockey-sized lad with a row of warts at the corner of his nose, said brightly: "Not me, captain. Kin I drive you somewhere?"

"Why, yes," the Dean said quickly. "Why, yes, you can."

We piled in his cab and were off in a serenade of gears. Seventy seconds later the cabbie pulled up behind a billboard and killed his engine. "I'm your man," he said casually. "You gotta be careful. You can't trust your best friend nowadays. What's stirrin'."

"What," the Dean asked, "did you do with the book?"

"Here's the story. You may like it and you may not. It can't be helped. This clerk calls me. He's implyin' he's snagged me some big business. He sends me after the book and I drove over and bring it back. Then he won't shell out the fare. Mr. Rock will pay you later, says he. When he pays the fare he gets the package, says I. I take it with me. The fare is six dollars and forty cents. You're sitting on the book. It's under the back seat."

"Here's your money." The Dean gravely counted out the exact change. A hasty examination showed the clipping to be intact. "Now," he said, "I want to tell you a little about ourselves. We're wanted by the local police and the local mobsters. The mobsters want us on general principles, the law for manslaughter and possible homicide. We're so hot—"

The driver interrupted. "Incandescent, eh?"

"Every bit of it. I thought you ought to know. Now do you want to play with us?" He took out the flashlight and a C-note. "Deliver this to police headquarters. The banknote is yours. Tell them that you found the light in an alley, last night, back of the Farmers and Commercial House. About midnight. You don't know anything about it, you just thought they might be interested."

"They will be." The cabbie stared blankly through the windshield. "You fellows," he said slowly, "have got me tangled. I can't figure you."

"Don't try." The Dean patted him on the shoulder. "Good luck."

Exhaust belching, tires scraping, the old heap rolled away.

WE LOST no time getting to work on Arnold Kutchin's scrapbook. The Dean slid a pencil beneath the Butcher Bird clipping, rolled it gently against the tabbed corners so that it was freed from the page. He placed a big palm over it and said: "Guess what?"

"Don't start getting squirrelly," I exploded. "A murder frame and you're asking guess what!"

We turned the clipping over and gave the back a gander. If the Dean was excited, he didn't show it. In fact, he was unpleasantly smug, as though the entire revelation only confirmed his suspicions. The back of the clipping said—

Mexican divorces are a source of bewilderment to the non-legal mind of your reporter-about-town.

The most recent sample is that of Lucinda Markham Pell, who, her friends inform us, has just taken the step away from her erstwhile husband, George, via a decree obtained in the Court of Gomez Marrija, Constitutional Governor of the State of Mangros, Mexico.

Miss Markham, it is whispered, is already brandishing a torch in a new direction—towards Manfred Frost, the popular turfman.

Just what is the percentage of validity in a "mail-order" divorce? Certain states, we are informed, do not give them "full faith and credit." In these states, the divorce proceedings, represented by an "attorney-in-fact," are considered without effect. In these states, the marriage contract is still binding.

So that was it. You couldn't tell what paper it came from or when it was printed—but the facts were there. Facts that could be easily verified. Lucinda wasn't married to Frost. She was actually married to a man named Pell.

"That explains it," I exclaimed. "Frost killed her to inherit. His inheritance is illegal—fraud as well as murder. Arnold

Kutchin sees the item in the paper—some old paper from out of town—dopes it all out. He tries to blackmail Frost and Frost knocks him off—like Mrs. Frost. Manfred inherits Mrs. Frost's wealth—"

"A run-down mansion and a jerry-built apartment house—"

"Something at least. Then he cashes in and grabs a train for New Orleans."

"The time has come," the Dean decided, "to get our fortunes told. Didn't we pass a chiromancer's someplace nearby?"

Invariably, in moments of crisis, the Dean's mind would show signs of going unbalanced. Afterwards, when you fitted it all together, it seemed the smart and logical course. I'd seen him do some loopy things—but I'd never seen him have his fortune told. I'd heard of readers that were actually hipped on their trade but I couldn't believe it of the Dean. Put it this way—the Dean could translate a half-dozen Eastern languages, he knew the Hermetics and their sources, the Kabbalists and the Chaldeans—and now he was suggesting that we consult some gyp that thought playing cards were invented by a sportsman named Canfield.

CHAPTER FOUR
FRAME FOR A FEE

WE SPIKED the set-up, down along the tracks, a district of back-fence gossipers and washing hung on lines. Out front, a messy child played in the gutter with a bantam rooster. A square of canvas depicting a giant hand in outline and bearing the ten-inch letters *PALMS READ*, showed through the bedroom curtains. The sagging steps to the porch were cluttered with blighted begonias set in coffee cans.

"Quaint," the Dean observed.

"It's a joint," I corrected. "Don't let the domestic touches fool you. They're just props."

The pony that answered our knock was about four and a half feet of surprise. She was built in high-velocity curves. Her bright red sport dress, plastered to her waist with a broad patent-leather belt, was like the page of answers in the back of the book. The belt and the dress yelled bargain basement but her hose were gossamer and her lizard pumps were custom-made. She looked up at us through a picket fence of long, tremulous lashes and asked us in.

You could see the wheels turn in her brain-box as she closed the door behind us. She was wondering. She wasn't steamed up over our visit. She acted wary.

The parlor was a flicker's nest, if you ever saw one. Paper hung in tatters from the ceiling, patched rat holes blotched the floor. The layout was entirely an inside room—no windows. The light came from an overhead bulb. Our hostess, the signs said, did a little medium work on the side. The Dean's eyes brightened with professional interest.

I settled down on a dilapidated horsehair sofa against the wall. The Dean seated himself in one of two chairs facing each other across a table skirted to the floor with sleazy cloth. "So you're the young lady that reads palms," he rumbled genially.

The pony's nervousness increased. "Excuse me a moment," she murmured. "The oven—I've something in the oven. I'll be right back." And she was gone.

"To change her dress," the Dean whispered. "She knows we're not ordinary customers. We've got her fuddled. She'll come back in something drab."

He was correct. When she returned, she was bare-legged, wearing straw sandals and a shapeless house coat. It didn't do much good. She still looked slow-fuse to me.

"You gentlemen wish your fortunes told?"

"No, my dear," the Dean boomed affably. "We hope for a little more than that. We understand you practice voyance. We want to ask a dead man a question." He was stealing Mervin Kutchin's thunder. "And we want honest answers. No *poltergeists*, please. We intend to pay—and to pay plenty."

She was like a rabbit in a cobra pit. Frantic but fascinated. She was money-greedy, you could see that.

"We'll get this over with dispatch," the Dean said smoothly. "No slates or knocks or darkened room. I just ask you the questions and listen to the answers. Can do?" The Dean laid his huge wallet on the table. "The spirit is Arnold Kutchin's. You remember Arnold?"

She wet her lips, tried to speak, nodded.

"Ask him about that lump of putty in the safe."

She was suddenly candid. "I'll level with you," she insisted. She paused, then went on. "They—the Kutchin boys—used to patronize me. But this is the first I ever heard of any putty."

The Dean appeared frustrated. "That's too bad. I really counted on your help. Who was Arnold Kutchin blackmailing?"

"So that's how he gets dough-heavy all at once!"

"That's how," the Dean confirmed. "You wouldn't know about that would you? You wouldn't have been advising him, would you. And maybe advising the victim at the same time—say Frost—to fork over?"

"No I wouldn't. I don't know what you're talking about."

"Did you know that Frost is down in New Orleans?"

HER EYES flickered. A crafty look came into the corners of her mouth. The Dean guffawed. "That's all I want to know. As I suspected, Frost is not in New Orleans. He never left town. He's right here in Palmersville now."

She got to her feet in a white rage. "I didn't say—"

"Let me see your hand!" Before she could evade him, the Dean spread it fan-wise, palm up, on the table. "Hum!" He scrutinized it. "Mercurian hand—avarice. Fingers set close together—reasoning power. Nails flat, broad, a little curved—guile. Middle finger, third joint, long—avarice again. My, my. Ring finger, finger of the sun, expresses criminal ambitions. Gracious! Do you see that? That star on the Mount of Saturn? That foretells painful death. The worst of all signs!"

She jerked her fingers from his grasp in fury. "You're wacky!" she grated. "It's all malarky. You told my fortune, now I'll tell yours. You're a couple of private dicks from out of town. You're smart—but not smart enough! You weren't sent for and you're not wanted. You're in the way."

The Dean selected a dollar bill from his leather, laid it on the table. "This is for information received."

"Information?" The edges of her mouth went white.

"Oh, come now," the Dean cajoled. "You told me the whole story—confirmed my wildest suspicions. It's as plain as daylight now. How's this?

"Palmersville is taken over by a new crime-lord. A maniac with an obsession for organized detail. The underworld is being put under new management, shaken down, weeded out, systematized. Mrs. Frost was in the way—so she went. Arnold and Mervin had to go. Christopher went. A vicious corporation is monopolizing. You are in the picture."

"That's not true," she whispered hoarsely. "Not a word of it."

Two men came into the room and deployed.

The first one to cross the threshold was Little Money Creegan, the out-to-lunch boy, the man who, according to Lieutenant Malloy, hadn't the proper nature for homicide. Creegan was carrying an Army automatic in one fist and a five-gallon container of gasoline in the other. Behind him pushed a cauliflowered thug with a furrowed brow. Neither showed any particular interest in us. They had a job to do and were going about it as impersonally as a couple of skinners on a silver fox farm.

Creegan said: "You wouldn't deal and you wouldn't scare. Now you take the black bottle and like it."

"Come in," the Dean invited. "Come in and bring your apprentice. Your name's Creegan. You come from New Orleans."

Little Money blinked. It wasn't a very big blink but it gave me the chance to slip my bulldog from behind my belt buckle and lay it in my lap under my coat. "She been gabbin'?" he asked coldly.

"Not me!" the girl burst out. "They're bluffing."

Creegan read her death warrant. "You're been a good finger. Your racket here has helped us get lined up with the locals. But you gab. You got to go, too."

The Dean was having the time of his life. I thought of the diamond cuff links and how he had promised me a jubilee. This was it. "That five-gallon can," he remarked politely. "Isn't that gasoline?"

The thug with the bum ear put in his helpful word. "We goin' to knock you off and then we goin' to incinerate the jernt. The boss says to. He thinks of everything."

The girl went berserk. Even the Dean was taken unawares. She snatched a vial of acid from the folds of her house coat, wheeled, and slammed it against the wall, missing the killers by five feet. Creegan shot her through the heart. The momentum of her twisting body threw her into him as she fell. He stumbled, raised an elbow to keep his balance—and the Dean's Magnum with its double powder charge plowed through his armpit.

The other lad squinted, hunched his shoulders as though he were a fighter coming out of his corner, and brought a pearl-gripped Mexican-style cannon with a chased barrel into the open. He was like a trained animal that knew a single trick and insisted on performing. I had no choice. I waited until he cleared his hip and laid in three where they would do some good.

OUTSIDE, ON the street, the gamin lookout with his bantam rooster was gone. We turned at the corner and glanced back. The palmistry banner in the window, the washing on the line, the begonias on the porch gave no hint of the shambles that lay inside. But the shooting had been heard. Uptown, sirens were screaming.

"That Alstetter dame!" I exclaimed. "How come she sends her gunmen after us?"

The Dean ignored my question. "There's real menace in this, Ben. It's far bigger than we supposed." He bared his teeth. "Lucullus Brant can help us here. We'll make a report to our client."

When the Dean contacted a client while a case was in progress it meant one thing. He was worried about his fee. He didn't want to get paid off in glass beads or popcorn balls. "What'll we report on?" I asked. "What have we to tell him?"

The Dean considered. "First of all we'll talk cold cash. Then we'll promise him to clean up his town—say in eight hours. We won't put out any information. We won't tell him we know who is behind this syndicate."

"Do we?" I inquired pleasantly.

"Of course we do. It can be only one person. This person has made two glaring mistakes. Either were incriminating. The two together give him completely away. Our case is actually on the verge of completion. We know the criminal. We know, beyond doubt, part of the motive."

"Then let's go to town. What's holding us?"

"The putty, Ben. It means something. Something criminal. It has to be explained."

"What about the frame we're in? What about the manslaughter charge?"

"Don't worry about that. We'll never see the inside of that jail. Depend on me."

LUCULLUS BRANT lived in a white cottage out Marshall Avenue. His diminutive yard was an eyesore of split-boulder lily pools and amateur Japanese bridges. The lawn was clipped down to the grass roots and conical evergreens were set out in arithmetical clumps. A gorilla in a gardener's jacket was on his hands and knees spraying an under-nourished malformed rosebush. He stood up as we approached.

"So it's you," I said. "I am deaf and dumb. I can neither read nor write."

"Quiet, Ben," the Dean interposed. "Where is the judge?"

The bodyguard was anxious to please. "He ain't here just now. He's been expecting you, though. He said if you was to come I was to take you in the house and ask you to wait."

Judge Brant's study was an 1897 nightmare—or as the Dean called it a fantasticism of bad taste. It was a small room, crowded with heavy teak furniture, hanging glass wind-chimes and moldy, mounted birds. Its raspberry walls were cluttered with steel engravings of dyspepsiac jurists. "Just sit," the bodyguard requested. "They ain't nothing to drink and they ain't nothing to smoke. He should be here soon."

The gorilla left us.

The telephone was on the floor by a stack of law books. The Dean lifted it to his lap. He made two calls. The first to Alstetter's funeral home—got no response. The second brought better luck.

"Superintendent Oliver G. Harmer," the voice answered. "Of Lockbridge Court. The Apartment House that Enhances the Joy of Living. Suites to accommodate all purses."

"Harmer," the Dean edged in, "this is Wardlow Rock. You remember me. What I'm about to say is going to embarrass you a little but that can't be avoided. It's this: I am a detective. I'm working on a very important case. Since I talked to you yesterday I have reason to believe that Manfred Frost has never left town—"

Harmer's voice was strained in its innocence. "Think of that!"

"—and you know it," the Dean continued, severely. "Now you don't want any notoriety. Let's get the straight of this business."

You could hear him gulp. "Mr. Frost seems to be afraid. He stays away all day and hides in his rooms all night. Every day and every night it's the same. He started it two or three weeks ago. When you offered me money just to see his empty room I couldn't see any harm in it. You won't mention it to him?"

"Of course not," the Dean said soothingly. "Now, we want to rent a room next to Frost's. I want it tonight. Can you fix me up?"

"Oh, yes. One of the nicest—"

"That's settled. One thing more. Did Frost have a friend with a Vandyke, a fat man?"

"I've never seen such a person on the premises." Harmer seemed certain. "Most of Mr. Frost's friends were what we men call the fair sex. Ladies. Not fat. No beards."

The boss hung up. He was grinning like a dog eating caramels. "It goes along, Ben," he said. "It approaches the blowup." He prowled nervously about the room, fingering bric-a-brac, peering into jardinieres.

I heard steps outside the door. "Here comes the judge," I said.

But it wasn't Judge Brant. It was his bodyguard and three plainclothes detectives.

"Help yourselves, boys," the bodyguard recited. "His Honor says hold 'em here for you, so I do. His Honor is always glad to be of service to the forces of law and order. You might mention that to the newspaper."

The Dean lashed out in a torrent of vitriol. "Tell that pigmy-brained ant-eater that hires you, that if he doesn't consult me within the hour, I'll wreck him. If I don't talk to him within the hour his campaign is over."

"Here! Here!" A big dick cut in. "No threats. Are you coming gentle?"

I turned to my boss. "Don't worry, says Wardlow Rock. We'll never see the inside of that jail. Depend on that."

THE LADS down at the city lock-up were decent enough, all things considered, but they were a harassed and harried lot and a tough crowd to stall. They felt their town slipping away from them and were trying against odds to keep it in their grip. They were all on a tension and outsiders like us coming in was the red flag. It was as honest an outfit as I ever ran into but Judge Brant's reform agitation had them stirred up and bellicose.

Four times—together and separately—they had the Dean and me up for the question-direct. Before long, one thing was apparent. They felt we were innocent of the Christopher kill. They realized that it tied up somehow with Palmersville's underworld. After the inquisition they locked us in a little office to cool off.

Fifteen minutes later Captain Kilroy paid us a personal visit. His dewlapped jowls were morose. "Just a couple of obstructionists," he grumbled. "You won't help us. I've a feeling that you know more about my town than I do." He studied us through rheumy eyes. "Wardlow Rock, you're the hatefullest man I ever saw." He sighed. "I had hoped to hold you till you opened up but I guess I can't. They's a caller outside wanting to see you. It's that durn old trouble maker, Judge Brant."

He paused and then went on: "You've been put in a frame for the Christopher kill. I know it and you know it. But dogged if I care. The reason I know it is this. The day after the death a cab driver came into the office here with a professional burglar's light that he had found at the scene of the 'accident.' They's professionals mixed up in this somehow and that lets you out. What it all tots up to is too much for me at present. But I'll work it out. One thing I want to know is *who made that light.* That man murdered Christopher. The scratches on your fender were just plants."

Reform candidate Judge Lucullus Brant was not pleased to be visiting at the city jail. The octogenarian was more repellent than ever.

"A man in my position," he quavered when we were alone, "can hardly afford to consort with criminals. Of course, if you wish to make a statement, a confession, to me, that is something extenuating. Otherwise—"

"You'll be lucky," the Dean said viciously, "ever to leave this prison. A man is wanted for a killing and you'll fit the picture."

The judge's cheeks glowed roseate. "What sort of fol-de-rol is this?"

Carefully, and with painful lucidity, the Dean told him about the construction of the burglar's light, how it had been made from a playing card, how it had been found at the scene of the crime. He explained how anxious the police were to identify its owner.

"All along," he concluded, "I have been way ahead of you. I knew from the beginning that you hadn't a shred of loyalty. This rig protects us from you, our client."

"And how," the judge sneered, "will that help you?"

"Ah! Wait until you learn!" The Dean chuckled. "The remainder of the deck of cards, including the trimmings of the shield, are plenty evidence of guilt. The remainder of the deck—including the trimmings—are hidden in your study! The police would be interested in learning this. I could tell them where to find them. Don't look for them yourself. I swear to you it would be a waste of time. Maybe they're hidden in that stuffed owl on your mantel. Maybe elsewhere."

"You unscrupulous scoundrel—"

"Now that's a compliment, considering the source. But to get back to the business in hand. My price is our immediate release here—you can swing it—and a ten-thousand-dollar fee dependent upon my settlement of the case by midnight. Do you accept my terms?"

Quick as a turtle, the judge snapped up the proposition. "I agree. You're dippy"—even the judge's slang was moth-eaten—"but dangerous." He was abruptly thoughtful. "Arnold Kutchin was a crank, too. Sometimes I've wondered if I wasn't a little hasty with Arnold."

"So now you tell me that you knew Arnold Kutchin!" The Dean was bleak.

"Of course, I knew him. He was as crazy as a loon. One day he came to my office hysterical with excitement. Wanted to sell me some criminal information. Claimed he knew of some important evidence hidden in a deserted farm house. Wanted five hundred dollars. Ha! I put him out of my office." The oldster paused. "Phoned me that night when I was at supper. Completely batty. Talked in enigmas. Said his hours were numbered. Said if anything happened to him I was to go to a place on the old pike *where a mule danced on its hind feet!*"

The Dean waited. The judge concluded: "Pure insanity. I hung up on him. That night he was killed in a hit-and-run accident."

The Dean winced.

"Get us out of here," he ordered. "We're wasting time."

DARKNESS HAD fallen by the time we were released. A fierce rain was whipping the little country town—exuding an odor of mown lawns and honeysuckle. The wind in the streets carried the lush burden of a potters-field.

Parked at the curb, in the silver drop of a streetlight, was Lieutenant Malloy's coupe. He threw open the door as we sprinted down the broad steps of the city hall and beckoned us in beside him.

"You knew we were being held," the Dean accused. "And you didn't even come in to say a good word for us!"

Malloy grinned. "How goes it?"

"Not so good," the Dean evaded. "What are you doing here?"

"Well, you might say, I'm on a kinda vacation."

The Dean followed his advantage. "You're trying to chisel in on my case! I solve your cases back home and now you follow me out of the city, out of the county, and try to hog me here in Palmersville. I declare, Malloy—"

"The commissioner sent me."

"The commissioner?"

"That's what I said. This case is bigger than you know. And it's to our advantage to have it cleaned up. Here's why. Somebody in this town is a broker in crime—not only local crime but nation-wide crime."

I thought I knew the angles, but this was a new one on me. "A broker?"

Malloy explained. " Some person in this town runs a criminal employment bureau. With a coast-to-coast hookup. Big jobs get started here. Cracksmen contacted. Fingermen supplied. Guns, tools, explosives and torches are furnished from headquarters here. The business is run on a percentage basis. There are immense profits. For some time we have suspected it. Now we're certain. The commissioner sent me over to work with you. Where do we stand? How much headway have we made, Rock?"

The Dean was absorbed. "So that explains the four lipsticks."

"Tell me this, Lieutenant," I remarked. "Does this person have to be a man? Say a woman undertaker was the spider in the web. She's got a hearse to haul stuff. She can bring the victims back to her parlors and maybe do some plastic surgery so they couldn't be identified. Then, too, her office is right across from the city jail—"

Malloy turned to the Dean. "What's he talking about. It sounds like he's needled."

The Dean covered up. "Just stringing you along. Just kidding." He opened the door and got out into the rain. "Tonight's the show-down, Lieutenant. There's a man named Frost that's been evading us. We've finally got him covered. I hope to turn him over to you by midnight. If you can get him to talk, he'll sew up your case for you. Meet me at a quarter to twelve. Lockbridge Court Apartments. The janitor will show you to my room." He took my elbow and steered me up the sidewalk.

"Wait a minute, blast you!" Malloy shouted.

We paid no attention.

CHAPTER FIVE

THE PLACE OF THE DANCING MULE

A HOLE-IN-THE-WALL chili shop seemed a quiet place to catch a little food. The rain was blowing and the restaurant window was filmed with a shifting lip of water. Before I could speak, the Dean had ordered our suppers—mine as well as his—a half-lemon squeezed into a cup of black coffee, no sugar. A harmless-sounding concoction that packs the authority of a pile driver. Gall in the mouth, fire in the stomach. But no substitute for a liver sandwich. "Food later," the Dean remarked. "No time now."

He called the counterman. "There's a cab driver in town with a row of warts on his cheek. Do you know him?"

The counterman was surprised. "You mean Joey Flahaven. You don't want that misfit. Customers always find him annoyin'."

"Tell him to meet me in front of the Alstetter home in thirty minutes."

"In front of the funeral home?" The counterman was sympathetic. "Have you lost someone near and dear? Was it maybe a sweetheart?"

"The best time to see your undertaker is before you lose anyone." The Dean smiled. "Like you do a doctor or a dentist. An ounce of prevention is worth a pound of cure."

The counterman boggled.

Wind and black squall filled the maw of the alley that led to the rear of the old Markham mansion. We felt our way along the fence until we came to the gate by the stable.

The gate was locked. The halter-catch had been replaced with a new padlock. The Dean growled angrily when his groping fingers touched it. "This is your job. Can you open it?"

"I'll try," I said. It had a five-pin tumbler cylinder. "You see what I meant," the Dean whispered, "when I said we were up against a maniac with an obsession for detail. The man with the mouth harp, the over-elaborate frame of manslaughter, that failing—the gunmen sent against us with their can of gasoline to burn the evidence. Take this lock. Put on since yesterday." He paused. "A genius must consider the essentials in relation to detail. This person is fascinated mainly by the detail itself. That is his weakness. What I'm trying to say is that our criminal slipped early in the game. Too much detail conflicts. I've known his identity for two days."

"Two days!" I exclaimed.

"Certainly. The lipsticks were the tip-off, Ben. Four different shades and *all the same brand.*"

"Were they?" I answered. "I hadn't noticed it. But it has an easy answer. Some girl, maybe that babe that told fortunes, is, or was, using Frost's room to disguise herself. From thence, she was wont to set out upon her nefarious—"

The shackle slid out of the case, the gate swung open. We stood in the backyard, at the corner of the carriage house, and got our bearings. There was no light in the shapeless old mansion. "Not the house, Ben," the Dean urged. "The stable. Get us into the stable."

The short cinder walk curved to a little door trellised with moon-vines. The door, itself, was a curiosity. Eighteen-inch oak planks, reinforced with criss-crossed iron lacing. It tried to look rustic but it looked like a fortress to me. The lock was a good one. But not too good. We were inside in a couple of minutes.

We found ourselves on what had been the old carriage floor. Ghosts of old fragrances welled out of the darkness—harness oil, clover hay. There were other smells. A whiff of embalmer's fluid, a suggestion of liquor and stale tobacco.

The Dean drew a plumber's candle from his coat and struck flame. We edged around a gleaming hearse and took timbered stairs to the upper story.

In the old days this had been the coachman's quarters. It had undergone alterations. It had been streamlined. And I mean just that. There were three rooms, each recently remodeled with an eye for comfort.

The little kitchen with its single unit range-sink-refrigerator was modern in black enamel. A bachelor's joy. Compact, neat, handy. The bathroom had a sunken tub and was tiled in glazed madder-yellow.

We entered the living-room and clicked on the lights. A millionaire's hunting lodge, right out of the Rockies. The wood-pegged, random-planked floor was gay with Indian rugs. Around three sides of the walls were ceiling-high built-in bunks. Enough space to accommodate half a dozen 'hunters.' Overstuffed chairs and taborets with decanters and sporting magazines.

"Egad!" I exclaimed. "A gentlemen's club in the old barn loft!"

The Dean was drawn with suppressed wrath. "A rats' nest, Ben. Here the out-of-towners meet, live, and enjoy themselves while they lay plans for bloody crimes. In this place they discuss wages, cuts, and distribution of loot. Killers peddle their wares in this room and cracksmen bargain with their chiefs." I was fiddling with something I had picked up on the arm of a chair. A little tin box which was lithographed with two encircling hearts and the words: *INFANTA BREATH PERFUMERS—VIOLET FLAVOR.* Unconsciously, I touched the knob behind my ear. So this was the hideout of the cokey that slugged me.

"What do we do now?" I asked.

"We get out."

I disagreed. "Shouldn't we locate the arsenal—that stock of tools and stuff Malloy mentioned?"

"No use looking. They're not here."

"In the funeral home, maybe?"

"No."

It took it a minute to penetrate. "So that's it." I got the idea. "That's what Arnold Kutchin had located in the deserted farmhouse. The cache of equipment. He had the dope on these boys—"

IF JOEY FLAHAVEN, master-cabman, was elated at seeing us he concealed his emotions. The rain had stopped and the thunderheads had gone into mackerel clouds around a luminous moon. Blinking puddles dappled the sunken sidewalks. Flahaven's taxi, engine running, waited for us in a shroud of shadows beneath a clump of maples.

Flahaven was singing the blues, talking to himself, as we approached. "—you're walking on thin ice, Joseph. Watch your step. These here guys are poison ivy. They come to town and act screwy—" Unassisted, we crawled into the rear. The Dean slammed the door.

"Joey," he said severely, "suppose you had a mule that danced on its hind legs. What would you do?"

The cab driver groaned. "See what I mean?" There was a moment's silence. "I'd call a veterinary. Mules are out of my line."

I could feel the Dean relax. "Son," he said gravely, "you've just punched yourself out a five-dollar tip. You're almost as valuable as Ben. Drive us to the best veterinarian in town."

"They ain't but one. He lives over on Dunlap."

Doctor Lynnly Hibbart displayed a brass horseshoe knocker on his door and a bridle foot-scraper on his front step. The vet himself opened to our rap. He was a vigorous little man with apple-red cheeks and a miasma of hair about his almost bald head.

"We won't come in, thank you, Doctor," the Dean remarked. "We want you to settle a wager. I'm taking your time and I realize it. I insist on paying your customary consultation fee. The problem I want to pose is this: What makes a mule dance on his hind legs?"

I cringed with embarrassment but the veterinarian was instantly intrigued. "Now that's interesting. Several things might cause it. Cockle-burr sprouts make young stock stagger and toss their heads. The purple shoots of water hemlock, found along streams and in wet places, is sometimes called wild parsnip. This makes animals twitch.

Horse-chestnut buds are poisonous, too. This, I'd say, is your diagnosis. Animals lift their front legs high, mincing-like."

"Thank you, Doctor." The Dean paid him. We perked up our ears.

"I had a case of a buckeyed mule, myself, about three weeks ago. Rather rare hereabouts. Farmer named Sylvester Bowman out on the old pike, pastured his stock on a vacant farm across the road. Mule cut up lively but I pulled it through."

Flahaven knew the Bowman farm. He wanted to haggle but the Dean was on the move. We drove past the city hall, turned at the iron statue in the park, Y'd off Cherry towards the suburbs. Suddenly, on the spur of the moment, the Dean called, "Stop!"

Joey screeched to the gutter. Lockbridge Court loomed in the murk. "Wait for us, son," the Dean commanded. And to me, "This is going to surprise you."

We caught Superintendent Harmer in a ski-type pajama outfit, sitting at his kitchen table. A flimsy booklet lay open before him and a cheap Hawaiian guitar was across his knees. He was giving himself lessons in music. A little row of pamphlets on the condiment shelf said: *Romance Languages—The Teach-Yourself System, How To Be Well Dressed, Five Hundred Parlor Tricks, Superba Muscle-Maker, Can You Mix A Gentleman's Salad?*—and so on. At least twenty of them.

The Dean was curt and swift. "We'll be back in an hour. If a certain police officer—Lieutenant Malloy—arrives, show him to the room you have reserved for me. The room next to Frost's."

Harmer wiped off a couple of glissandos and laid down his steel. "He's upstairs now."

"Good. We won't go up. Now here's what I want to ask you. You say Frost comes back here every night, hides out in his room? Are you positive?"

The superintendent was positive. "If you'd see the laundry bill for sheets and towels. And the empty bottles and such. And the shameless girls parading the halls!"

"You've actually observed Frost himself, in person?"

"Frequently!" Harmer considered. "Not exactly seen or spoken to him," he corrected, "but it must be Mr. Frost. Who else would use the room? Who else would have the keys? I tell you that room is used every night."

The Dean radiated satisfaction.

Harmer gazed at us in rapt ecstasy. "Detectives," he murmured. "Two of them here in my own kitchen." He flushed. "Would you consider me forward or presumptuous if I offered you assistance?" Before we could answer, he had a coffee can down from a cupboard and the lid off. Buried in the coffee beans was an old pistol. The firing mechanism was fused with rust, the barrel was clogged and scaley. The monstrosity was fully loaded and the cylinder was corroded with verdigris. "You may borrow this," he said self-consciously. "It's deadly."

"It emphatically is," the Dean agreed. "Thanks. If we should need it we'll say so. It's a thrill just to look at it."

OLD PIKE was a four-mile section of backroad, meandering through brushy swamps, which had been cut off from contact with the world when the big highway had been straightened. It was a ghost road, desolate, isolated. Every third farm was vacant. We drove over corduroy bridges, through fungoid woods, along snake-infested sloughs. The air was dank and steamy.

"The next place on the right," Flahaven announced, "and we're there. That was Bowman's we just passed." He cut his wheel, pulled into a locust lane and stopped. "All out. We have arrived. Take it away. It's yours."

The residence, originally of brick, had, years ago, been enlarged with a frame annex. It had evidently been long abandoned. The marsh had grasped out to reclaim it. From its sunken foundations to the last square nail in its roof beam, it was sagging with decay. The cabman flashed his light about, sprayed a twisted malform orchard grown with weeds, a slime covered springhouse.

"What's them white things in the fence corner?" Flahaven inquired tensely.

The Dean chuckled. "Tombstones. That's the old family burial lot." He added brusquely: "What we want is inside the house. Let's get started. Joey, are you coming or staying?"

"I'm coming, chief." He took a set of brass knuckles from a bracket under the dash and dropped them in his pocket. "My lucky piece," he proclaimed.

"Lucky piece?" The Dean couldn't resist the temptation to expound. "A protective talisman, according to the ancients, was a complicated thing to compound. You must go into a red room on Tuesday, at eight o'clock in the evening, burn a perfume of hellebore, powdered magnet and gentian root made into a paste with wolf's blood, take a little disc of iron—engraved with a mystic sign—and enclose it with a ruby, together with certain odds and ends such as spiders and nettles, in a red bag sewn with red thread."

We pushed forward through the scrub and briars. Flahaven tagged silently at our heels.

At the far side of the building, flush with the brick facing and hidden from the road by the jutting wing of the frame annex, was the entrance to the root cellar. Four slippery steps descended to an arched areaway.

"Do we pass this up?" I asked.

"No," said the Dean. "We do not. It looks promising."

Believe it or not, it was down in that evil smelling entranceway to the old cellar that we found the answer to Arnold Kutchin's lump of putty.

I worked about seven seconds on the lock before I realized that it was jammed. It was an old warded lock set on the outside of the door. You know the type. A cast-iron box that is screwed on below the knob. Absolutely worthless for an outside exposure. I flipped a telescopic screwdriver out of my key case and had the whole thing apart in an instant.

We gaped when we got a look at the inside of it. The lock had been deliberately gaffed. Putty had been tediously crammed into the key-hole until the space between the ward and the bolt was completely blocked.

Brother Arnold, in his ignorance of locks, actually thought he had jinxed it.

The Dean said placidly: "So that's it. He came out here the afternoon before he was killed, jammed the lock to secure the contents of the cellar—the evidence—and phoned Judge Brant. Distracted, he took the remainder of the putty home with him and cautiously locked it in his safe."

Suddenly we knew we were in the presence of death.

We were completely inside before we discovered the corpse. The vault was walled with field rock. Flahaven's flash swung across the dripping stone—passed over a high, small window—and came to rest on a crumpled hulk of mildewed clothes that lay in the corner. It was a gruesome sight. A man of some kind. A dandy. You could make out his fawn-colored spats. A sporty whipcord raincoat was folded neatly at his feet. Atop the coat sat the gentleman's Homburg.

The whole thing fitted itself together in my mind. "George Pell!" I whispered.

The Dean was taken aback. For a moment he was genuinely flustered. "Who? What did you say?"

"That's the solution! That's the body of George Pell."

"Stop talking wildly and explain what you're trying to say. Who's George Pell?"

"George Pell. The husband—the real and first husband—of Lucinda Markham. Don't you remember the clipping? They had to kill him, too. He was the rightful heir. It all fits. It's all over now. All we've got to do is go back to Lockbridge Court and catch Frost."

The Dean gritted his teeth. "Please be calm. You had me off my trolley for a minute. I'd forgotten all about Pell. He's out. He doesn't come into this. Forget him. This is the man that counts. This is Manfred Frost."

"Frost?"

"That's right. He was killed elsewhere and brought here. Hidden. Note the coat and hat. Arnold Kutchin learned of it. Maybe he witnessed the murder and trailed the killer here. Childishly, he jammed the lock and tried to peddle the contents. Yes, this is Manfred Frost, and he has been dead, I should judge, several weeks. Rather revolting, isn't he?"

Flahaven laid his torch on the floor, walked to the door and gagged. The action saved his life. A shotgun charge from the outside channeled through the high ventilating window and blasted the flashlight to oblivion.

The Dean's great arms came out of the blackness, en-circled me, threw me bodily through the entranceway, out of the angle of fire. Volley after volley detonated in the small cellar as the killer swept the chamber with his slugs. The bull-throated explosions roared and reverberated like great war drums.

"Let him have his fun," the Dean said amiably. "We've got the chair all wired for him."

CHAPTER SIX
THE FOUR LIPSTICKS

ON **THE** drive back to town, we were all pretty quiet. The Dean had as good as said that Frost had been out of it all along. I worked on this for a while and couldn't do any good with it. "Does that mean Frost was innocent?" I asked.

"Far from it," he answered. "Frost came up here from New Orleans with his wife. He looked Palmersville over and liked the set-up. Somehow he contacted someone and together, no doubt, they worked out the criminal employment bureau scheme. This partner was the one that had the big ideas. The syndicate expanded too rapidly and on too large a scale for Frost's comfort. He got scared. To make matters worse, Lucinda got wise and objected. The partner then started his killing chain and took over."

"One thing more," I put in. "I've been wondering. Did you actually plant that deck of cards in the judge's study?"

The Dean was irritated. "Of course not, Ben." He tapped his pocket. "They're right here. They are too valuable to part with—yet."

Joey Flahaven kept his eyes on the road. He was swathed in meditation. Finally he joined the conversation. "Where do I get hellebore?" he inquired.

"I beg your pardon?" The Dean was polite.

"Should I want to make one of them little red lucky-charm bags, where do I get the hellebore?"

"Oh," the Dean smiled. "So that's it. Stick to your brass knuckles. They're much more effective, in my academic opinion."

Palmersville had a good police force but the department, like many others, had its leaks.

We hit a filling-station phone at the edge of town and tipped Captain Kilroy that the showdown was at hand. By the time we had reached our destination, before Kilroy could arrive, Judge Lucullus Brant was waiting for us. The judge had his pipeline, a big one complete with valves and faucets, right into the heart of headquarters.

The first thing that filled our eyes as we slewed up to Lockbridge Court was the Alstetter hearse—parked before the building. Judge Brant and Jane Alstetter climbed down from the driver's seat as we approached.

The girl was trembling like a leaf. Her eyes were blazing with a hot mixture of anger and fear. She was wearing a short-skirted dress of foamy voile with a summerish school-girl collar of pleated lace. She walked stiffly, her hands clasped before her. As she came into the glare of our headlights we could see that her frock was rumpled and that she was wearing ten-cent toy handcuffs. The judge trotted possessively at her side, a leer of self-approval on his goatlike old face. "I was told I'd find you here," he called. "We have a prisoner."

I had those cuffs off her slim wrists before she could realize it.

"What does this mean?" the Dean said quietly. "Judge Brant, give me an explanation and make it good. I've had enough of you so be careful what you say."

The oldster blustered: "I've saved myself your fee—that's what it means. While you've been fumbling around, I've gone out and solved our case. This woman, this female undertaker, is behind it all. I've got my spies"—a smug expression settled in his jowls— "and they've been working. They've learned things. Suspicious characters, criminal characters, go through that little gate by the old Markham stable. I'm an old barrister. I've got a legal and logical mind. I put two and two together and decided she should be in custody. I arrested her."

The Dean said gently: "So you've arrested her. On what authority?"

"He's got a badge," the girl cried out. She huddled like a frightened animal close to the Dean's great frame. "He tried to make me swear to things I didn't know."

"Let's see this badge."

The old man had one. Solid gold. He displayed it proudly. Obverse, it said *Honorary Deputy*. The back was engraved: *In Greatest Esteem To Judge Lucullus Brant—HE RID OUR COMMUNITY OF SMOKEHOUSE THIEVES—From The Women Of The County, Oct. 17, 1897.* The Dean returned it to him. "As worthless as a beer-bottle cap. Judge Brant, you've got yourself in a hole."

The old man spluttered: "A private citizen can arrest a criminal—"

"—acting as his own agent. A false arrest under these circumstances is extremely grave. I advise this girl to sue you down to your last penny." He patted Jane Alstetter on the shoulder. "Come with us, my dear."

We left the stuttering octogenarian on the sidewalk.

INSIDE THE apartment, the halls were dim and shadowy with feeble night-lights. The Dean crowded the girl into a dark corner. "What's your story?" he breathed grimly.

Her poise was perfect again, she was almost insolent. "Don't pant on me. I'm not afraid of you—just that terrible old man." She faltered. "I've decided to take your advice and come over on your side."

"I hope it's not too late," the Dean answered. "Tell me about Little Money Creegan and the furnished rooms in the stable. Make it honest and to the point."

"The rooms were there when I bought the place from Mr. Frost. But I didn't know it at the time. I just saw that there was garage-room downstairs and let it go at that. The gangster, Creegan, came right after I set up shop." She shuddered. "He just moved in. I was afraid. They told me not to worry. To just continue my business and to let them alone. I don't know who they were or what they were doing. Is it all over?"

"Just about," the Dean answered. "Now do what I tell you. Look up the superintendent, get him to show you to my room upstairs. There you'll find a policeman, Officer Malloy. Tell him I said you were in danger. Wait with him. I'll be with you shortly."

Obediently, she turned and left us. For an instant there was the clean, fresh scent of sandalwood. The Dean—wagged his bearish head. "A mortician—a Callipygian Astarte—trailing the suggestion of lavender and old lace!"

We went back along the corridor, through the parcel delivery, out to the vacant lot at the rear. We stepped back and studied the face of the building. It was almost completely dark. A fire-escape zigzagged to the roof, cutting through the glow of a single light—a room on the third floor. I indicated the yellow window. "Malloy is on the job," I remarked.

"I sincerely hope so," the Dean said queerly. He was silent for a moment. I could tell from the way he swept his eyes from ground to cornice that he was counting, checking. "As I feared," he observed at last. "Malloy sits in the dark. That light is from the suite of Manfred Frost. I can't believe it. Things have gone entirely wrong. I fear we're late!"

We got our second shock when we reached the foot of the fire-escape. The last iron step overhung the ground by about eight feet. A stepladder stood in position beneath it. The red tip of a cigarette smoldered in the grass by my shoe.

"Up we go," the Dean said placidly. "Be careful. Some-one's waiting for us."

He was. He crouched on the second-floor landing, gun in hand, hoping to blow off the tops of our heads as they rose before him like clay pigeons. I didn't see him until we were almost on him. Only the shifting shadows and his poor marksmanship saved us. Catlike, he arched his back, thrust out a pallid hand and slammed four jacketed slugs clanging into the ironwork around us.

There was the scuffle of his feet as he scurried up the steps. The Dean was frozen in immobility. A window squeaked as it was raised. "He's going into the room—Frost's room. Hurry."

Then we heard it—the new sound. It came out from the open window—a clattering, treble rattle—long-drawn, vicious.

I recognized the sound as surely as if I had been up in that little room where it had happened. The little auto-matic with the extended magazine, the pigmy machine gun, that we had seen on Judge Brant's claw-and-ball table in his slummy office. We were up the last flight and in the room before we were expected.

THE BEDROOM-LIVING-ROOM was unchanged. Chiffon hose hung from the doorknob, the Spanish comb lay on the dressing table and the five gal-photos were still plastered around the mirror. A new item of interest had been added, however—and not by any interior decorator. A dying man lay on the floor.

It was my old playmate, the cokey, the lad who liked breath perfumers, the boy who had slugged me out because I would not accept his ten grand. His chest was riddled. His lips were working silently. Before we could reach him, he died.

Judge Lucullus Brant sat on the edge of the bed, his venomous little gun beside him.

"How," the Dean asked quietly, "did you get here so soon?" Then, before the old man could answer, he changed his question. "What are you doing in this room?"

"I have information—I have my spies—"

"So you mentioned before." The Dean cut him off. "You appear to be guilty of murder and trespass. Can you defend your position?"

"There was shooting outside. He came in the window with drawn weapon. He's a notorious desperado—a wanted man. I shot him."

"Now we'll take that other question," the Dean said softly. "How did you get here?"

Brant shifted his obnoxious, watery eyes. "I followed the girl."

"But she didn't come here."

"She's in the next room. Sitting in the dark with a man. This door was unlocked, so I stepped in—"

"—to eavesdrop. You'll make quite a mayor, Judge Brant. You're one of your own best spies. But here, my friend, you've slipped your leash." There was commotion in the hall. The door was flung open. Lieutenant Malloy and the girl pushed in. A second later they were followed by Captain Kilroy, Superintendent Harmer—in a fluffy candlewick bathrobe—and Joey Flahaven.

The custodian pointed sternly to the body on the carpet. "Who did that?"

"Yes," Malloy chimed in. "What goes on?"

Captain Kilroy glanced at Flahaven with troubled eyes. You could tell he recognized him, was trying to place him in the pattern.

The Dean was serene. "Captain Kilroy," he suggested, "deprive the judge of his weapon." When this was done, he made a little speech. "As most of you know, I am a detective by trade, a fortune teller by choice. Criminology and investigation are my bread and butter, divination is my nectar—"

"He's doing it again," Jane Alstetter muttered to me from the corner of her mouth. "He's talking stagey."

"Rarely, very rarely indeed, do I encounter a case that permits me to apply the field of fortune telling to its solution. When such a case arises I am, of course, delighted. This case appears to have reached an impasse. I shall, in the next few seconds, solve it by the ancient art of stolisomancy." He seemed pensive. "First, however, let me lay a bit of background.

"There are many, many branches of ancient magic. There is low magic and there is high magic. To the ancients all earthly appearances were manifestations of supernatural order. It is from this supposition that omens derive their importance. There is divination from the howling of dogs which is known as ololygmancy. There is divination from the appearance of wine which is oenomancy. There is divination from strewn pearls which is margaritomancy. This is but to name a few."

The Dean paused. "Then, too, there is stolisomancy. That mantic art which foretells from garments and clothes—from the manner of dressing. Does anyone wish to volunteer for an observation?"

"Batty as they come," the judge quavered. "Watch him! He's dangerous."

The Dean beamed on Superintendent Harmer. "How about you? I'd love to work on that bathrobe. I've been wondering, for instance, what you are wearing beneath it."

THE TRANSFORMATION was ghastly. The little superintendent's face twisted in harsh fury, a killer's gleam whipped itself into his glassy eyes. Cornered, trapped, he went completely, gibbering mad. I remembered what the Dean had twice said—that we were up against a maniac. It was unholy to watch. Spasmic with passion, he slapped his pocket, clawed for a gun. He didn't have a chance. Four of us were ready and waiting.

Captain Kilroy shot him between the eyes.

The Dean bent over the lifeless figure, turned back the dressing-robe. Harmer was fully clothed. There were swamp burrs and beggers-lice on his trouser cuffs. "An hour ago he was in his pajamas. Twenty minutes ago, he was out on Old Pike blasting at us with a shotgun."

Malloy frowned. "What does this get me?"

"This is your man. The syndicate is broken. No more employment bureau. This apartment was the clearing house. Someplace in this building you'll find their supply room. Guns, explosives, tools and torches."

"The Alstetter funeral home," the judge interrupted. "Why—"

The Dean turned to me. "Frost doubtless knew Harmer in New Orleans. Imported him. They had criminal contacts. They remodeled the stable and built this apartment house. The nature of their business required two establishments. Early in the game they must have discovered the necessity of keeping their workmen separated."

"So," the Dean continued, "the stable was indispensable to the organization. Now, as I have said, Frost got cold feet. He sold the mansion to Jane Alstetter with the intention of clearing out. Harmer killed him before he could dispose of the apartment."

Kilroy was stunned. "Frost dead?"

"That's right. Just hold your horses. I'll elucidate. Arnold Kutchin was lured into the affair by—ahem—certain information that fell into his hands. He learned of Frost's murder, possibly witnessed it—Ben will clear this up for you later—so Arnold had to go. Harmer, a screwball on trickery and detail, rigged up this room with an amorous atmosphere to explain Frost's absence. The lovelorn 'darling widower' note, the female apparel, were elaborate theatricals. I knew this, of course, when I first saw them."

"You mean you guessed," I put in.

"I mean I *knew*. Yesterday morning, here in this suite, we found the clue that blew up the case. Four lipsticks, all the same brand. For four different complexions. Here Harmer's oversubtle nature slipped up and set a deadfall for him. It was straining coincidence to expect four assorted ladies to prefer the same brand. Those lipsticks were bought by one person in one purchase.

"If the lipsticks were fakes then it was all fake. Who wanted us to believe that Frost was unfaithful to his dead wife, a libertine? Obviously not Frost himself. Who, other than Frost, had access to the room? Harmer. How could Harmer perpetrate this deceit? Only if Frost were out of the way and he, Harmer, knew it. It all fitted yesterday morning. Harmer was the man we were after. But he had to be trapped."

Kilroy was frisking the body. "Yah!" he grunted. He held in his hand the deck of cards, slid the scraps and trimming out in his palm. "Here's what I've been looking for. They were in his shirt! This bears you out, Mr. Rock. This here is the bird that made that light. According to my notion, he bumped off Christopher."

Judge Lucullus Brant gulped. The Dean looked mildly interested. "I could have told you that this afternoon, Captain. Christopher was the judge's confidential secretary. He tried to turn a double trick, frighten the judge and frame me. And that, gentlemen, clears up the case."

Captain Kilroy hesitated. "We surely thank you, you and the lieutenant. You've cleaned up our town. I'll keep it clean." He was embarrassed. "There's something—one thing—that's got me stumped. A clue I've been holding out on you. Maybe you could help me."

"What's that?" the Dean inquired.

"It's a sorta scrapbook. The boys picked it up at the scene of a shooting in a joint down by the railroad tracks this afternoon. Found it laying in a swelter of blood on the floor. Like somebody threw it away and lammed. Now this joint was a fortune teller's and I thought, being as you're a fortune teller yourself, you might be able to show me what it's all about."

"Sorry, Captain. Can't help you there." The Dean was staring at Jane Alstetter. "My!" he said suddenly. "That's a pretty frock you're wearing. I hadn't noticed it. I like it. I certainly do!"

She gave him her slow, inviting smile. "Let's go outside and talk it over," she laughed. "This is just a little public for a discussion of stol—stoliso—whatever it was."

"Stolisomancy," Joey Flahaven supplied. He turned brightly to the Dean. "Can I drive you somewhere, chief?"

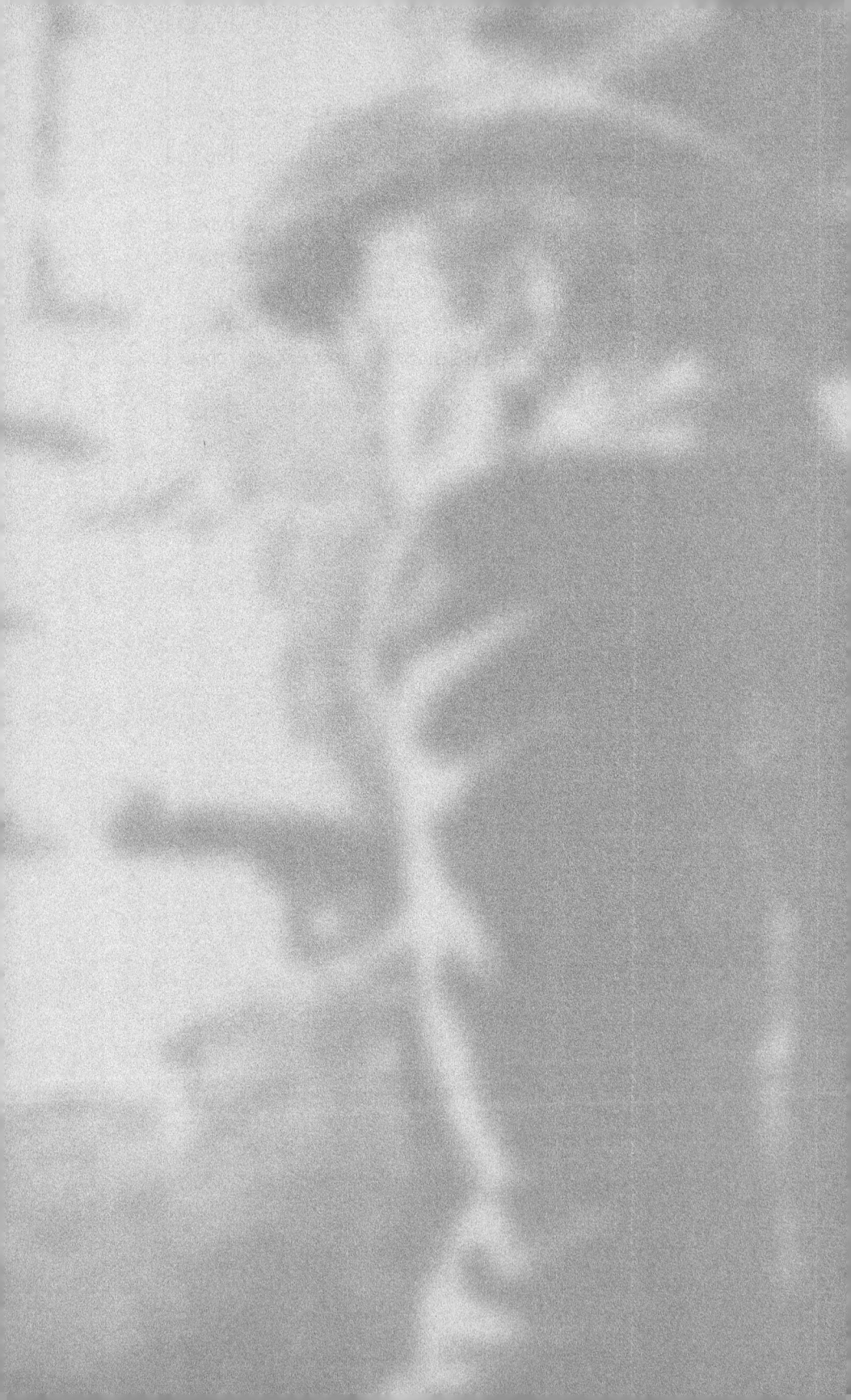

ONE CORPSE TOO MANY

IT STARTED OUT AS A SIMPLE SMASH-AND-GRAB—THE LOOT, FROM A LEPIDOPTERIST'S FIELD KIT, THREE NICE BIG SPOONFULS OF KCN—AND IT ENDED WITH A TRAINED NURSE KEEPING A MIDNIGHT DATE WITH A CIVIL WAR ADMIRAL IN THE PARK. THE PARALYZED DRUNK WITH THE PET PIGEON, THE FINGER-EXERCISING PUG AND THE TOAD WITH THE GOOSE-QUILL IN HIS MOUTH WERE JUST SUPERNUMERARIES IN THE CHASE AFTER THE MARQUISE GIRDLE, HELPING THE DEAN BRING THE CORPSE-TOTAL TO THE MYSTIC COUNT OF SEVEN.

CHAPTER ONE
THE POISONER

THE DEAN and I watched the smash-and-grab from across the street. The whole operation—break, steal and getaway—clocked about five seconds. We couldn't have stopped it if we had tried. It was a nimble job and, to tell the truth, it caught us flat-footed.

We were headed for the waterfront to examine a rock-crystal sphere we'd heard about, owned by a Chinese scryer. The Dean is a private detective who practices as a professional fortune teller. Crystal gazing is one form of soothsaying the Dean won't touch—he considers it dishonest—but good rock-crystal balls are scarce and he was curious to take a look at it.

We never saw it.

The district was dingy with small shops and narrow cobblestone alleys. We had just rounded a corner headed for the river, when we ran into action. A lumpish looking drifter in a shabby plaid topcoat was standing on the opposite curb halfway down the block. He was staring into the show window of a tiny store. In the crook of his arm he held a loosely wrapped newspaper. A familiar picture. It should have registered instantly. The man, the bundle and the store window. I'm tenderloin born and raised and plenty familiar with the set-up. Suddenly the bimbo pulled a paving brick from the paper, stepped back and heaved it through the plate glass. Quick as a cat, he made his grab—and was gone.

The Dean tensed. I grinned. "Don't try to catch him," I advised. "You can't do it. He'd make a fool of you. Those smash-and-grab boys may not be criminal aristocracy but they know their game. They learn it the hard way."

"Ben, we must check that man—" The Dean was white around the lips.

"Impossible. He's got his throttle wide open."

"Do you realize," the Dean asked quietly, "what we have just witnessed?"

"I think so," I answer. "A very low and harmless variety of petty larceny. Ten to one there's nothing in that window above two bucks."

"Harmless?" The Dean seemed harried. "Let's see."

We crossed over. I had to admit it was screwy. A little card in the mailbox said the shop was closed for the afternoon. A big sign said:

BUTTERFLIES
Bought & Sold
WE PAY MARKET PRICES

The show window itself was about the size of a pool table and almost bare. Standing at the back, to catch the eye of the passerby, was a panel of six giant moths. A couple of butterfly nets were propped in a corner. In the center, facing us, was an open tin box containing some odds and ends: long, slender mounting pins, a pair of tweezers, labels. A little ticket informed us that we were looking at Jenkins' Handy Field Kit and that we could take it home with us for $1.85.

The Dean's face was bleak.

A small knot of bug-eyed bystanders, attracted by the crash, gathered at our shoulders. A young patrolman appeared, bustled about asking questions. The Dean beckoned to him. "Pardon me, officer, let's step over here a moment."

The cop was intelligent and friendly. The Dean gave him our names and address. "Now mark this," he advised, "and you're in line for a quick promotion. We saw it happen. A half a block away. The man had on an old plaid coat."

The policeman became wary. "What the hell is this?"

"A promotion," the Dean repeated. "Take it or leave it. See that box there in the window? That's a lepidopterist's field kit. Something has been stolen from it. A killing jar. A killing jar is a wide-necked bottle which contains a disc of blotting paper and about three nice, big spoonfuls of potassium cyanide."

IT LOOKED from this as though the Dean was giving the affair the brush-off, that he couldn't smell a fee so he was turning it over as a thank-you job to the law. I should have known better. That night, after supper, he brought up the subject again.

I've been working with the Dean for some time now. He picked me up when I was down and out and gave me wages and bed and friendship. I happen to know a little about guns and locks. I hate to think where I'd be now if he hadn't stepped in just when he did.

As long as we've been together, I've never been able to figure him.

The Dean poses as an affable crackpot and carries a shouldergun, point three-five-seven, that can knock over a Sonora grizzly. It's hard to learn much about his history but now and then a story seeps through to me. I've heard in a roundabout way that he solved a tong case in Frisco

The blast of his Magnum was swallowed by the roar of
the 12-gauge tearing into the floorboards.

by carving a counterfeit soapstone seal, and broke another
in New Orleans when he got a job with an old French
costumer, sewing sequins on Mardi Gras gowns. He likes
to pretend—even to me—that he has a hinge loose—which
makes him a little hard to live with. His genius ranges
from steganography to lens grinding but his obsession is
divination.

We had a little three room apartment in a grimy brick
rooming-house down in the slum section of town. Fortune
tellers, as a rule, fall into two classes: the cultists and oc-

cultists, who practice in rosewood paneled penthouses, and the smart-apple boys who hang out their shingles on the edge of shantytown. We had a modest layout but it brought in a turnover that rushed us twenty-four hours a day. The shop acted as a front for our investigations and we worked under the secret sponsorship of the police commissioner.

I was in the kitchen, scalding the supper dishes, when the Dean gave a halloo and called me into our office-bedroom where he lolled in his broken Morris. He licked the snipe of a thin black cigar, got it going. "I wish, I fervently wish, that you'd burn that apron. I know it saves

your clothes but I can't stand those frills and lace insets—
don't interrupt! I'm perfectly aware—"

"Wait a minute," I cut in. "It was your idea in the first
place and you know it. If you think I like—"

"Exactly. I was just going to suggest your replacing it
with, say, an artist's smock or perhaps a dentist's jacket. I
flinch when you pass my line of vision. Be that as it may—"
He leaned back and closed his eyes. "I've been thinking,
Ben. I've been thinking about *veneficium.*"

"*Veneficium?*"

"That's right. The term, which means the art of poisoning, is in little use nowadays though the practice persists.
Of all methods of murder there is none so inept, so childish, as the employment of poison. Certain definite mechanical limitations make this true. Take, for example, the
procurement of the agent and its administration—both
highly vulnerable to investigation, both leaving traceable
trails."

"You're speaking, perhaps," I suggested, "of that busted
window—"

"I'm speaking of the art of poisoning which is no art at
all. It is far simpler to solve a complex poison case than
an impassioned hatchet slaying. The typical poisoner is
almost invariably out for profit. He is more interested in
his goal than in covering his trail, more interested, that is,
in the *result* than in the *method.* Now consider the man in
the plaid coat. He, we must conclude, is not a typical
poisoner. This worries me. An imaginative poisoner is a
dangerous animal to be loose."

I agreed with enthusiasm. "A little gem worthy of Lom-
broso, sir!" And added servilely: "Can I go back to my
kitchen?"

The Dean hunched forward and glared. "No, blast you. Not until I get this thing worked out. It's nothing to clown about. And there's a big fee somewhere in the offing."

"Of course," I murmured. "Ah, the human brain. A little too much fatigue, a wee bit of strain and blam!—it shoots the works. Would you like me to rub your temples?"

He gave me a nasty, mawkish smile. "Just wait. Just wait and see."

AS USUAL, he was right. Twenty minutes later the case began to break in our laps. The Dean was pulled up to his work-table, reading proof on a pamphlet about Mayan sacrificial knives—a clutter of corrected galleys around his ankles—when Ernie Van Deman and Consolacion Honda came in.

They stood in the doorway plenty worried. I staked them in the reception-room and called the boss.

My information on Ernie was pretty vague. He'd been in town seven months. The story around the cigar stores was that he had dropped off an airliner one night about 8 P.M. and by dawn had organized the local gamblers into the strongest syndicate our town had ever known. He was rated as a lad that could take care of himself.

Honda was a West Indian, an ex-fighter, smalltime cardman, who appeared to be enjoying prosperity since he had joined up with Van Deman's board of control. He went in for navy blue shirts and oxblood shoes.

"Gracious sakes!" The Dean was genuinely astonished. "To what do I owe all this?"

Van Deman grinned. "Don't look at me. It wasn't my idea. Ask Consolacion."

Nodules of sweat glistened on the fighter's meaty cheeks. He was in a quandary. He wanted to speak and distrust checked him. The underworld had no particular love for the Dean.

"Well, speak up," the Dean commanded impatiently. "Speak up or fan out of here. I've work to do."

Honda managed a gesture of conciliation. "We're clients. We want your help. We're in a hole."

Van Deman demurred. "Scarcely that, Mr. Rock. What Honda is trying to say is this: a bit of a difficulty has arisen in which he believes you could assist us. There is quite a legend about you around the spots. It is my personal opinion that you are superlatively capable—"

"Thank you."

"—and to be perfectly frank, we could use a little capable advice."

The Dean shook his head. "I've known Honda for seven years and don't like him. You, I've never seen before. But I've heard about you. Don't ask me for advice. Don't tempt me."

Van Deman was unruffled. "Let me present my case before you pass judgment."

It made a weird sketch. They had been framed. Ernie gave it to us candidly and in detail. A couple of weeks ago a retired manufacturer named Bogess Newcome had contacted Honda and put out feelers: he wanted to pool his way into the gambling trust. The syndicate, composed of three men—Van Deman, Honda and Julius Brennan—hotly discussed the advisability of accepting the new member. Brennan blackballed him. For two weeks he refused to alter his position. Tonight Brennan had suddenly changed his mind. He had phoned Van Deman and Honda at their bowling alley and told them to meet Newcome at White Pickets and incorporate him. White Pickets was a tourist camp at the edge of town.

Just as Van Deman got wound up in the tale Honda chiseled in and took over the narrative. They drove to the camp, located cabin Number 9, and entered—according to arrangement. Manufacturer Newcome lay sprawled on the bed. His throat was neatly cut from ear to ear.

Honda reached his climax. "It was very unsightly." The fighter beetled his brows. "It's a frame."

The Dean sat through the recital completely bored. "You're positive in your identification? The man is Newcome?"

They nodded. "It's Newcome, all right." Honda was grim. "It's the man that's been trying right along to buy his way into us."

"But why a frame?"

"Brennan knew we were meeting him. Brennan sent us."

The Dean seemed unimpressed.

"We found two trinkets in the death room." Van Deman clinched it. "Item one: a fountain pen, named in gold, C. Honda, under the corpse."

The fighter blustered. "I never had no pen like that—"

"Item two: this!" Van Deman held out a hammered coin-silver case for a folder of matches. The Dean took it from his fingers and examined it. On the back was engraved: *Ernie from Theophilo Ottoni.*

"That was on the floor," Van Deman said dryly. "Now here is an interesting point. It's mine, all right. I didn't know that I had lost it. That engraving has been put on since it left my possession. When I had owned it it was blank. I never heard of any Theophilo Ottoni. Neither has Honda. Someone is going to pay for this monkey business through the nose."

"You should have left them where you found them," the Dean said rudely. "I don't think I want to represent you. I may change my mind tomorrow."

Van Deman froze. "So that's your answer. After we count on your decency. I'm not surprised. I understand it's a favorite trick of yours—insult clients and then boost fees."

That hurt. It was the truth and we all knew it.

The gambler continued: "Every man to his own racket. But just don't get out beyond your depth. You can catch me tomorrow at my hotel."

The Dean went white to the eartips. "Get going." His voice was low and gentle. "Before you bring on added misfortune."

AFTER THEY had left, the Dean complained: "This isn't working out. Maybe I'd better call Homicide."

But Homicide called us first. It was Lieutenant Malloy. "Stay where you are. I'll be right out. I want to talk to you."

The Dean hung up. He showed relief. "That's better. That's the way it should be. That's why I gave that policeman our names."

Both of them came—Malloy and Captain Kunkle. They burst through the door like they were consulting a doctor. The Dean was one man that Lieutenant Malloy didn't fool. He knew him for a dangerous rival. When the boss and Malloy were on a case together they were as jealous as a couple of ringmasters. The captain was a little over-fond of publicity but otherwise easy to get on with. He kept close-hitched to Malloy and managed to ride through the press in an atmosphere of glory.

Kunkle looked bewildered. Malloy was uneasy. "What's this all about?" he asked hostilely. He laid a brown paper parcel on the reception-room table. We unwrapped it. It contained a shabby plaid topcoat rolled around a wide-necked bottle. The bottle was empty.

"Exhibits A and B," Malloy said. "Let's have the explanation and have it quick."

The Dean was amused. "Just why, may I ask—"

"Don't stall." Malloy meant business. He spoke clearly and loudly, as though he were testifying from a witness chair in a crowded courtroom. "This afternoon there was a smash-and-grab over on Union Street. You see it. You tell the officer that the guy is wearing an old plaid coat. You point out to the officer that the guy stole a poison jar from the window." Lieutenant Malloy paused.

"A coupla hours later a gal drops into H.Q. with this bundle. She claims her aunt seen a man in a wheelchair hide it in the shrubbery over in the park—"

"A man in a wheelchair?"

"That's what she said. The bottle was empty when we got it. Doc Engles says he found heavy traces of potassium of cyanide."

"Why come to me?"

"Because of this." Malloy unfolded a square of tweed-style, deckle-edge note paper. "In the pocket of that coat there's another little pocket—you know, a change pocket. In the change pocket we found this. You're a so-called expert on ciphers. Let's see you do your stuff."

The letter, scrawled in brown ink, said:

Dear Avery:

Today's the day. I'll take care of the shop. You take care of Newcome as per plan.

P.S. He'll have on him a marquise girdle trimmed with a cluster of 12 caliber rosettes. Don't pass it up. We'll add it to other stuff. It's worth the price of a kill in itself.

The Dean whipped out his glasses, clipped them on his nose and inspected the missive over Malloy's hairy wrist. "Who's Newcome?"

The lieutenant gave him a quick flick of the eye. "You make out you don't know. I hope for your sake you're telling the truth. Newcome's a stiff. He's just been reported in from White Pickets. Found in a cabin with his neck sliced. This nutty note ties in. What do you make of it?"

Captain Kunkle put in his oar. "It's too much for us. I'm sure the commissioner would appreciate—"

"Glad to help if I can." The Dean shut him up. "In the first place, the subject has used a highly flexible pen-point upon an unlined paper—two valuable aids in a reconstruction of a psycho-diagnostic assumption. The affected brown ink and the elaborate texture of the paper are also rich in personality implications. The letters themselves are sinistrogyrous, or backward sloping, and the individual terminals are in general drooping—"

"That's—ah—all very interesting." Captain Kunkle beamed. "And we all have the highest opinion of your—er—fortune telling. But what we want to know—what I want to say is, well, what in the hell does the postscript mean? A marquise, as I remember it, is a noblewoman one step above a countess. My wife says that rosettes don't come in calibers like pistols. And a man wearing a corset! Of course, I've heard of such things—but—it must be code."

"It's not code," the Dean said gravely. "It's good old straightforward English. It means just what it says." He watched their faces expectantly. "Is that all, gentlemen? Well, then, good-night."

I couldn't go to sleep. I picked the far side of the bed and tucked my face to the wall but it wouldn't work. I kept seeing a picture of a fattish manufacturer with a beribboned corset. I saw him lying there on that cot in that cabin in the woods. The thing wouldn't leave my mind, let me relax.

"Boss!" I called softly. "Wake up. I hate to do this. But it's getting me down—"

I heard the bedsprings squeak. The Dean's genial voice came out of the dark. "It's quite all right, Ben. I know just what's bothering you. You're having nightmares over that note. Don't."

He paused. "It's perfectly consistent with the facts of the case. There is, however, one thing that troubles me. It's that man, our murderer, being in a wheelchair. That's absurd. That's inconsistent with the facts. You get my point?"

"No," I answered. "And don't trouble to amplify. It just gets worse."

CHAPTER TWO
THE KNIFE

B Y THE time we had finished breakfast the next morning, I had a little better idea as to what it was all about. Guava jelly and bacon had put the boss in an expansive humor and he launched into an explanation. "You're still fumbling with brother Newcome's girdle." He guffawed. "This is going to be a busy day. Call up the commissioner and see if you can get the address of the girl who brought in the coat. And see if you can catch Mort Hobson at his room."

The girl lived at 117½ Market Alley. Hobson didn't answer.

"We'll start the day by dropping in on Mr. J. Brennan," the Dean decided, wiping his mouth with the hem of his napkin. "Brennan's the kingpin here."

"I get it," I said. "This Brennan has a bum steal the poison. He's trying to monopolize the gambling field. He's going to kill off his partners."

"No, Ben. Please! In the first place the poison is going to be hard to explain. You can be sure of that. I have a feeling that the murderer expects its use to pass unnoticed. This poison will be the key to the whole case. When we find out what the poison is used for—then and only then will we be ahead of the game."

Anyone from the district attorney down to the hatcheck girls in the cellar clipjoints, would have told you that looking for Julius Brennan was a waste of time. Little was actually known about him. He made it a practice to keep out of the public eye and he simply couldn't be located by inquiry. He owned a half-dozen establishments, was reputed to be fanatically proud of their reputation for honesty. His operators and strong-arm men were imported. They were a clannish, loyal lot and kept tight mouths.

"Can you do it?" the Dean asked. "Can you bring me to him, face to face?"

"Sure," I said. "Easy. Give me twenty minutes."

"Fine." He was jubilant. "I'll be over at the public library. I want to look at a map of Brazil."

"That'll have to be postponed," I corrected. "You're coming along with me."

I had already decided on *The Smokery*. The Dean stationed himself in a barber shop next door and waited.

The Smokery was rumored to be Brennan's pet. It had been owned by his father before him and he had slept as a baby in a beer-keg cradle at the end of the old bar. It was in this neighborhood of pawn shops and tenements that he had got his start. It seemed a good place to cross his trail.

I stepped out of the bright sunlight into the dim, long room. It was mid-morning and there was a lull in trade. The only customers were three guys sitting around a wire-legged table in a corner playing "fingers" over tumblers of sour wine. They gave me a hard inspection as I entered. I'll swear the decorations hadn't been changed in forty years; there was a penny grip-testing machine on a cast-iron pedestal just inside the door and the backbar was hung with an old oil painting of an Amazon wrestling with a centaur.

I stepped up to the bar and went to work. "I want the best you got. Money no object."

"Rye, Scotch or bourbon?"

"You heard me," I repeated quarrelsomely. "The best you got. Money no object."

The bartender reproved me with a cold, colorless eye. "That ain't no way to order." He placed a glass and bottle before me. He was a big man and moved like a wrestler. After I had downed my drink, he reopened the conversation. "You loaded with dough, eh?"

"Not at the present. But I'm headed in the right direction."

The barman raised his eyebrows politely. I could see curiosity eating at the back of his brain. I lowered my voice and leaned forward. "I'm from St. Louis. We're set to take the town. Me and my brother. It's been a long build-up but we're ready to touch it off."

He thought I was needled. He tried to bait me. "Yeah? You better go back to St. Looey. This here's a tough town to take."

"Not for us. We've got a system. Bud gets a job. He's a croupier. He works a while and then calls me in. One night—just one night—and we clean the joint across the table. It's like taking—"

"Who does your brother work for?"

"A big-shot in town. A fellow named Brennan."

The barman wrung out his towel and laid it on the brass drain. He strolled to the back of the room, opened a closet, took off his apron. Whistling through his teeth, he wriggled into a natty cheviot coat, placed an expensive felt on his bald head. He came around the corner of the bar throwing a shell into the chamber of a big blue automatic. "O.K.," he said, dropping the gun into his side pocket. "We're on our way. Don't give no trouble, just do as I say." He spoke to the three customers. "Tend business for me, boys. I'm called out."

It was that simple.

Outside, on the sidewalk, the Dean stepped up to us smiling. "Is it all fixed up?"

"And how! Be circumspect. The gentleman's got a gun on us."

The bartender nodded sagely. "So this here's the brother, eh? He kin just join the party. Mr. Brennan'll want to talk to him."

We walked a half-block and flagged a taxi.

THE HOUSE our guide took us to handed me quite a surprise. I thought I knew the criminal mind like a book but the gambler had figured out a new angle. It was a brick bungalow out in the university neighborhood, on a street that faced the sleepy campus. Old elms arched above the flagstone walk. A little bronze name-plate on the door jamb said: *Julian Browne*. Ivy grew to the eaves, framing diamond leaded windows in waxy leaves. The Dean's eyes brightened in admiration. "Charming."

The babe that let us in changed the picture. Red hair and a jaw like a carpenter's mallet. She wore a maid's uniform and high French heels but I've seen too many trained nurses not to recognize the profession when I meet it. This gal wasn't hired to take calling cards. Brennan had her here to wrap a quick bandage when, and if, necessary. And to dress gunshot wounds.

"Morning, Chain Locker," she greeted the bartender. "J.B. is finishing breakfast." She completely ignored us.

The barman nudged me in the ribs. "Down the hall. And be good."

The room was a solarium-conservatory. Lemon-yellow sunlight beat through the windows upon a thumbnail jungle of giant ferns and blossoming flowers. Brennan reclined in a fan-backed wicker chair before a little teak taboret, containing an empty plate and a litter of egg shells. Hardboiled eggs for breakfast! Wow! The gambler in an old corduroy dressing robe lay stiff-necked and rigid, watching a pink-breasted pigeon strut in and out of the shrubbery. My first impression was that Brennan was paralyzed. Later, I realized my error.

Chain Locker burst into his story. "They come quiet," he concluded.

Brennan's glazed cheeks broke into a mechanical grin. "Let's hold it until we hear what they have to say." His voice was ready, metallic, as though it came from a microphone deep in his chest. More and more, as I studied him, I felt we were facing an automaton. "It looks, my friend, like you've been taken. It's phoney." He rotated his head slowly until he focused upon the Dean. "What's behind all this malarkey?"

Suddenly, I knew. He was paralyzed, all right. Paralyzed drunk. Only his brain was alive, but it was ticking away like a Swiss watch.

The Dean studied him carefully, taking his mental weight. "I'm Dean Wardlow Rock, private investigator," he declared. "This is Ben Matthews, my assistant. We had to get in to talk to you. About the murder of an associate of yours, a Mr. Newcome."

Brennan wiggled his thumb at Chain Locker. "Out!" he ordered. "So what?" he asked.

"So you knew Newcome was murdered?"

"I can read the papers, can't I? Newcome was no associate of mine. I didn't like him and said so."

"I understood you changed your mind on that point."

"Well, I didn't. And I haven't. I don't know where you get your information and don't much care. The facts are that he was nuttier than a Bellevue runaway and I didn't want any part of him."

"You mean he was unreliable?"

"Unreliable? Ha!" Up came that stiff, glazed grin. "I put a tail on him to see how he spent his time. Guess how he spent his spare time. He had a filthy little room down by the waterfront called, of all things, the Florabelle Studio, where he mended Oriental rugs. And him a millionaire!"

The Dean got out his cigar snipe, screwed it into the corner of his mouth. "You didn't like Newcome. That seems to be your summary."

"This gambling business, Rock, is like banking. The depositor has to have confidence in the house. A gambler has to be dependable and honest. A breath of scandal can wipe out his entire business. He can't go in partners with no lunatic." The pink-breasted pigeon swaggered out of the fern fronds, hopped on Brennan's knee. "But that wasn't no reason for me to knock him off. If you ask me, Van Deman did it."

"I didn't ask you," the Dean answered curtly. "But I will ask you this: did you phone Honda and Van Deman at their bowling alley last night?"

"Not then nor any other time. There isn't a phone in the house. I don't use them. I won't talk to anybody I can't see face to face." He paused and added: "I haven't left this room for six years."

Julius Brennan pressed a buzzer with his toe. The red-headed maid appeared in the doorway. "Natalie, show the gentlemen out."

I ASKED at lunch: "What did you expect to locate on that map of Brazil—a nice, reconditioned Baluchistan prayer rug?"

"Don't scoff, Ben." The Dean was smugly complacent. "It marches along very satisfactorily. We've cut sign on a mighty big fee. This is real money."

"So I believe you have already hinted. Is it unseemly to ask a question? Who's retaining us? Who *is* this generous client?"

"Mort Hobson. Watch his face when I talk to him. It'll be a kick in the pants!"

This should have cleared up a lot of this that puzzled me. But it didn't. In a way, it made things worse, fogged me down. Mort Hobson was sort of a general utility man for three large insurance companies. His specialty was paintings and holographs and family heirlooms, stuff that had a fluctuating value and was impossible to replace. Say someone stole a presentation copy of *Huckleberry Finn*. Mort would dig around in his brain for about ten minutes, catch a train for Nashville, Tennessee, and bring it back. Or say a dowager set up a howl that her ivory chessmen were missing. Mort would drop around to her home and find them for her—right on the second shelf of the gold-leaf cabinet where she always kept them. You see what I mean? A valuable man.

But he was hard to do business with. He'd haggled and horse-traded with so many gyps and cranks and fences and freaks that he thought the world was composed entirely of chiselers. We caught him at the bus terminal inspecting the passengers as they poured off the out of town buses. He wasn't pleased at seeing us.

He put his hand up to his mouth and talked through his spread fingers. "Scram! Leave me alone. Beat it. I'm on a job."

We dropped down beside him on the bench. "This'll only take a second," the Dean said amiably. "Ben, here, wants to ask you about something that's been puzzling him."

"Not me!" I exclaimed. "I'm satisfied if I never speak to—"

"Of course you do. It's been worrying you to death. It's this, Mort: what is a marquise girdle trimmed with a cluster of twelve-caliber rosettes?"

Hobson glared. "You know as well as I do. A marquise girdle is a style of gem cutting. The top of a brilliant is the crown, the lower facets constitute the pavilion. The largest circumference—the division between the crown and the pavilion—is the girdle. A rosette, too, is a type of cut. Caliber-cutting is cutting in proportionate dimensions—

as when a number of small gems are arranged in a design about a large one. The thing you're describing may be a clip or brooch, I'd say brooch, made up of a large marquise-shaped stone, trimmed with a cluster of twelve smaller rosette-cut stones. Now blow."

"Certainly," the Dean said rising. "If that's the way you feel about us. Come, Ben—"

A flush of blood reddened Mort Hobson's baggy cheeks. "Wait a minute. Hold on! I make it now. You're talking about the Marlowe blue diamond. What's your angle in this?"

"I infer the piece has been stolen?"

"Three weeks ago. At Miami. You're bluffing. This is some of your infamous chicanery. The piece doesn't exist anymore. No one would hold the Marlowe marquise. It's been broken up, recut, reset. Too dangerous."

"Of course," the Dean agreed heartily. "That's logic." He got to his feet. "Sorry to have bothered you."

We separated at the corner. Frequently in the middle of a case the Dean would offer some vague apology and go wandering off into obscurity. It always seemed to happen when the going got the hottest. He'd mutter something about taking a little stroll and getting some air—and leave me with a load of trouble. Usually, during such occasions, he was on tour, contacting his network of friends and informers. Over a long period of time, with infinite patience and no little personal expense, he had built up a human file system cross-indexing the town in all its phases. It really brought in results.

He never volunteered any explanation of these pilgrimages and I never pried into them. The Dean wouldn't have told his dying grandmother the name of any one of his informers.

"I'll be leaving you here, Ben," he remarked absently. "Going to stretch my legs a bit, get a breath of fresh air." He hesitated a minute, frowned. "May I ask you to do me a favor? I really should take care of it myself but I'm going to be tied up for the afternoon. You remember the girl Malloy spoke of? The one that brought in the coat and bottle? I believe you have her address down in Market Alley. Run out and interview her for me, will you? Find out *about that man in the wheelchair.* He's a blot in our picture. He doesn't fit. In fact, he's impossible!"

NO. 117½ Market Alley was a welding shop. A brawny bozo with a tattooed forearm was laying metal in the open doorway. He stopped his work and glared. "Not here, brother. Does this look like a residence?" When he had me completely rattled, he added: "I get the same question a dozen times a week. Each time it's from some fancy Don Juan like yourself that should be holding a torch or catching rivets like a decent man instead of chasing wrens that's hardly out of high school. I'm getting tired of being interrupted. I'm going to get me a sign painted: *Notice! Man at work. Do not disturb.* Velma Dolan does not live here. She resides in rear. Take passageway by rain barrel."

I took the passage by the rain barrel, a rotting boardwalk that pushed its tunnel-like way between the dank side of two dilapidated warehouses, and came out in Miss Dolan's front yard. Smack in the center of a dozen wrecked and rusty automobile carcasses was a little tin-can and tar-paper shack with cherry red curtains at its windows. It was pretty hard to express but that touch of lively color made you know that the occupants enjoyed life. The Dean would have called them hedonists.

A girl was sitting cross-legged on the narrow front porch, peeling potatoes. She put aside the pan as I appeared.

"How did he act this time?" she asked.

"Who?"

Miss Dolan pointed toward the welding shop. "Chuck. He's my fiancé. He always insults my gentlemen callers."

Ah! I thought, well he might! Velma Dolan, circum sixteen, with her blued eyelids, false lashes, her tinted toenails blinking from her gold-paper sandals—was as pretty a candy doll as ever decorated a five-tier wedding cake. "I'm from the police," I explained. "Well, not exactly the police—what you might call the *special* police. I'd like to talk to your aunt. The one that found the package in the park."

"Aunt Dora? She's over on the south side today, visiting Cousin Dolbert."

"Is that so? That's too bad. I'm sorry I missed her. Maybe you can help me out." She perked her chin attentively as I continued.

"We want to know a little more about the man in the wheelchair. You said your aunt saw a man in a wheelchair hide that bundle in the bushes. Did she happen to get a good look at him?"

Miss Dolan went into peals of laughter. "Them cops! They can't never get nothing straight. I never said no such thing. It was my *aunt* was in the wheelchair. She's crippled. Every day I push her out in the park to sun. What I told the officers was that my aunt seen a guy, sitting in a wheelchair, see? She's sitting by the duck pond, the guy's over by the flagpole—too far to make out. He pokes this stuff down in a bush. Aunt Dora gets curious, rolls over and finds the coat and things. We decide I'd better turn it over to the cops."

So that was that.

Miss Dolan considered the conversation ended. She picked up her pan and put it in her lap. The pan contained six peeled potatoes and a paring knife. It was a mighty ritzy paring knife. It had a bright red handle with a shiny aluminum butt. Unconsciously, my eye lingered on the slender, four-inch, saber-ground blade. I boggled. The blade had a blood-vein.

Miss Dolan was paring her potatoes with a razor-edged, Swedish steel *hunting knife.*

"Where did you glom onto *that?*" I demanded. "Don't answer. I'll tell you. You found it wrapped in the coat."

She looked startled, bit her lip and nodded. "It wasn't stealing," she insisted. "The man didn't want it. He threw it away."

I wrapped it in a handkerchief and laid it reverently in my pocket. "Wasn't it a little—er—sticky?"

Miss Dolan made a pert grimace. "Awful! But I gave it a good scrubbing."

I patted her hastily on the head. "Good-bye, my child. And enjoy your potatoes."

CHAPTER THREE
SUICIDE JOKE

I EXPECTED the Dean to pop his valve when I brought in my trophy. He didn't. He scarcely looked at it. After an absent-minded glance at the knife, he clucked his tongue, murmured something about its being a "foul toy," and tossed it in the corner of the dresser drawer where he promptly forgot it.

"It's the murder weapon, all right," he decided. "The one that killed Newcome. It was a valuable find—and an afternoon well spent. But probably for a different reason than you surmise. The knife itself as a clue or evidence is completely worthless. Absolutely untraceable—manufactured and sold by the hundreds. Fingerprints, of course, are out." He gave me a quick, wolfish grin. "But all this is trivial. The important point seems to have escaped your notice. It's this: Auntie saw the murderer in the late afternoon, in the sunlight, *after the commission of the crime.* The weapon was freshly smeared with blood. Therefore the slaying took place some hours before Van Deman and Honda found the corpse at White Pickets.

"Thanks to your little adventure, the case is distinctly on the upgrade. We can now fill in a fairly authoritative hypothesis. These things we can deduce with comparative safety. First, that the gambling angle is of secondary importance. The field of action, the murder, only *appears*— because of certain incidental contacts—to be a consequence of gambling enterprise. As a matter of fact, Newcome was not slain because of any gambling association. The motive for his murder was theft. Theft, pure and simple. Do you follow me?"

"I refuse to answer."

"Good. Let's go on. From Mort Hobson we learn that the Marlowe brooch possessed by Newcome at the time of his death was hot. Newcome, the respectable retired manufacturer possesses a piece of stolen jewelry. If a single piece, why not several? The 'Dear Avery' note said the marquise group *alone* was worth a murder. This implies the existence of other loot." He paused, and went on.

"My conclusion is this: Newcome was dishonest. He was in all probability more than that. He was a cunning, but obscure, jewel thief. We may conjecture that it was for this reason he was murdered. He was uncovered, slain, and robbed of his stock in trade."

Events were to prove that every word of this was true.

"In that case," I exclaimed, "we'd better hotfoot it down to that rug mender's shop, that studio, that Brennan told us about. A good frisk might turn up something."

The Dean objected. "No hurry. The shop will wait. I conclude it can tell us nothing we haven't guessed." Events were to prove here that he was gravely in error.

For a full hour after supper, the Dean brooded. He took out the proofs on the Mayan pamphlet, put them away. He prowled about the room, fussing with the bric-a-brac, adjusting his tie, glancing at his heavy silver watch.

"So we're expecting company," I declared. "Is it a girl?"

He grunted.

"In that case, perhaps I should slip into my leopard skin—it shows off. Who is this girl?"

"Listen, Ben." The boss was under strain. "Don't annoy me. Don't catechize me. It's not a girl. I'm expecting Mort Hobson. He's fighting with himself now—trying to make up his mind. He's a lone wolf. He shudders at the thought of splitting his commissions with anyone. But we've swung the bait in front of him and he'll show up slavering at the dewlaps."

WE GOT our company. But it wasn't Mort. It was Van Deman, trailed by Consolacion Honda. Van Deman was in an ugly mood.

"You've had enough time to think it over, Rock," Van Deman snarled. "What about it? Yes or no? Are you working for us or does your interest lie somewhere else?"

The Dean listened with good-natured composure. "We got off last night to a bad start. My feeling at the time was that it was *you*, not Mr. Honda, who wished my services. Despite your dissimulation. I detest a client who doesn't trust me. And I can't work without facts. After you left I did a little fancy guessing about you."

Honda shifted nervously. "What," Van Deman demanded, "did you decide?"

"This: that you are a strong man but there is a chink in your armor. That you are alarmed over something and that something is not the frame of Newcome's murder. I would say, offhand, that your greatest desire is to keep your past life a secret. Your association with *any* crime and the threat of police investigation disturbs you. *There is something in your life you wish to remain hidden.*"

Van Deman's control was an education to watch. He got out his engraved matchbox and lighted a cigarette. The man was a born gambler. "A murder frame is a nasty thing," he said quietly. "But I can take care of it. You're entirely correct. I don't want the police prying into my history. They'll find five blank years. I'm getting set in this town. I'm branching out into real estate."

Honda wedged into the conversation. "It's this way, Mr. Rock. Ernie spent them five years in the Sudan, shooting tigers."

Van Deman's eyes turned to blue ice. "He isn't being funny. He's trying to help. He's told that story so many times I'm getting to believe it. Sometimes it's the Sudan, sometimes it's the Congo. The truth of the matter is that he doesn't know any more about it than you do. But he's going to hear now, and so are you. I spent those five years in jail."

"That's a little better," the Dean said pleasantly. "If this case is handled properly it'll never come out."

Van Deman said bleakly: "I owed a debt to society. I paid it. It's over now. They can't mortgage my life."

"Exactly!" the Dean assured him. "Dismiss it from your mind."

Half an hour later I made my evening trip to the corner drug store to pick up a paper. There was a gleam of white in our mailbox. A personal check, for one hundred dollars, payable to the Dean and signed by Van Deman. He must have stopped on the top step on the way out and left it.

The second late development was a story boxed on the front page of my newspaper. I pointed it out to the Dean when I returned.

GRUESOME HOAX

The discovery late tonight by a dock watchman of a woman's shoes, hat and purse on the pierhead of the West End wharf led the police to suspect, at first, a case of suicide. This suspicion was confirmed by a note found in the purse which read: "Everything is futile. Death beckons and I must answer. Good-bye. (Signed) Avery."

Alert and efficient investigation by Police Captain Kunkle of a dyer's mark in the shoes identified the owner as Myra Finley, waitress at White Pickets, local tourist camp.

"It's beyond me," the little waitress asserted to the police. "The clothes are mine all right, but I don't know how they got there."

Captain Kunkle, asked for a statement, declared: "We are working on this brutal joke. The note is a vital clue. Handwriting is a valuable aid to the reconstruction of a psycho-diagnostic assumption. It's a deep study and I don't want to bore you. Did you know, for instance, that some letters have drooping terminals? We expect an early arrest."

The Dean puckered his face in angry distaste. "The faker! Putting out that hokum. He picked that up from us. He doesn't know a drooping terminal from a paraph!" He closed his eyes. "This takes looking into. It's getting grisly. I think we'd better go out and get this girl's story." He reconsidered. "No. You go. I'd better wait for the spirit to move Mort Hobson."

WHITE PICKETS, at midnight, was lighted up like a county fair. I stopped in the shadow of the rose-arbor gateway and took stock. I didn't care for my job. A conviction had been growing on me, and now, somehow, as I looked over the layout, I felt that I was right. The Dean had sent me out *to check on a dead girl.* I had sensed that from the way he had acted when he read the story in the paper. In spite of the police, in spite of the newspaper, I'd bet my shoestrings that right at that moment Myra Finley lay in some hidden grave. What it was all about I hadn't the slightest idea, but one thing I was certain of: the phoney suicide was a cover for a kill.

The camp was a murder nest, if I ever saw one. A graveled lane led from the highway, through a trellised arch, into the grounds. A group of three small buildings—a filling station, a lunchroom-tavern and the manager's residence, fringed an oval parking lot. Back of these buildings, extending into the black cloudy night, were the patches of second-growth woodland that secreted the scattered cabins.

I walked through the powerful floodlights, across the parking lot and entered the tavern.

The place was really going to town. Overhead lights were shaded with hoods of blue crepe paper. A three-piece orchestra, in burlesque hill-billy costume, was banging away from an unpainted pine platform at the rear. The walls were lined with curtained booths and waiters with orders shoved their way through dancing couples. Tourist camp? Ha!

A vicious-looking rat with plucked eyebrows and a mismatched vest stood just inside the door picking his teeth with a goose quill. His eyes were on me before I crossed the threshold. He sauntered over and blocked my way. "Don't I know you?" he asked.

"I hope not. Where's the manager?"

He thumbed his chest.

"Fine!" I made my voice unfriendly and it wasn't hard to do. "I'll just trouble you for that ninety-six dollars and seventy-five cents. I don't want to get tough but I will if I have to. You people can't push us around. When she signed that little coupon she signed a contract. We made the delivery, now we want our cash. We're tired of being stalled. A ten-volume, quarto, half-morocco, de luxe *Decline and Fall* ain't hay."

It was one of the Dean's pet tricks and it looked like it was going to work.

The manager wavered. "Now wait a minute, pal. You're blowing your top. You've got the wrong party. What's it all about?"

"The books," I said. I spoke with a pretense of painstaking clarity. "There's a waitress here. Myra Finley. She's bought a set of books from us and won't shell out. She gave the management as reference."

The hood's short grating laugh clinched my hunch. "Try and collect. She don't work here no more." I knew we were talking about a corpse as surely as if I had seen it disinterred. "She quit here just tonight. Right after somebody played a practical joke on her. Maybe you read about it in the paper. She packed her bag and hit it for the sticks. That's the way with these gals from the junctions—here today and gone tomorrow."

"If it's all right with you," I suggested, "I'd like to take a gander at her sleeping quarters. That *Decline and Fall* is valuable merchandise."

It took him a good two minutes to decide. "Why, sure, pal." He was suddenly seized with a spasm of good humor. "Why, sure. Go ahead. She lived in the third cabin to your right—number 9. You can't miss it. It sits in a clump of brush and scrub, down in a little hollow."

THE PLAY, from his angle, wasn't too bright. A moron would know that the cabins were for paying guests, not the help. It was like asking a hotel clerk the whereabouts of a chambermaid and listening to him say: "Perhaps she's resting in her room. That's the bridal suite overlooking the lake."

Cabin 9, I remembered, was the one in which Newcome had been found. Stepping from the clearing in among the trees was like being suddenly blindfolded. What I mean, it was dark. Wild grape-vines, looping from the oaks, cut off the weak glow of a watery moon with filaments of shadow. There was the stale odor of rotting logs and slimy fungi in the still stagnant air. The path twisted over the crest of a knob, descended towards a ravine. Here, I located my cabin.

An indistinct bulk in a cavern of foliage, I nearly skipped it. It set back some yards from the trail and I would have missed it entirely if it hadn't been for the violin.

The weird muted minors of a plaintive dirge came through the leaves to meet me.

Someone was in there, *sitting in the dark, listening to a radio.*

I made a snap decision. Pushing through the briars, I circled the building in a wide arc and sidled up to the back door. Through the rusty screening, deep in the vague interior, I saw the red ember of a lighted cigar. It was about knee high and perfectly motionless. There was something wrong about that cigar. It was a little too motionless, too lifeless, as though it had been propped on the arm of a chair for my personal attention. Suddenly—too late—I knew I had been trapped.

"Just like a homing pigeon!" I felt a cold lip of metal behind my ear. "Walk inside—and be careful." An arm snaked across my ribs, a hand patted my pockets, snatched my belly gun from my belt. I stepped inside. The lights went on.

I took a look around. On the little brass bed, where Newcome's corpse had lain, a portable radio gave out with *The Old Refrain*. The floors and walls were bare planking. A cheap race-horse print hung above the dummy fireplace. A telephone sat on the corner of the bureau. White Pickets had room service!

My playmate closed the door, pulled down the shades, turned off the radio. He had coarse, pinched features. His knotty billiard-ball head, clipped to the crown, was topped by a tangle of greasy red ringlets. Two things told me I was facing a veteran, a bruiser of the old school: first, the haircut, and second, his hands. A heavy cylinder gun hung loosely in his bare left fist, his right hand was empty but *gloved*.

I got the whole set-up from this. I was in for a shellacking. By an expert. The old kid glove boys were about gone but now and then one pops up. I saw an eager look in his eyes and knew I had him whipped. He was too hungry for blood, too anxious.

There's one—and only one—way to beat a man at this game. Catch him on the pistol-whip.

"I'm Myra Finley's brother," he recited. "An' I'm goin' to learn you to keep away from her. I'm—"

"You're just another tramp," I said. "Give me back my gun and get out of here while you can still walk."

"You're asking for it," he snarled. "Ten days in the hospital." His gloved fist came up from his ankle. He was quicker than I expected. Tight leather burned across my cheek. His elbow smashed me on the backlash with a rabbit punch that knocked me to the wall.

He hit me three times and each time, through a fog of blood, I grinned at him.

And then it came. The pistol-whip. I grabbed his gun hand, jerked him to me, and laid a good old-fashioned sea-going Danish kiss under his jaw. His eyes went blank, he pulled the trigger once, shot the race-horse print through the withers, and sagged to the floor.

A quick frisk of his pockets revealed a pair of lopsided dice, a plug of tobacco, a carved peach seed—prison work—and a little heart-shaped brass padlock about the size of your little fingernail. The kind that you see on these fancy cedar chests that the gals keep their love letters in. I took the lock, returned the other stuff and left.

The Dean had retired by the time I returned. I washed my cut and swollen cheek in the bathroom and reached for the iodine in the medicine cabinet. The Dean had scrawled in soap on the mirror: *Have turned in. Hope they didn't treat you rough.*

THE NEXT day wound things up. The morning started out with a telephone call. The Dean was out, down to the corner grocery buying a breakfast fish, when the bell rattled. I lifted the receiver. "Hello?"

The voice was raspy, disguised. "I'll do the talking. You just listen. This is a friend. I'm giving you some good advice. Lay off the Newcome case—"

I cut in politely: "Whom did you wish to speak to?"

"Isn't this Wardlow Rock?"

"No," I said. "Mr. Rock is occupied. He is in the workshop filing a Maltese cross on the nose of a Magnum slug. Shall he call you back?" I eased down the prong before he could answer.

When the Dean blew in, I gave him a transcript of the proceedings. "Good!" He waggled his big hand. "They're coming into the open." He sobered, studied the blunt tips of his competent, stubby fingers. "The sooner the better. I don't like girl-killers."

Mort Hobson's morose presence fastened on us as we were finishing our coffee. The insurance man, bleary-eyed from lack of sleep and the torture of perpetual suspicion, pulled up a cane-bottomed chair and groped for words.

The Dean offered him an opening. "What's on your mind, Morton? Not worrying about that Marlowe brooch, I hope."

Hobson clicked his teeth. "Lieutenant Malloy's right. You should be sequestrated. You're a menace to society. I've been actually dreaming—" He left the sentence unfinished. "Tell me, Rock, truthfully and honestly—have you a line on that piece?"

"Yes," the Dean answered pleasantly. "I expect to have it in my hands some time today."

"Well, that seems to settle it." Mort made up his mind. "This is going to be the hardest thing I've ever had to do. It's a disgrace to the name of Hobson but I can't see any way out." He leered at the Dean in distaste. "I'm hiring you to work for me."

"Thank you," smiled the Dean. "I accept. Now I'll tell you what you expect me to do. You want me to recover the Marlowe piece, of course, but there's more than that in the air. You have reason to believe that when I recover the Marlowe piece I will inadvertently uncover a cache of stolen diamonds. It is actually these gems that you are anxious to locate."

Hobson nodded glumly. "We're flooded with losses. Diamonds are better than currency these days. Transatlantic shipments are interrupted and prices are high." Mort Hobson volunteering information was a pathetic sight to watch. He decided to spill it all.

"There's a crooked merchant, a big one, that's got a standing order out at fences from coast to coast. He'll take anything they can get. Who this man is, we don't know yet but we do know that he works out of this very town. When you find the Marlowe you'll find the other stuff. You can be sure of that."

"I'll work on the customary percentage of value recovered," the Dean laid down. "Take it or leave it. I'm to work as I please and guarantee to have it cleaned up in twelve hours. If I need you, I'll call you in but it looks as though Ben and I can handle it alone."

"Tell me this," Hobson asked. "Did I give you anything you didn't know?"

"Very little," the Dean answered. "We know the man and his hideout."

Hobson appealed to me. "How does he do it?"

"Black magic," I explained. "It's his trade."

CHAPTER FOUR
MRS. DUFFY'S SORCERY

ABOUT MID-MORNING we paid a call on Consolacion Honda at the Happy Hour Bowling Alleys. In the cab, on the way, the Dean prompted me into repeating to him—for the third time—the account of my experience at White Pickets. He took the little brass lock from his pocket, rolled it thoughtfully between his fingers. "If you'll permit me to advance a theory," he remarked at last. "I submit that it is this lock that explains the theft of the poison. Now it is you, not I, who are the expert on locks. Please explain to me the probable use of such a lock."

"Well," I considered. "They use those little fellows on several things. On cedar boxes, like I told you. They use them on the hasps of diaries." A thought suddenly occurred to me. "And on dog collars." I gave him a quick glance. "Is that any help?"

"Plenty. I was just waiting to hear it from your own lips." He lay back and relaxed on the cushion. "That's all we need. It sews up the case."

The Happy Hour was not large but it was select. Sandwiched in between a poultry store and a hock shop, about forty feet wide and three stories high, its upper floors housed a warren of lodging rooms. The old Chinese restaurant which had occupied the ground floor when I had peddled papers in the district as a kid had been remodeled as a bowling alley. It was this firetrap which Van Deman was fond of referring to as "my hotel." As a matter of fact, I happened to know it was owned jointly by Ernie, Honda and Brennan. A sagging green door set in an areaway to one side bore the sign: ROOMS—UPSTAIRS.

Honda seemed pleased enough at our visit.

We caught the big fellow as he was just getting up. His little cigar-box room, back in the bowels of a dark, evil smelling hall, was lighted by a weak, fly-specked ceiling bulb. The Dean stiffened with amazement at the spectacle that greeted us as we entered.

Honda, his swarthy torso naked to the waist, sat on the edge of a cot, in a tangle of filthy bedclothes. He was taking exercises. Hand exercises. In the palms of each fist he had a ball of crumpled newspaper about the size of an apple. During the entire span of our conversation with him, he kept these balls in constant motion, kneading and squeezing them. It was an old fighters' method of strengthening your fingers. On the floor by his pointed oxblood shoes lay a long-legged cloth doll. Another, a yarn-haired French grisette, sprawled in a corner. A Mammy, a Sun Bonnet Sue, a lavender giraffe, a leather blackjack and a Smith and Wesson with an eight-inch barrel were lined up on the dresser.

"Good morning," the Dean said quietly. "I had a list of questions to ask you but they must wait. Where did you get all these dolls and why?"

Honda grinned. "Cute ain't they? I stole 'em. Or, as we used to say down in the Caribbean, I thiefed 'em."

The Dean floundered. "Why? Why on earth—"

Honda flexed his wrists and resumed his perpetual squeezing. "Myra, a chippie I used to go with, had a set just like 'em. Even down to that screwy-looking giraffe. I'm sentimental, see? Myra skips town. Last night I run into these out to Brennan's. They ain't nobody looking so I stick 'em under my coat. I like 'em around." His mobile face saddened. "She was a swell kid. I wish I knew where she went."

"If you're talking about Myra Finley," the Dean said roughly, "—she's dead."

"Naw," Honda corrected, "she ain't dead. She's went back home to the farm. I wish I knew where that farm was." He pulled down the corners of his mouth.

"Tell me this," the Dean asked. "Did you kill Myra Finley?"

There was a long silence while we waited for him to answer. When he did it gave me the surprise of my life. I knew in a flash that there was a brain in his skull. Abruptly, he dropped his mask of stupidity. "Wardlow Rock," he grunted thickly. "*Dean* Wardlow Rock, the busybody. You make a juicy living here in town—and so do I. I come to you for help the other night and now—already—you're trying to push me around. Don't ask me questions like that."

We groped our way along the iron pipe banister, down the steep stairs, to the street and fresh air. For a moment we stood on the sidewalk, then, at a sign from the Dean, we turned into the bowling alley. Van Deman, wearing a green eye-shade and a bookkeeper's sleeve-guards, was leaning on the cigar counter, checking racing entries. He stuck his pencil in his vest and raised his eyebrows. "Up and at it so early?"

"It's that engraved match-box of yours. Theophilo Ottoni is a strange name. You say you don't recognize it?"

"I said that the other night. Now, it might be a different story. I think I've got a lead. I figure it was put on for a purpose and I think I can find out why." He tossed the Dean a quizzical glance. "Are you a gambling man?"

"Why, yes," The Dean answered ponderously. "At least I like to fancy myself a bit in that light. What are you getting at?"

Van Deman pushed back his eye-shade. "This. I'll bet you five C's I finish this business up before you do. No arrest and conviction necessary. No questions asked. I'll take your word and you take mine."

"That's fair enough," the Dean responded. "I believe I'll copper that bet."

LUNCH TIME caught us in the neighborhood of our apartment so we came home for a slice of cold beef and a cup of tea.

Mrs. Duffy, our landlady, was sitting in her bay window, watching for us through the slot in her lace curtains. This was a sign that we had long since learned to recognize as important. When Mrs. Duffy was in her crow's-nest, a critical situation of some sort was at hand. As we let ourselves into the hall she intercepted us. A half-dozen things, the extra layer of orange rouge on her chubby cheeks, her quilted satin slumber-jacket with its collar of ostrich feathers, informed us that this was a court occasion. As usual, she was soaked with lilac perfume and bristling with conspiracy.

She handed the Dean a fifty-cent piece.

"I did one myself," she whispered. "It was easy. Like playing a parlor game. But the money's yours. Yes, sir, I did one all by myself."

The Dean coughed. "Good for you. You're a little wonder. Er—what was it you did?"

"I told a fortune. Such a nice lady. She's in there now. She stayed for lunch. She made the cinnamon toast and I brewed the tea. She raises chickens."

"Now this lady—"The Dean brought her firmly to the point.

"—has been seeing ghost lights. She noticed your sign outside and came in for advice. You weren't here and she was so worried and all so I just took her into my living-room and did it myself."

Mrs. Duffy was blissfully unaware of the fact that she was on dangerously thin ice. The Dean was a professional diviner but he had his own code—and it was an extremely strict one. He'd made a lifelong study of the mechanics of ancient magic—he read a half-dozen Eastern languages—and was interested in the subject entirely from a rationalistic viewpoint. He loathed flummery and always informed his clients that fortune telling was hokum. He gave Mrs. Duffy a veiled glance. "I didn't know we were quartered in the same building with a rival operator. How did you tell this fortune? Coffee grounds?"

"Oh, no," Mrs. Duffy informed us. "I did it with the Bible. The way my grandmother used to do. I stuck a silver knife in the Bible, opened it, and read the passage. It's a marvelous way to get good advice. It told the lady in Apocrypha: *Remember that the convenant of the grave is not showed to thee! Ecclesiasticus fourteen, twelve.*"

Relief spread across the Dean's face. "That's about as honest a method as any. It's called, in case you didn't know, sortilege. Its tradition is a long one. It goes back to the days of parchment and probably beyond—to the days of papyri. Its power is supposed to derive from the sanctity of the written word. The written word, historically, is the priestly word. Mohammedans practiced sortilege with a dagger and the Koran. Your particular form is known as *sortes Biblicae*. Sortilege was a favorite method of prophecy and instruction with the ancient Romans who used the works of Vergil and Homer: *sortes Vergilianae* and *Homericae*." He placed a kind hand on her excited shoulder. "It was certainly worth fifty cents but I think we'll return her money to her. Can I come in for a minute and meet her? I'd like to hear about those ghost lights."

The customer's name was Katie Tripps. She was a little wizened old maid with a face like a dried apple. She lived out on Snake Creek with a flock of Plymouth Rocks and she had quite a tale to tell. It seems like a couple of years ago the county had put in a new bridge across from her place. It was built of rock and the workmen, when they were erecting it, had mortared into its base some old broken tombstones that they had discovered in the weeds of an abandoned cemetery nearby. Miss Tripps had objected at the time but all she got was a great big scoffing laugh from the foreman. After that, for two years, she had sat out there in her little cottage waiting for the supernatural visitation that she knew was bound to come.

Finally it happened. In fact it happened twice.

Several nights ago, two to be exact, just after dark, she had gone to draw a pitcher of water to take her nightly stomach powders. Gazing towards the creek, she had suddenly noticed it. A blob of orange light, fuzzy and malevolent, way back under the bridge.

A night later, she had seen it again. This time early in the morning, before daylight, when she went out to check on the temperature in the brooder house. Again it was way back under the bridge.

The Dean beamed. "A long and wandering story, madam, but highly engrossing. Permit me to say that I am the only man in the world who knows what it was that you witnessed. Here's my advice: dismiss it completely from your mind. You were watching the red glow of a flashlight dimmed through the fleshy fingers of a man. There was nothing supernatural about it. It will not occur again."

Miss Tripps was dubious. "A man back under the bridge? That's silly. There's nothing under there!"

"I'm afraid you're wrong," the Dean corrected gently. "Why not spend the afternoon here with Mrs. Duffy while the police drive out and have a look-see?"

ACROSS IN our apartment, he grabbed the phone, got Homicide and asked for Malloy. "It's the *corpus delicti*, Myra Finley," he told me over his shoulder. "It can't be anything else. The time tallies for both nights."

"Both nights? I don't get this. Last night, yes, could be Myra. But the other night—"

"This is gruesome, Ben. As bad as I ever ran into." The receiver clicked. "Hello? Lieutenant Malloy? Now listen carefully. Here's a chance to show up your captain. Remember Myra Finley, the fake suicide? I have reason to believe she was slain. Murdered *prior* to the phoney suicide set-up— Yes, yes. I know the police talked to her afterwards. But they were taken in. They talked to a substitute. Myra had already been killed. Captain Kunkle's identification of the shoes threw the murderers into a panic. They scurried around and dug up a double. Where did the identification take place? You called the tourist camp and she came down to H.Q.? Someone out at White Pickets intercepted the call. This double is going to be hard to trace."

I could feel the explosion of Malloy's angry voice shaking the diaphragm.

"Now wait a minute," the Dean insisted, "and I'll tell you all about it. I'm offering you a trade. Here's what I want. Sometime today, when we're together, I say to you: 'Did you get an answer to our cablegram?' Then you hand

me a blank sheet of paper. Get it? Do you agree? All right."
He then told about Miss Tripps' visit and the bridge. "It's
sheriff's office—out in the country—but it's a city kill.
You'll find the girl there—and something else. Something
pretty horrible, I imagine. Sorry can't go along but I'm too
busy. I'll call you back later. Bye."

Hardly had the Dean put down the instrument when
Julius Brennan paid us a call. He came forward off-balance,
walking on his heels, clutching the arm of Natalie, the
maid. His clothes, from spats to collar-rim, looked glossy
and new. It was as though he had been lifted out of a coffin,
set on his feet, and propelled across the room.

The girl handed me a jolt. Somehow, when she was
dressed in street clothes, you didn't notice her aggressive
jaw. She stood there, lithe and slim and supple, supporting
her boss with a slender wrist. Her little blue jacket with
its white stock wasn't much bigger than a cocktail napkin.
Only her midget shoes, with their trim, low, military heels,
confirmed my original impression of her—that she was a
professional nurse.

"Come in, come in!" The Dean waved them to seats.
"And what is it, Mr. Brennan, that coaxes you out of your
sanctum? Six years, I believe you said, in monastic retreat.
That's an extraordinary record and now you're breaking
it."

"Things are cooking." Brennan's waxy, mechanical grin
got into action. "All hell's stirred up. I had to get out to
see you. It's a case of self preservation. I've come to ask
you this: how are you coming on the Newcome kill?"

"It's in the bag," the Dean said confidently. "It was
clumsy work from the first. We've found the little brass
lock. Moreover, we've found the girl."

"Don't give me a song-and-dance. I want facts. Have to have 'em." Brennan fumbled stiff-fingered for a cigarette. The nurse slipped it out, lighted it for him. "I don't know—or care—about any lock or any girl. What I want to know is who killed Bogess Newcome?"

"Don't get steamed up. You'll find out. At the proper time. Why the sudden interest? I thought you didn't care, that you very definitely considered it good riddance."

"Listen, Rock," Brennan answered in that queer microphone voice of his, "don't you speculate too much on my interest. Leave me out of it. The less you get to wondering about me the better." He tried to sneer. It was too much work and he gave it up. "What's this hooey about a girl?"

"That's what I want to know." The nurse's cool, low words broke into the discussion. She had been listening, taut and intent, with narrowed eyelids. "When things are going on around me I like to be informed."

"Who doesn't!" The Dean gave a short, quizzical laugh. "Goodness, yes!" He eased off the subject and worked around to a new point of attack. "You know, Brennan, I've been wondering about that tourist camp—White Pickets. Can you tell me, in confidence, have you heard whether or not it might be in the rackets? Its manager, the lad with the plucked eyebrows and quill toothpick—" I gasped. The Dean had never laid his eyes on the man. He was repeating my description of him. "—somehow strikes a response in me. I haven't placed him yet but somehow I have a definite impression that—well, he has a record."

"He has," Brennan said curtly. "I know because he's on my payroll. White Pickets belongs to me. I don't get the slant." The lacework of veins on his cheeks flushed. "Yes, I do," he amended. "I'm beginning to see. You're selling me down the river. You're stringing together a string of coincidences and accidents and making out a brief for prosecution. Here's your case: I own White Pickets. I make an appointment with Newcome in cabin 9, have my manager bump him off. I call Van Deman and Honda—"

"And try to frame them."

"And try to frame them!" Brennan juggled himself to his feet. "It won't work. It's lousy."

"Of course it is," the Dean agreed affably. "It's not my case at all. My case is simple. And foolproof. A schoolboy could solve it with an ordinary map of Brazil."

Brennan pawed for the arm of his escort. The redhead braced herself, caught him on the sway. "That's all," he said. "I just wanted to make myself clear."

The pair of them, gambler and nurse, tottered from the room.

THE DEAN said grimly, "It's the Florabelle Studio. Time is slipping!"

The city directory gave us the address. We flagged a cab at the corner and made the crosstown trip in twenty minutes.

"I was just thinking," I said as the taxi swooped from the curb. "There is more in this business than meets the eye. It's subtle. Get what I mean? Say Newcome was a jewel thief. He had a girl friend. He knows he's on the spot. What does he do? He hides his gems. Where? He hides them in Myra Finley's dolls. Those rag dolls on Honda's dresser are stuffed full of diamonds!" I let the idea set. "How does it sound?"

The Dean listened with fatherly attention. "It sounds demented. But I can see you're trying. Some day, perhaps, you'll be a great detective. Who knows?"

The Florabelle Studio, the little shop where millionaire Newcome, according to Brennan, was wont to while away the hours at the whimsical trade of rug mender, was a front basement in a mouldering flophouse. A strip of yellowed cardboard in the window said:

FloRABeLLE STUdio—ORIENTels REPARed

The letters were hard to read. All in all, it was as poor an imitation of illiteracy as I have ever seen. It was the kind of printing you see on kidnap notes and poison-pen letters. Before we had entered the shop we could see that Mr. Newcome wasn't on the up-and-up, that he was trying to cover something shady.

The lock gave me a bit of trouble. It was a tumbler job and the cam held out on me for a while but finally I heard the bolt give. I turned the knob and opened the door.

"What was the matter?" the Dean asked. "Was it stuck?"

"No," I answered patiently. "It was locked. There is a difference, you know."

In the murky light of the crusted, cob-webbed window, we gave the room a quick once-over. Patches of plaster, as big as turkey platters, had dropped from the ceiling, leaving rotted lath exposed. Underfoot, the warped and shaky floor was littered with rubbish which had been swept half-heartedly into the corners. On the back wall was hung a dusty, cast-iron wash bowl and above it was tacked a gaudy, new travel poster depicting moonlight on Bagdad.

"It's not an attractive place," the Dean remarked. "It's not supposed to be. The whole setting is staged to discourage trade. When an assertive customer insisted on leaving a rug to be mended, Newcome no doubt sublet the order to some professional. But such occasions, I imagine, were rare. We can safely assume that brother Newcome, hidden in this hole, was left pretty much alone—as, of course, he wished to be."

There were but two articles of furniture in the room: an old shoemaker's bench and a broken-down milking stool.

The Dean muttered to himself. "What we want is here—it has to be. If we can only find it. The man was much cleverer than I had at first suspected."

"What are we looking for?"

"We're looking for a dop and a skeep."

"It's a funny thing, boss, but it sounded like you said we were hunting a dop and a skeep."

"I did." The Dean pummeled the back wall with the heel of his hand. "There must be a concealed door in this wall. It's just a little too solid to match the others. A dop is a cup-shaped instrument with a handle. A skeep is a horizontal burnishing wheel of soft iron. They are the two essential tools of a diamond polisher."

I lifted the creases in my trousers and perched on the corner of the cobbler's bench. The rack at the end contained a single awl. Now, I don't know much about awls but I never saw one like that one. I lifted it out of its bracket and looked at it. It had an ordinary knoblike wooden grip and a stubby *copper* blade. "Look," I called. "I've found a dop-skeep!"

Wham! It dawned on me. I knew what I was holding. "So there's a hidden door in that wall." I got to my feet. "Kindly step aside."

When you knew what you were looking for, it wasn't hard. It took me about a minute to spot the object of my search: a little hole. About shoulder high. "Before I do this," I said to the Dean, "I'm going to make a speech. Just like you do. We're facing an electrically controlled door. I stick this copper prong into this hole, it makes contact and completes a circuit. Thus—"

A section of the wall, about two feet wide—the wash basin and the poster—swung inward. We entered a little workroom and closed the panel behind us. "This," the Dean whispered smugly, "is more like it. We are in Newcome's diamond-cutting shop. As I surmised, he was more than a jewel thief—he was an expert cutter. Here is where he did his bruting and his slitting and his polishing. Here is where hot diamonds changed their shape and became brand-new trade goods."

CHAPTER FIVE

THE EXTRA CADAVER

THE DEAN bent over a heavy table and eagerly inspected its jumble of tools. "This power-driven belt turns the spindle. Here"— he touched a thin disc of bronze about four inches or so in diameter— "is the buzz saw that makes big ones into little ones. The edges of this disc are charged with diamond dust to give it cutting power. This iron thing is the tongs, the tool that controls the angle of the facets—the new facets."

"What's this?" I asked. I kicked a five-foot chain on the floor just inside the door. The end of the chain was bolted to a metal plate set in the baseboard. "It looks like a dog-chain."

The Dean wheeled. "That's it!" he exclaimed. "It's the last nail in our killer's coffin. We'll hang him with that chain!" He tried to take it easy but he couldn't hide his excitement. "Here's the way it happened. Before, it was a guess, now, it's a fact. Newcome kept a valuable supply of stones in this room. No doubt his entire collection. Two killers, working in unison, worked this business: one poisoned the watchdog with the potassium cyanide and lifted the loot from this room, the other trapped and slew Newcome at White Pickets. Remember the note: 'I'll take care of the shop. You take care of Newcome as per arrangement.' It was a fiendish business and it hasn't stopped yet."

"If the dog was knocked off here, where is he?"

"He was taken away. To forestall investigation. A carcass decays, you know. Odor is far-reaching."

There was a drawer in the table, an empty drawer with a false bottom. The compartment beneath it, too, was empty but for an oil-cloth covered memo book. "Looted," the Dean affirmed. "Bare as—whoa! Let's take a look at this."

The notebook contained lists, item after item, page after page. With dates. The first page started off:

10/30/37	Pr. pendants, pendeloque—St. Paul
10/30/37	Sunburst, 10 rose coupee—Denver
11/12/37	Ring, Old Mine—Chicago
12/2/38	Circlet, 8 keystone—Cleveland

The last entry in the book was dated four days ago. It said: *12/11/40 Brooch, marquise, 12 caliber rosettes—Miami.* It was our old friend, the Marlowe piece.

The Dean closed the book, slipped it into his big, leather wallet. "Wait until Mort sees this." His eyes took on a voluptuous glaze. "He'll go into convulsions! He'll have apoplexy!"

He took a last look around, opened the panel. "Let's be moving. We've seen everything."

Seen everything? Ha!

Two old chums of mine were waiting for us in the front room.

The manager of the tourist camp, the toad with the fancy eyebrows, squatted on the broken stool. The goose quill was jammed between his front teeth and a sawed-off 12-gauge with a home-made pistol handle gleamed in his lap. The kid-glove bruiser, the lad with the bumpy neck, leaned against the wall. He was tapping hot licks on his knee cap with a cheap Spanish automatic and arguing with his boss. It seemed as though they had trailed us into the basement and we had vanished on them.

"—come into this very dump and then—hocus-pocus! They're gone." The bruiser was talking. He was scared.

The hood with the feminine eyebrows attempted a condescending laugh. "There's nothing to it. It's just a trick. You gotta know how, that's all. If Houdini can do it, why can't Rock? We'll wait. They'll be back."

The Dean closed the door softly behind him and stepped into the room. He kept his empty hands in plain sight. He stood in front of me, a little to one side, so that his shoulder blocked my gun arm from their view. It was a risky play—it depended upon the Dean's gift of gab—but we had managed it before. "You're just the lads I want to talk to," the Dean said affably. "No need to get alarmed." He bared his teeth. "Unless, of course, you feel so inclined."

The manager swung the shotgun to his thigh. "Funny stuff, eh? Where you guys been?"

The Dean addressed the thug against the wall. "I have eighty-two dollars in my wallet. It's yours if you answer me one question. Did Myra Finley give you that brass padlock?"

"Don't be a sap!" His pal tried to shut him up. "It's yours anyways. You can take if off him after the kill."

The bruiser smirked. "And split with you? Not me. I'm putting in a option. Here's what happened, cap. It's a coupla nights ago. I'm playin' checkers with Eddie here. Myra calls, gives me the number of this joint and says bring around a car. She's waiting outside at the curb when I get here. They's a dead dog lying in the shadows in the doorway. We pile it in the back seat, drive out in the country and hide it. Next morning when I'm cleaning the floorboards I find that little padlock. Myra musta lost it. Maybe it come from the dog. Is that worth eighty-two bucks?"

"It certainly is. Where did you end this pastoral excursion?"

"I drove Myra around to Avery's and left her. He was waiting for her?"

"And who on earth is Avery?"

"That's the chief. We call him Avery because it's a sissy name and it ribs him. If you want to know his genuine, certified name you'll have to ask Eddie. You tell him, Eddie."

It was the tip for the fireworks.

And about as subtle as sending up smoke signals. It gave me a good three seconds to prepare. The bruiser snapped a shot at us but I stepped out and spiked him with three quick ones before his hammer struck the firing pin. There was a blink of light on the shotgun breech and I saw the Dean hunch his shoulder. The blast of his big Magnum was swallowed by the double roar of the 12-gauge as it tore through the floorboards. Eddie hurtled from the stool with a hole above his eye.

The Dean replaced his weapon in his worn leather shoulder holster. "Let's be moving," he said. "We're in for action now. We're running their trap-line and they know it."

Two blocks away we slowed our pace, caught our breath. "Listen," I said. "I've seen you make that draw time and again—"

He put me off with an angry snort. "Just a matter of concentration. There are dozens of skilled trades—watch repairing or wire-walking, for instance—that require a far greater refinement of physical dexterity."

THE DOWNTOWN library was a quarter of a mile from the rug mender's. We took it at a hunter's walk. I had been in the big stone building with the Dean before and I always felt foolish. Guns and locks, I know moderately well, but the longest book I ever read from cover to cover was a leaflet I once picked up on a railroad platform called *Dredged Through The Brimstone Of Hell or A Burglar Reformed.*

The Dean was top man on these visits. The help around the place almost held a party when he entered.

The spinster behind the desk jerked back her lips in a toothy yawn of welcome. "Good afternoon, Dean Rock. You're just the man I want to see. Miss Mettlefinger, over in reference, has on a new blue blouse. I say it's sky blue and it's the color for Sagittarius. Her lord is Mercury and that means her planet is in exile. She says the blouse is iridescent and that the color *is* Mercury. Now would you be kind enough to settle—"

"Somebody seems to be color blind," the Dean said genially. "I'll look into it if I have time. I want a good atlas. With a map of Brazil."

The librarian nodded. "I happen to have a copy right here at the desk. Unusual thing. A sickish-looking man"— she described Julius Brennan— "and a horse-jawed woman came in a little while ago asking for the same thing. They pawed at it and argued and scolded. They seemed very angry. They couldn't find what they wanted." She batted her eyes. "What's going on in Brazil?"

"They've discovered coffee in the hills just back of Santos," the Dean answered sententiously. He ran his finger rapidly down a printed column, made a note on the back of an old envelope:

municipio—Minas Geraes, state,
pop. 163,000

"Thank you," he said. "And now this, please." He thrust a sinewy arm through the wicket and dragged out the desk phone.

The spinster sat stunned. The Dean made his connection. "Mort? Things are turning. The Florabelle Studio is the place you've been looking for but stay away from it. Right now it's hotter than a basket of imps."

The Dean was an accomplished opportunist. When things began to break, when he had a case on the run, he pushed his luck for a quick crackdown. We hit the sidewalk. Dusk had fallen. The deserted streets, abandoned by the last straggling office worker, were engulfed in that breathless silence that arrests a city at supper time. It was the hour so sacred to mankind, the hour of liver-and-onions. I brought up the subject with a bright smile. "I'm hungry."

"So am I. But we'll have to wait."

"And thirsty."

"Chew a bullet. If it was good enough for General Custer it's good enough for you. We've got a little unfinished business to take care of. Do you know, by chance, a certain Doctor L.B.S. Grinnell? No? Then brace yourself. This is going to be an experience. He's eminent."

DR. GRINNELL lived in a seventy-thousand dollar Georgian mansion just next door to his hospital. I got a glimpse of the gentleman through the window as our cab came to a stop—a pompous little man with an imperial, eating in his formal, wainscoted dining-room, alone. Just a flash of silver and snowy napery and the prim, munching imperial.

The Dean told the driver to wait. I sized up the impressive porch with its stagey, two-story pillars. "Have you an appointment?" I asked. "If not we might as well go home. This is going to be a hard drum to crack."

"Not so. Not so, Benjamin, my boy." The Dean chuckled. "The more pretentious the person, the more numerous his weaknesses. Now let me see—" The Dean got out his old-fashioned clip-purse and riffled through his assortment of cards. It was his conscientious habit to pocket every calling card that passed through his hands. His collection ranged from titled cards with crests to solicitations for dry cleaning. "Where is it?" he muttered. "It's here somewhere. Hah!" He plucked out the object of his search, returned the others to his purse. The card said:

TUKE MANUFACTURING COMPANY
Artificial Hands—Arms—Legs
Broughton Tuke, Pres.

He uncapped his pen, dashed across the back: *Let's avoid any unpleasantness.* "That'll bring him out of hibernation," the Dean decided.

We didn't appeal to the menial that answered our ring. He made a mild moue as though we were crusty at the seams. "Patients next door. And, of course, the doctor never—"

The Dean handed him the card. "I can give Grinnell three minutes," he grated. "Get on your broom and gallop."

The doctor met us in an alcove in the baronial hall. He grasped a salad fork. His face twisted and jerked with annoyance. "I've never heard of you, Mr. Tuke—nor do I care to. What is the meaning of this unwarranted interruption? When I am at table—"

"Do not call me Mister Tuke. I am Wardlow Rock. Private investigator. The reputation of your hospital is in question."

"Be good enough to amplify."

"Consider this hospital of yours, this humanitarian creation of a single brain—yours! Let's put it this way. Where would this town's medical profession be today if it weren't for you? What one man, by sheer power of personal charm and keen scientific insight, controls the destinies and directs the work of so many nurses and associate doctors as yourself?"

"What you say is quite possibly true." Dr. Grinnell was listening attentively. This was the kind of conversation he enjoyed. "In fairness to myself, I must admit that I have done, in a modest way, my own small bit to improve—"

"The preachers shout it from the pulpits. The newsboys cry it from the streets. Now, Doctor, I'm in a little difficulty. I come to a great man for guidance."

Dr. L.B.S. Grinnell was effusive. "Come in, sir. Join me in a coffee. Guidance? Well, well. At your service, sir."

The Dean hit his stride. "It's about my dear friend, Mr. Fuller." He bowed to me. "Mr. Fuller is a homesteader from Alaska. He has come here to take unto himself a wife. Lonely in his little Alaskan cabin, he suscribed to a marriage bureau—*The Heart Renewed Service*—and was soon corresponding with a young lady, a nurse at an address in this town. The girl's name is Natalie and her letters are sent care of Julian Browne, 1487 University Place. Can you give us any information concerning this maiden?"

Dr. Grinnell rocked on his heels. "Officially, no." He gave us a sly look. "Unofficially, it's lucky you came to me. The girl is Natalie Anderson, a highly trained and competent nurse, whom we were forced to discharge some time ago. It was alleged that she was alienating the affection of a staff doctor from his wife—or was attempting to do so. Taken from our lists, she went from bad to worse. At the present, I understand, she's attending an underworld person, a dipsomaniac. Mr. Fuller, she's an evil person." Dr. L.B.S. Grinnell shook a warning finger under my nose. "Go back, Mr. Fuller, and seek out some wholesome, upstanding daughter of Alaska's prairies. You can never be happy with Natalie Anderson."

THE DEAN was unbearably priggish over the result of the incident. We climbed into our cab and slammed the door. I gave him a piece of my mind.

"What did you do before you met me? You got along all right, didn't you? Stop foisting me off to strangers as though I were a diseased kidney in a bottle of alcohol. Mr. Fuller, the homesteader from Alaska!"

"You befuddle me." The Dean pretended regret. "And I'm not referring to your unfilial rebellion. You heard the hoodlum at the rug mender's confess that Myra Finley robbed Newcome's shop, slew the dog, took the carcass to the country to conceal it—yet you evidence no interest in this weird revelation. Don't tell me you guessed it from the beginning because I'm certain you didn't. Aren't you curious about the waitress and her association with the case?"

I sulked. The Dean continued: "The little girl from the country was the killer's accomplice. I see her as a dominant thread in this murder tangle. It was she who actually put Newcome on the spot, she who, somehow, probably through amorous device, drew the secret of his trade from him, learned the mechanics of his locks, poisoned his dog and robbed him. It was she who wrote the unsigned note about the marquise girdle—that death warrant which told her principal that the time was at hand to steal and slay. The next day this principal, this person known to us as Avery, grew distrustful and eliminated her also."

I nodded. "Just about as I said. The ice will turn up in Honda's dolls. You wait and see!"

"Quit harping on Honda's dolls. They have no significance whatever. It is Brennan's nurse, the evil Natalie Anderson, who has the diamonds. Tricking her into releasing them is going to be, I'm afraid, quite a job." He leaned forward and spoke to the cab driver. "Find a drug store." Our teeth rattled as the car went into a gambado and floundered to a stop. "I'll be right out. I want to call Honda and ask him to meet us."

An instant later he was back beside me, a brown paper sack in his lap. "Sandwiches," he explained. "I caught him. What'll you have—chicken salad or tuna fish?"

"Where are we meeting him?" I asked.

The Dean shifted a generous bite to a pouch in his cheek. "The morgue." He brushed a crumb from his lapel. "Here comes Bill Malloy. Don't let him take your appetite."

The lieutenant was visibly shaken. "Move over, you guys, and let me in. I want to sit down. We've been looking for you from hell to breakfast." He got in, took a ham on rye that the Dean proffered him, ate half of it in moody silence before he continued.

"We went out to the Tripps place on Snake Creek, crawled back under the bridge—like you said. Rock, it was horrible! I've been on the force for thirty-five years and before that, when I was a brat in knee pants, I shined up the old gaboon by the sergeant's desk and curried down the mare that pulled the patrol wagon. I've seen trunk murders and torch murders and torso killings. But I never saw anything like this. This here is one of them crazy cult slayings. There was an extra corpse under that bridge." He stared blankly at the toes of his easy-comfort shoes. "There was a girl, Myra Finley—we got her identified positive this time—*and a dead dog.*"

"One thing at a time," the Dean requested. "First, it is not a cult job. It's the good old murder-and-robbery motive. It's dressed up a little so you missed it. Secondly, and most importantly, while there *is* an extra corpse, you have your cadavers mixed. It's the girl and not the dog that is the extraordinary element. Because it was the girl herself who killed and hid the dog there."

"Hold on!" Malloy was again his official self. "That needs explaining."

"Doesn't it though?" the Dean agreed smoothly. "I know just how you feel. I felt the same way all morning. You'll be astounded when you work out the solution. We were, weren't we, Ben?" He called to the cabman. "Let's go out to White Pickets, driver."

"Lieutenant," I queried. "Here's a puzzle for you. Did you ever hear of a man named Ottoni?"

Bill Malloy was a cop with a camera eye and a memory like a filing machine. He remembered every crook that had ever crossed his path, every picture that he had ever seen, every alias and racket that he had ever heard about. He ran my question through the channels of his mind, rejected it, shook his head. "Never heard of no Ottoni. Who is he?"

"Nobody," the Dean cut in angrily. "Absolutely nobody. I wish to heaven that Ben wouldn't attempt to free-lance."

Discussion lagged. The lieutenant seemed uninterested in our destination.

"A funny thing happened a little while ago," Malloy said casually. "A basket peddler selling shoestrings and kitchen stuff was working the waterfront neighborhood when he went down into a basement area of a place called the Florabelle Studio, saw the door open and stuck his head in. They was two dead gunmen on the floor and the air was blue with cordite fumes. You wouldn't have any data on that affair, would you?"

"That depends. Who were these two characters?"

"An old time habitual named Red Shawney out of Cleveland and a local boy, Eddie Watts, with a record as long as your arm for unlawful conversion."

The Dean laughed. "You don't say! I can hardly believe it!" He lowered his voice to a mock whisper. "Those boys are cogs in the Newcome-Finley case."

THE CAB driver first called our attention to it. A fire, and a big one, out in the north end of town. The faint pink blush in the night-sky reddened and spread, threw the black housetops into stark relief as the blaze gained in fury. Soon we were close enough to hear the crackle and snap of burning embers and the clamor and din of fire engines. "If that ain't the place we're headed for, I'll eat the chromium angel on my radiator cap." The cabman sighed. "What shall we do now? Would you gents desire to drive out anyways and sight-see?"

"Straight ahead," the Dean ordered. "And help yourself to the traffic—you're on police business."

The jalopy curvetted from the highway onto the graveled drive, skidded under the trellised arch into the grounds and shuddered to a vibrating stop. "The Seven Wonders of the Ancient World!" the driver announced in a loud, theatrical voice. "All out."

The place was a shambles of destruction and confusion. The camp was outside the city limits and the firemen were having difficulty in finding sufficient water. A small knot of employees, their faces enameled by the fierce glow, stood in a helpless group beyond the line of hose. The manager's residence was a billowing inferno. Sparks in swirling clouds had spread the fire and the roof of the tavern was sheeted in a single lip of roaring, orange flame.

Malloy's wise eyes wrinkled. "It's a touch-off. It's an arson job. That building caught at all four corners. It's—"

The explosions cut him off in mid-sentence. There were three of them, hand-running, deep, cavernous, like three earth-shaking coughs from the pit of some bottomless well. My eardrums felt as though they had been kicked. My knee was on the ground and the back of my hand was scratched. I staggered upright and looked dazedly around. The burning buildings had vanished. The detonations had cleared them from their foundations.

"It's all over," the Dean remarked quietly. "Our criminal was too quick for us." He was taut, pale. "I blame myself for this delinquency. Shall we go back to town?"

Social relations on the return were strained.

"You had a tip," Malloy accused. "You knew it was due to happen. That's why you took me out. I want the story— the whole story, now—and none of that high pressure salesmanship of yours. What was it? Insurance fraud?"

"No," the Dean answered slowly. "It wasn't insurance fraud. The fire was set to destroy evidence. What evidence, I don't know and don't care. We don't need it. We've got an ironclad case without it."

Malloy's jaw went rigid. "Who's got what case?"

The Dean continued: "Newcome was a dealer in hot jewels. He used cabin number 9, here at White Pickets, for his drop. The stickup lads and fences from coast to coast came here to deal with him. Myra Finley, a waitress at the tavern, learned his business, tipped off an accomplice who murdered him. The girl, in turn, next day, was slain by her accomplice. Red Shawney was in on the deal, as was Eddie Watts, who, incidentally, was manager of the tourist camp. You have told me that these two were slain this afternoon. The murderer, frightened at the death of his aides, fired the camp to obliterate any possibility of their association with him."

"You're trying to muddle me. You're deliberately putting everything hind-end first. Who did these killings?"

The Dean sizzled. "Don't press me. Don't rush me. I've given you three-inch banner headlines and a four-column spread already. It's as much as I can offer now. Meet me at the home of Julian Browne, University Place, at exactly midnight and you can make your arrest."

WE DROPPED the lieutenant at headquarters, swung around the corner to the morgue.

The building, a phantasm of Moorish tile and yellow brick, basked in the faint light of a single blue bulb, like some eerie night-monster, gorged and sleeping.

Consolacion Honda waited for us on the stone step. The gambler was barbered and powdered. A crushed-raspberry scarf was knotted about his neck and an ivory-headed walking stick was in the crook of his arm. He made no attempt to conceal his hostility as we approached.

The Dean pounced. "I asked you to meet me here for a rather abominable purpose. To prove an assertion I made to you this morning. I repeat, Myra Finley is dead. Her body lies inside. Would you care to come in and confirm my statement?"

Honda hesitated. "Yes, I would," he decided. "But I'll go alone." His manner became steady, assured. "I think you're a liar by the clock."

He was gone twenty minutes.

The Dean peered into the dim corridor. "I wonder what's keeping him?"

The gambler's return completely flabbergasted us. He reappeared with Natalie Anderson. Brennan's nurse walked, softly weeping, at his side. The big man's heavy-muscled face was as blank and lifeless as a shaman witch-mask.

The Dean lifted his hat. The little redhead joined us. Honda, in his trance, continued past us. We watched him march down the steps out of our circle of vision, blended into the shadows. "What's the matter with the man?" I asked.

"He's been signing papers," Natalie Anderson explained. "Releases. For the girl inside—arranging for an expensive funeral. She was his wife. They didn't live together but he loved her."

The Dean blinked. "Wife?"

The nurse gave a low, antagonistic laugh. "Don't stand there and gawk at me that way. You rigged the whole cruel set-up and you know it."

"But not your presence here," the Dean lashed out. "What brings you here?"

"A premonition. Myra was my best friend. Every day we had lunch together. Several days ago she brought over an armful of old dresses, her boudoir toys, a fur neckpiece she was through with—stuff like that—and gave them to me. She was terribly excited. She said she was on the verge of making a fortune and leaving town. I didn't like the way she was acting. It scared me. Two days and I didn't see her. I became alarmed and came here. No sooner had I—"

"You're rattling on like a low-grade opium dream. This is no time to distort the truth. You're at the foot of the scaffold. There have been two murders and there will be more. You're covering for someone. Don't do it. It's risky." He slammed his words at her. "The police want you this very minute. They want you for that substitution. Why did you go to headquarters and fake an identification of Myra Finley's purse and shoes?"

The redhead stared at him dumbfounded. "You get around!" She drooped her lips in a derisive curl. "You're turning out to be as tough as your reputation. Let's go somewhere and get this straightened out."

"First," the Dean said. "Let's spend money!"

CHAPTER SIX
IN THE ADMIRAL'S HAT

THE DEAN seemed in no hurry to start his cross-examination. He led us on a tour of the city as though we were wealthy relatives. He was killing time—though I didn't realize it at the moment. He assumed a new personality, and I thought I had seen them all. This one was sort of a matinee idol routine, charming, boyish, entertaining. The expedition lasted for three hours and I swear I never had a more pleasant—or goofier—evening.

We took in four night clubs and a penny arcade. We went down to *Journal* and watched the presses roll. We window-shopped a Chinese herbalist, listened to a pitchman lecturing on human anatomy and bought the nurse a snakeskin belt and a horsehair watch fob in a hole-in-the-wall pawnshop.

We wound up at the Kollege Kat, a coffee and dance den for students, out on University Place—about a half block from the cottage of Julian Browne Brennan.

Wedged into a corner booth with her, I finally cleared up an impression that had been growing on me all evening: Natalie Anderson was a subtly exciting person. In her quiet, modest way she threw off an allure as physical and disturbing as Mrs. Duffy's high-test lilac perfume. She was the mouselike kind of wench that splits happy marriages and keeps the turnover moving in the divorce courts.

She gave the Dean a warm, svelte smile. Our excursion had thawed her considerably. "Tell my fortune," she begged. "I'm a sap for fortune tellers. I believe every word they say!"

"No you don't," the Dean contradicted genially. "You're playing me six ways to Christmas. Or trying to. However, I will make this observation. You have red hair. That branch of the divinatory arts which is known as physiognomy holds that a possessor of red hair is either all good—or all bad."

He settled down to his steeple-chase. "I feel sorry for you, my dear," he began. "It's impossible to consider you innocent. You have been exposed in an act of guilt. It's going to be interesting to hear you explain it. How can you deny that you went to the police station, posed as another girl, identified her clothes as your own?"

The nurse had her answer. "I was tricked," she stated. "Here's the buildup. I'm a trained nurse and I like my work. Some time ago I was connected with a large hospital, in a good position, pointing to promotion. A doctor's wife claimed I was estranging her husband. She filed a complaint—threatened to go to the law. The superintendent called me into his office, yelled at me for ten minutes and fired me more times than a repeating cap-pistol."

The Dean appeared absorbed in her tale.

"I've had a hard time getting by. It's tough for a nurse without references." She faltered, took a deep breath. "The other night I got a message. The sender claimed that he was Doctor L.B.S. Grinnell, the institution's big-shot. He promised to take me back into the official fold if I would do him a favor. He asked me to assist in a practical joke, a fake suicide. I was surprised to be asked to impersonate Myra but I didn't see any harm in it and the stakes were high. I wanted to get into accredited work again. I did what he said. The next day I got in touch with Grinnell. He flatly denied the whole business. I was hooked."

"You certainly were." The Dean pondered. "Now wiggle out of this one: you have, at this moment, in your custody, a small package—left in your care until asked for. I haven't the slightest idea what you suppose this package to contain but, for your own information, it contains cut gems. Stolen diamonds worth many thousands of dollars. Who gave them into your trust and where are they?"

She flushed, started to speak, changed her mind and gave us a languorous, puzzled frown.

"Keep silent if you wish," the Dean said heartily. "I know the answer—both of them." He opened his massive watch. "Well! Much later than I thought." He beamed. "Perhaps we'd better break this up and be taking you home."

Miss Anderson objected. "I'd better go alone. For special reasons. It's a short walk. Thanks for a lovely evening."

She picked up her gloves, tucked her sporty patent leather pocketbook into her armpit. "I guess it's good-bye."

WE WATCHED her slim, straight back as she left us. "This is a desperate strategy," the Dean revealed. "Pray that it works. She's got the wind up. She's worried about that ice. She's going home to change its hiding place." The girl passed through the door. We got a glimmer of her face through the plate glass as she swung along the sidewalk. "Through the kitchen!" the Dean urged.

A flabby, unshaven chef stood at the sink. He gave us a stunned, adenoidal smirk. "The back door!" the Dean demanded. "Quick! We're sick." He shot it at him in a volley of assorted languages. "Krank. Enferno. We've got to go! *Iu hong li–tsih!*"

The night was as black as charcoal. We circled the building, paused in the gloom of a hedge. The Dean surveyed the shadowed pavement that stretched towards Julius Brennan's. It was as silent as the tomb, deserted. "Where did she go? She can't have disappeared."

Then we heard her hasty, clicking footsteps. Sounding behind us. *Running in the opposite direction.* There was a quick glimpse of her under the arching elms as she crossed the street beneath a distant arc-light. "This affair is taking surprising turns." The Dean was suddenly concerned. "Hurry! Sit on her wake. She mustn't get out of sight. Look—she's entering the college grounds!"

It was a nutty jaunt. Several times she almost eluded us. A big campus in the dark is like a cemetery. We trailed her as she looped around the Law School, skirted the girl's dormitory, pushed through the landscaped evergreens and headed for Science Lab. Here she changed her course. She pulled up by the ornamental flower-plot in front of the museum. It seemed to be her journey's end.

The thick, curdy clouds thinned before the moon, gave us an indistinct view. In the center of the star-shaped flower-bed, on a granite base, stood a metal, life-size statue of the campus hero—a portly Civil War admiral. We could make out his posture in the vague light—chin up, one hand on sword pummel, the other, clutching a plumed iron hat.

The nurse threw a look about her, seemed satisfied that she was unobserved. She unfastened her pocketbook, fumbled in it. Abruptly, lithe as a cat, she scaled the stone pedestal. For a long instant her blurred outline merged with that of the statue. Then, lightfooted, she dropped to the ground and was gone.

"For heaven's sake!" the Dean ejaculated. "She had them with her all the time!" He shook his head. "If she can climb that thing," he marveled, "then so shall I." He slipped away.

When he reappeared, he was a little short of breath. "Let's have some light," he said. I flipped on my pencil torch. The Dean held in his hand a small chamois bag. He uncorded its mouth, poured half its contents into his cupped palm. Diamonds. About a whiskey-glassful. They caught up the pale beam of the flashlight and tore it into coruscations of colored fire. "Newcome was killed for these." The Dean himself was impressed. "Mort Hobson wants them. Natalie Anderson hides them—in the admiral's hat!"

JULIUS BRENNAN'S ivy-clad hermitage was stirred up about something. Every window, from cellar to dormer, was highly lighted. The cottage looked as festive and friendly as Hobby Night at an Old Ladies' Home. The Dean didn't like it. "I don't know what it means," he complained. "It gives me a feeling of acute danger. Perhaps we'd better case the outside before we face the showdown. We'll prowl the backyard first."

There was a new sport model in the drive—Van Deman's. We passed it up, entered the garage, and discovered a second car—a rusty, battered coupe at least ten years old. The Dean snarled when he encountered it. "Mort Hobson! What's he doing here?" He took a plumber's candle from a pocket, lit it, looked around. "That's just what I hoped for."

A ladder, built to the wall, led to an overhead trap-door. We ascended it to an unfinished, half-story attic. "There we are." The Dean pointed to a tiny cob-webbed window set under the eaves. "I thought I noticed this the other morning."

The dusty pane looked directly down into the gambler's solarium-conservatory. Mort Hobson was relaxed in the fan-backed wicker chair, joking with Ernie Van Deman, who was facing him across the teak taboret. Natalie Anderson, again in her maid's costume, starched cap, spiked heels and all, sat holding a highball glass upon her crossed knee. The host himself was nowhere in sight. "They seem to be enjoying themselves," I said. "Where's Brennan?"

"Where's the pigeon?" the Dean countered. "The pink-breasted pigeon. Ah!"

Julius Brennan's pet bird strutted around a potted cactus. It picked its way over a white goatskin rug, made a beeline for the far corner of the room, swaggered behind Hobson's wicker chair—and hopped up on an old house-slipper sticking out of a clump of giant ferns. A red carpet-slipper—*on a human foot.*

"That answers your question," the Dean said calmly. "Brennan's there. Concealed behind that curtain of fern fronds. As dead as a quarter's worth of lamb chops. Let's get inside and bring this thing to an end."

The nurse met us at the door as though we were complete strangers. "Mr. Brennan's out at present." She seemed genuinely perplexed. "He rarely—"

"We'll just step in and wait." The Dean pushed by her. "I'd like to see him."

We weren't received with open arms. Van Deman appeared irritated at our arrival. Mort Hobson was polite enough but there was a harshness about his lined face that was new to me.

"Didn't know you boys were chums," the Dean remarked. "Where's Honda?"

"We're not chums." Van Deman rejected the idea with distaste. "Or anything like it. It's Brennan's behavior that's bothering us—"

"He won't bother you any more," the Dean informed him affably. "He's been taken care of. He's behind that chair, flat on his back."

They took it as though he were posing a knotty problem. No one seemed interested enough to get up and look. Hobson studied the tips of his fingernails, Ernie buttoned and unbuttoned the top button of his vest. Nobody said anything until Natalie Anderson offered a suggestion.

"Maybe we'd better search him. Maybe he killed himself. Maybe we'll find a message—"

The Dean overrode her dourly. "It would be a waste of time. There are more pressing matters—" A bell in the hall buzzed and chirped with noisy insistence. The Dean glowed with satisfaction. "The police," he announced. "Perhaps the maid had better let them in."

LIEUTENANT MALLOY, in an ugly mood, drifted through the door. Consolacion Honda was at his elbow. "I brought this guy along," the detective explained to the

Dean. "He comes to headquarters and complains—" He broke off, leered at Natalie. "Hey! That's the dame that gives us the false identification—"

The Dean seemed unconcerned. "She is the one person in this room whom I must demand you completely absolve—before we get down to business." He paused. "Do you agree?" Malloy gritted his teeth, nodded. "Excellent. This has been a case in which the murderer has been in the limelight at all times. Ben." He turned to me. "Who is the extra person in this group—the person that doesn't quite fit?"

It hit me with a shock. "Mort Hobson, boss."

"Could you explain to the lieutenant on what you base that rather surprising conclusion?"

Everyone has had at some time the experience of listening to words coming from his own mouth, words of astounding wisdom. That's what happened to me. I said things I swear I hadn't been aware of until that moment. "It fits mighty neat," I said. "Who knew all about Newcome and his collection of gems? Hobson. Hobson didn't come to us. We went to him, accidentally tipped him off that we were on the trail of the Marlowe brooch. He thought it over, came around the next morning to hire us. To buy his way in with us to keep in touch with our progress—"

Van Deman interrupted. "It's a pleasure to listen to you lecture but it's costing me money. I happen to have a half-grand bet with Mr. Rock and I hope you'll excuse me if I seem anxious to collect it. As a matter of fact, my stake in this is even greater—it's personal." He dropped his languid manner. "There has been double-crossing going on and I can't use it. I've been framed, my partner's been knocked off—" He controlled himself, added formally: "I charge

Consolacion Honda with murder and petition that I be allowed, here and now, to prove my charge."

The Dean spoke to Malloy. "Did you get an answer to that cablegram we sent to Brazil?"

Malloy was caught off balance. "Did which?"

The Dean gave him a baleful glance. "I said,"—he spoke as though he were addressing a child—"did we get an answer to that cablegram we sent to South America?"

"Oh. Yeah! Sure. I get you now." Malloy fumbled in his pocket, handed the Dean a folded sheet of paper.

The Dean flicked his eyes from side to side, moved his lips soundlessly, as though he were reading to himself. "Just as I expected. Listen to this. It's from the town of Theophilo Ottoni, in the diamond district of Brazil's state of Minas Geraes. It says: 'Man you refer to well known in police circles and gem trade throughout Brazil as notorious thief and diamond expert. Practiced shady business in this municipio for five years. Dangerous. Exercise caution in arrest.'" The Dean looked up. "Too bad, Van Deman. You made too many blunders—"

Ernie fooled us all. He jerked a midget automatic, a palm-sized gambler's gun, from inside the V of his vest, wheeled—and shot his partner, Honda, three times in the belly. There was terror in his eyes as he pulled the trigger. The big man caught at the air, stumbled and collapsed. "One down," Van Deman whispered hoarsely. His gun-hand trembled. "Don't move—any of you."

The Dean rebuked him mildly. "You killed Honda first. You were afraid of him, afraid he was about to learn that you murdered his wife. Was she infatuated with you?"

"She was nuts about me." Van Deman gave it a nasty slur. "She helped me rig the whole play." He spoke to the nurse. "Get me that package. And don't stop to ask questions."

Mort Hobson yelled, "Calm down, Ernie. I'll make an offer."

AN UNHOLY thing happened. Honda, his eyes filmed with death, his loose lips edged with bloody froth, moved on the flagstone floor. A hairy hand, the hand that had been corded to whip-leather by squeezing paper balls, lifted a Smith and Wesson and blasted out with a single, wavering round. The slug got Van Deman below the kneecap. He buckled, cursed. Lieutenant Malloy nailed him before he could recover. Nailed him for keeps.

"Talk, somebody," the detective ordered. "Fast and convincing. It's too much for me."

"To the contrary," the Dean remarked. "It was one of the simplest cases I've ever undertaken. It's the only major crime I've ever encountered that could have been solved by a blind man."

I rebelled. "A blind man?"

"Yes. Just that. I'm being perfectly serious. Now here's what happened—as it occurred. Van Deman himself smashed the window and stole the poison so that Myra could kill the dog. He met her, gave her the potassium cyanide, then, still disguised in the old plaid topcoat, he went to White Pickets and knocked off Newcome. This was late in the afternoon. Later, he discovered that he had dropped his match folder at the scene of the crime. He was fully prepared to convert this error to his advantage. It may be safely assumed that he had in his possession a previously prepared pair of pens—stamped with Honda's and Brennan's names—for just such an emergency. Honda's pen now came in handy. After concealing the topcoat and knife in the park, he returned to the *Happy Hour* where Myra called him. He took the call, pretended it was Brennan, lured Honda to White Pickets. Here, together, they discovered the corpse. This gave Ernie opportunity to locate his silver matchcase and plant Honda's pen. This brought Honda into the picture, established Ernie's innocence in Consolacion's mind—"

"You've been suppressing evidence," Malloy ground out. "Haven't you heard about the law that—"

"Later," the Dean suggested. "Tell me about it later. As I was saying, the job was getting out of control by this time. One thing imperiled the whole affair. There was one fact that must not come to light. This was, of course, Van Deman's past life. Knowledge of his former trade of diamond thief in Brazil would give away the set-up. He gave us a yarn about a prison term—"

"Do I get this right?" I asked. "Theophilo Ottoni is a town—not a man?"

"Certainly. You can find it on any good map of Brazil. Now, the fake suicide—"

"I don't understand—" Malloy began.

The Dean went on: "First, why the phoney suicide? It was doubly necessary. A day's pondering on her crime had given Myra the jitters. Van Deman eliminated her, hid her body with the dog beneath the bridge, placed her purse and shoes on the wharf. Through a slip—Miss Dolan—the 'Dear Avery' note had gotten into the hands of the police. Van Deman, himself, of course, was Avery. This suicide of Avery was supposed to run the police into a blank wall. This plan, too, miscarried. You know the result."

"About the blind man," I persisted. "How, in the name of heaven, could a blind man solve—"

"By sense of touch. In our first conversation with Van Deman he claimed the engraving on the silver matchcase was brand-new. A blind man, with the ball of his thumb, could have exposed this lie. There was no burr on the cut, no sharp ridge to the engraving. As a matter of fact, the case was probably given to him on his departure from Minas Geraes by some of his crooked friends—"

Natalie Anderson put in her question. "Who murdered Mr. Brennan?"

"Again Van Deman. To keep him from chiseling. Brennan was getting hep."

"That's true," Mort Hobson agreed. "That's why I am here. Julius sent for me. Said he had a tip."

"He was knocked off just before you arrived." The Dean was gazing at the nurse. The girl was making a decision.

"The diamonds," she decided. "They go back to their rightful owners."

Malloy perked up. "What's she talking about?"

"Who knows?" The Dean gave her a hasty cover. "She's unstrung." He produced the chamois pouch and the little oil cloth memo book, handed them to Hobson. "Split my piece into two checks. Seventy per cent to Wardlow Rock— thirty to Natalie Anderson." He gave her a little bow. "You can build your own hospital now, my dear," he added. "If the whim should strike you."

THE PUZZLE OF THE TERRIFIED DUMMY

THREE MONEYED MANNEQUIN-MAKERS DIE "ACCIDENTALLY" WITHIN A YEAR, A SCARED SEXTON BEGINS TO SEE VAMPIRES IN THE GRAVEYARD, AND THE GIFT-CARD-POET HUSBAND OF AN HEIRESS GETS HEEBIE-JEEBIES. THEN, A SCULPTOR WITH THE SHAKES ASSEMBLES SOME "SHOOKS" AND DIGS TWO GRAVES, WHILE HIS WIFE GETS DRUNK AND DIGS DITCHES, AND A PAIR OF IMPORTED PUNKS RUN MURDER-RAMPANT. WHO BUT THE DEAN COULD MAKE SENSE OF A CASE THAT'S BATTIER THAN THE CARLSBAD CAVERNS?

CHAPTER ONE
THE STAKED GRAVE

DON'T THINK the boys that make their living outside the law don't have their own social register. And every page repeats the same sermon: it's a life of dog eat dog and nothing succeeds but success. Dorvin Gartell was item one in the underworld bluebook.

Teacher Gartell was the most ambitious crook in the city and, all in all, the most talented. A middle-aged ex-principal of a back-country school who had come to the metropolis with some new ideas, he had started cleaning up the instant he had crossed the corporation line. Blackmail, extortion and forgery were his trinity.

He was the last man in the world the Dean and I ever expected as a client.

Dean Wardlow Rock's my boss. He's a private detective that practices, with the *sub rosa* sponsorship of the police commissioner, as a professional fortune teller. He's easy talking with a foggy manner that makes him seem battier than the Carlsbad Caverns, and carries a shoulder gun, a Magnum .357 that does business with a muzzle velocity of about a quarter mile per second. The Dean picked me up when I was down and out and gave me a job. I've been with him from that day to this, and from that day to this he's been as big a riddle to me as one of his favorite Chinese scrolls. We have a dingy apartment, not squalid, not swanky,

in an old brick rooming house down in the slums. The turnover it does would knock your eyebrows off. The chief's interests include about everything, Assyrian lithoglyphs to glass blowing, but his real obsession is divination.

Me, I just know two things. Guns and locks.

The heavy pistol blasted
once and Teddy's right
eye went into vapor.

   We had just taken our bedtime showers and were relax-
ing a bit in our office-bedroom before we turned in. The
Dean lolled in his broken down Morris under the green
student's lamp, deep in a tome on fabulous medieval mon-

sters. I was on the edge of my bed, a bowl of crackers and milk on my lap. It had been a routine, noneventful day and we were both bored.

Suddenly the Dean became excited. "May I break in upon your reverie? I've just come across a new word. New to me, that is. It's a thing of beauty and a joy forever. I don't see how up to now I've managed to get along without it. Gad, language is a wonderful thing!"

"What is this word?" I asked warily. "Am I old enough to hear it?"

"Therianthropic."

"I'm sorry. But you're lecturing to an empty hall."

"The word is therianthropic," the Dean repeated patiently. "It means combining human and bestial form. Like a centaur."

"Like Jo-Jo the dog-faced boy?"

"That's right. It's a valuable word to know. There are times—" He paused. An intent look came into his eyes. He was listening.

Then I heard it. The soft opening of the kitchen door. The light footsteps across the linoleum. "Haw!" exclaimed a smug voice suddenly from somewhere behind our backs. "May I come in?"

The entry was typical of Dorvin Teacher Gartell: oversubtle, cautious and illegal. He was a plump little man in funereal blue serge. He had a loose nervous mouth and bushy senatorial eyebrows. He bubbled physical allure. Women, and men too, for that matter, went for him on sight. I didn't like him. Behind his bulging eyes lay the dark sneer of perpetual contempt for his fellow man. He just couldn't get out of his mind for an instant how good he was.

"I surprised you, didn't I?" he purred. "First thing you knew and here I was!"

The Dean was ominously quiet.

"Just a little joke. And besides, this visit must be confidential. No publicity." Teacher Gartell glowed charm. "Back doors are more private than front doors."

"What's this confidential visit about?" I asked.

Gartell seated himself on a chair, pulled it up close to the Dean's knees. "Well, here we are at last." He winked slyly at the chief. "I've been waiting for this for a long time. You and me together, working in the same harness! You know," he rolled his frog-eyes—"you know, I've never mentioned it before, but you and I, Mr. Rock, have a lot in common. I've often thought about it. We're, you might say, replicas of each other. We both have genius, both are erudite, we both work with our eye on the old bank account. There's no doubt about it: Dorvin Gartell's a thumbnail Wardlow Rock!"

IT WAS wonderful to watch the Dean. Blood drained from his lips in white rage. He remained silent.

"What was it you wanted?" I inquired.

Teacher Gartell took a slip of paper from his billfold and laid it on the arm of the Dean's chair. The paper was about three inches wide and about eight inches long. It lay on the flat surface with a crimp, as though it had been curled around a pencil or something and then straightened out. The Dean motioned to me. I reached out and picked it up.

"What is it, Ben?" he asked.

"Well," I answered, "it's a check. It's perfectly blank."

Teacher Gartell attempted to look owlish. "Turn it over. Read what's on the back!"

There was a note scrawled on the reverse. I read it aloud: *"They're all gone, all three. Let's wind up this business. I've got the shooks. That's all. It's unsigned."*

Gartell amplified. "It must be a mistake. He means he's got the shakes—and I don't wonder. There's big money in this, Mr. Rock. Honest money. But—"

The Dean frowned at me. "What's he wheezing about?"

"Search me," I said with heavy emphasis. "I think the man's completely therianthropic!"

Teacher Gartell became insistent. "You better tie in with me. Let me tell you the story about that note. I have a little office in the Elman Building. Ramshackle and old-fashioned but genteel. The building has no mail chute. We put our outgoing letters in an open box outside our door. The janitor collects them from each office just before mail time and takes them to the street, to the curb box." He hesitated and went on.

"Last Thursday the janitor knocked on my door and handed me an envelope. He was just about to drop it into the box, he said, when he happened to notice that I had forgotten to stamp it. Well, I thanked him and laid it on my desk. After a while I got looking at the address and it didn't strike any memory chord. I couldn't place this party. I slit the envelope and took out this note"— Teacher Gartell cast down his eyes— "I had committed a grievous error. A gross breach of ethics. The janitor had been confused. He had brought me another man's mail. I had opened a stranger's letter. Think of that!" He screwed up his face to indicate concern. "I deduced the sender."

I interrupted. "You did what?"

"I deduced the sender. It must have come from my floor, the third. There was only one other office on that floor— and it, at the present, is not doing business. I'm referring to the Amberton Mannequin Company. It's beginning to sound sweet, isn't it?"

The Dean spoke laboriously to me. "Ben, tell the visitor—"

Teacher Gartell cut in on him. "I've heard you were eccentric, Rock, but I didn't expect anything like this. I don't appreciate your manner a bit. You act as though you were too good to talk to me. It's Ben ask him this, Ben ask him that. Do you want in on this thing or not? Answer me directly." He whipped out the words as though he were talking to a half-bright child.

"All right." The Dean smiled at him. "A direct question deserves a direct answer. This is it: get out of here so we can burn a couple of sulphur candles and fumigate."

Scorn smouldered in Gartell's eyes. "You're ordering me out?"

"I am. You've got some filthy squeeze in mind. I don't know what it is but I don't want any part of it. You can't play it yourself or you would never have come to me. You're a crook and a not very smart one at that. You're playing us for suckers. You think we're a couple of wrap-ups.

"Giving me all that story about the janitor and the unstamped letter. I'll tell you how you got that note. You stole it like any street gamin. See that curl in the paper? That's where you've left the mark of your trade. You prowl the foyers of apartments and office buildings and rifle mailboxes of outgoing mail. Those letters that promise to have checks in them, you take home with you. There you get to work. You take the check out without breaking the seal on the envelope. Later you will replace it and mail it intact. As it was. It isn't the check you want but the information the check contains. You copy the signature. The face tells you where the person banks. Later you will get a check from that bank, fill it out for a generous sum—you have a way of even finding out the depositor's balance—and forge the name. You pass the check with little difficulty. No one knows how it happened—"

"The crimp in the paper," I asked. "I don't get it."

"The envelope looked as though it had a check in it. As a matter of fact, the writer simply used his personal check pad for notepaper—I've done it myself. Gartell took it home, inserted a thin wire tool under the top corner of the flap at the back of the envelope. There's a little space there where the glue doesn't reach. He caught the paper in the tool, twisted around and around and slid it out. It's a professional sleight. Anyone can learn it."

TEACHER GARTELL'S face grew hard. "So I did. O.K. I admit it. So what of it?"

The Dean waved his hand at me. "That's your cue, Ben. Turn off the dictaphone."

I went into the bathroom, closed the door and counted to seven. We don't have any dictaphone.

When I came out Teacher Gartell was gone.

"Sit down," the Dean said, "while I get organized. That imbecile left me tangled." He furrowed his eyebrows. "This business will take a little filtering."

According to the news accounts of the past year, Amberton was just another way of saying hard luck. The Ambertons were like the old poem, gone were all the old familiar faces. There had been three of them and they were one of the town's few traditional families. Actually, they had been a pretty tepid tribe and would never have hit the front page if they hadn't begun to kick off so regularly in such strange ways. The Amberton Mannequin Company had been started as a tricks-and-novelty house back in the eighties by old J. Waldo who had founded the business in his basement workshop by turning out satin shamrocks for Irish lapels and penknives with fancy handles.

When his two sons came into the business they made some changes—they specialized. For the past eight years the Ambertons produced but one item: a cut-rate *papier-mâché* mannequin for the small town trade. Back-street department stores and small shops from the Great Lakes to the Gulf featured sleazy models in grimy windows on Amberton heads, torsos, calves and hands.

The Amberton estate was plenty wealthy. For eight years they had been running a monopoly.

The avalanche of disaster had started a year or so ago with the death of Bart, the oldest son. Bart, the police report affirmed, had returned from a billiard match when death tagged him. Stopping his car in the drive, he had got out to open the garage doors when he thought he observed a prowler at the basement door. There was an old Spanish-American War revolver in the car compartment. He took out the gun, held it over his head and fired a shot in the air to frighten the intruder. At least that was his intention. The gun went to pieces like a hand grenade. The police gunsmith later explained it as caused by "an untrue alignment of cylinder and barrel produced presumably by defective—" etc. His father, old J. Waldo, was sitting in the car and witnessed the whole thing. He testified as to the episode.

Lee, the second son, died two months later. Hunting rabbits. The breech of his shotgun blew up in his face. Police reconstruction, with the aid of Mr. Amberton, Sr., who was on the party, proved it an accident. It seems that Lee, who was in his cups, had rested the barrel on the thawing ground and had picked up a muzzle full of mud.

The violent demise of old J. Waldo, himself, came six months later and wiped out the clan.

The death of Amberton, sire, appeared at first to be a run of the mill accident: an oldster searching for a leaky gas pipe in the cellar of a vacant house with a match—and finding it.

But this case proved not so simple. Investigation disclosed two facts. There was no gas in the house, the flow having been previously cut off at the curb. Moreover the old man had definitely, beyond any shadow of doubt, not used a match in his quest—but a flashlight. It was difficult to explain. The newspapers were still yelling their heads off.

"I've been trying to keep out of the Amberton case," the Dean reflected. "The method of murder employed is, of course, transparent but the affair has a certain unholy quality about it that repels me. From beginning to end—"

"Just a minute," I said. "Let's take this a little slower. What's this about the method of murder?"

"The guns, the pistol and the shotgun, were doctored with Nobel's oil. They must have been. It's devilish."

It was a new one on me. Firearms are my big yen. "Nobel's oil?" I asked. "I've never heard of it. What is it—some hex ointment?"

The Dean guffawed. "You know it very well indeed. You just don't recognize it by its proper name."

I objected. "I don't believe it. What about the old man in the cellar? More oil?"

The Dean's face became abruptly grave. "I'm afraid so, Ben." He stared at his blunt fingertips. "Well," he said at last. "This is none of ours. Let's go to bed."

We were, however, thwarted once more. We had hardly clicked out the light and closed our eyes when there was a hammering on the reception-room door like the Yukon thaw. I cursed. "Drunks. It's too late for palm reading. Let them bang."

"No." The Dean switched on his bedside lamp. "No. Let them in. I remember that gavel fist. It's the law."

IT WAS. Lieutenant Bill Malloy and Captain Kunkle. They burst into the room like a couple of berserk barkers. Bill Malloy was the smartest cop on the force. He was so smart, in fact, that he made the Dean uneasy. He bore a perpetual gripe against the Dean—based on the Dean's access to the police commissioner—and the Dean resented Malloy's advantages of a well organized department. They were as jealous of each other as a couple of chick peacocks with their first tail coverts. Captain Kunkle was pompous, garrulous, and would co-operate with anyone as long as it paid him headline dividends.

The Dean sat up in bed, got the snipe of a poisonous Cuban cigar into action, and waited.

Captain Kunkle angled his heels, strained the chest buttons of his tunic, and gave forth in an oratorical voice that sounded like a fish peddler yelling in a well. "When, in the course of events, I run into the supernatural I am, quite naturally, somewhat at a loss." The captain's jowls beaded perspiration. "Mr. Rock, we do, I pride myself, our work well. But spirits and demons are outside the metropolitan jurisdiction—"

The Dean shook his head in bewilderment. "I wonder how he does it."

"It seems," I suggested, "that certain demons are throwing a crime wave—"

"It's nothing to joke about!" Captain Kunkle glowered uncertainly. "Take my wife's sister. She lost a diamond earring. Mrs. Haggerty, our neighbor, is a seventh daughter. She said just look behind the geranium. Well, there it was! You can scoff if you like—"

"Listen," the Dean cut in. "Observe me. I'm in bed. Preparing to go to sleep. Don't meander. What's this about your wife's sister?"

The captain made a new start. "No. Not her. That was just an illustration. To get you in the proper frame of mind."

Malloy took over. "Rock," he asked, "do you believe in vampires?"

"No."

"Neither do I. So let's do business. Maybe I can clarify the captain's statements. Here's what he's driving at. You're supposed to be an authority on black magic. We want your advice." Lieutenant Malloy chose his words carefully. "The sheriff's office has just received a report of a strange act of vandalism and turned it over to us. Maybe you remember hearing about the Amberton deaths? The bodies, the three of them, were buried out near S-Iron, the old family homestead, in a little country churchyard. We've never completely dropped that case." He took a big breath. "Well, tonight it popped up again. The sexton, wandering around among the tombstones, got the shock of his life. Someone had desecrated old Waldo Amberton's grave, had driven a wooden stack smack down into the center of it! How do you dope it?"

"There is but one explanation." Captain Kunkle elbowed his way back into the conversation. "Vampire. Though you may not suspect it, Mr. Rock, I'm a bit of a litterateur in odd moments. What I mean is, I read books. Take the vampire. Lord Byron says: 'The freshness of the face and the wetness of the lip are the never failing signs of the vampire.' Now that's a perfect picture of the late Mr. Amberton, Senior. There's one way, and only one, to remove the menace of a buried vampire. The vampire marauds after death. That way is to drive a stake in the grave. As I've been telling Lieutenant Malloy, the way I figure it is this—"

"Foosh!" The Dean snorted rudely. "It's perfectly human. Offhand, I'd say this: that the stake was driven into the soft earth of the grave by someone who wanted to make sure that there was a coffin actually there. Do you see? A sort of a sounding rod."

Malloy batted his eyes. "I think you've got it!"

"Could be." Captain Kunkle faltered. "But who—"

"And now, gentlemen," the Dean concluded the party, "good evening, if you please."

After they had gone, his big face crinkled in a grin. "I've got them walking on their heels! They're hauling a load and don't know where to deliver it. It's a great life, Ben!"

I washed my wrists and neck in cold water, crawled between the sheets and was instantly asleep. Almost as instantly, I woke up. "Listen, boss," I urged. "This is too good to keep. I know the answer to everything. It came to me just then in a dream and don't laugh. Would you like to hear it?"

The Dean's calm gentle voice came quietly through the dark room. "I'd be delighted."

"Well, it's this way. There isn't any case at all. Ha! Old man Amberton was the murderer. Bart and his pistol and Lee and his shotgun—both times the old man was on hand keeping a weather eye cocked. The old man kills off his sons and then commits suicide. There haven't been any killings since then, have there?"

"No. But there will be. Your solution leaves out the staked grave. And—very importantly—the man with the shooks."

"You mean shakes."

"I mean shooks."

"Nuts. Wait and see. This business is finished."

That night Teacher Gartell was murdered.

CHAPTER TWO

CORPSE IN TRUST

THE NEXT morning the Dean got up in a playful mood. When I'd ask him about the case he'd say what case, and when I'd refer to our last night's visitors he'd pretend he didn't remember. It got me down. I never could take ribbing before breakfast. I withdrew into myself, as they say in the books, and held it through bacon and eggs and three cups of coffee. And still the Dean kept up his clowning. It looked as though I were going to have to take a walk to cool off.

The telephone call from Homicide snapped him out of it.

The department experts were in the Elman Building offices of Amberton Mannequins. They were devoting their time, attention and affection to the corpse of Dorvin Gartell. It appeared to be a baffling situation and they felt they had reason to believe that we were not entirely unaware of certain contributing circumstances. Would we be good enough to grab our hats and run over? Lieutenant Malloy desired to interrogate us.

"That settles it," the Dean decided. "We'd better go. We're in it now whether we want to be or not. It's our own necks now—and I don't mean from the police." He closed his eyes, frowned. "What do you know about movies? Neighborhood houses. From the managerial standpoint?"

"Nothing, suh. Nothing at all."

"Then I'll have to handle this. Pray for the best."

"I don't like to criticize," I remarked gently. "But it seems to me that if you really intend to mess in this thing you've muffed a golden opportunity."

The Dean looked startled. "How so?"

"Gartell," I explained. "He held all the clues of entry. You should have asked him one question: to whom was that envelope addressed?"

"Goodness." The Dean showed relief. "You had me caulked for a second. Don't worry about to whom the letter was addressed. We'll find out *who wrote it*. That's what's really functional."

He drew the phone to him, lifted the receiver, gave the operator an unlisted number. Almost immediately he was talking to the police commissioner's private secretary.

"Miss Blythe!" he exclaimed. "How are you? So you've been intending to call *me*. I'm indeed flattered…What?… Oh, you're having a party and you want me to suggest a fortune-telling game?" I listened with my mouth agape. The Dean takes his divination seriously. It's hokum, and he'd be the first one to admit it, but he doesn't feel it should be practiced by incompetent amateurs. One sure way of striking his tinder was to refer to the ancient art as a frolic. His eyebrows drew together. "You want an icebreaker, eh? I know just the thing. Why not try viscera? The Romans did a nice job of fortune telling with chicken intestines… What? What did you say? I see. Don't get excited. Maybe you're right. Now here's what I wanted to ask *you:* Is there anyone, anyone at all, connected with the Amberton case who is an artist?" He beamed. "Fraley Wilkes, 378 Front Street. Thanks."

"There you are." He hung up and grinned. "There's the man who wrote the note. Get ready for the street. We're going into action."

THE HOTEL just missed being a flophouse. I had passed by it dozens of times before but, to tell the truth, this was the first time I had ever noticed it. It was just a single row of rooms, down an alley, over a squalid all-night drug store. A homemade cardboard sign in the front window said: *Special Rates for Resident Guests.*

We felt our way up the half-light of the odorous stairway to the second story. A dim matting-carpeted corridor stretched from the dirty bay window that fronted over the street, back into the murky gloom of the building. A line of varnished, numbered doors ran down one side of the hall; the other was blank plaster wall. A blowzy dowager, her foot in a plaster cast, was sitting at a card table in the light of the bay windows. She had a box of chocolates, a pekinese and three tattered magazines in her ample lap.

The old lady watched our approach with beady, suspicious eyes. "And what," I asked, "brings us to this dump?"

The Dean ignored me. He turned to the beldame, his hat lifted about four inches above his head. "The fascinating proprietress of this hostelry, I presume?"

No comment.

I could see the boss was flustered. His glance lit on a magazine. "Whiling away the tedium with the pleasant pastime of reading, I observe. They're old copies, I see, but still vigorous. That serial, *Ashes of Heartbreak*, is a sad sweet tale. It gets under your skin, doesn't it? Surprising ending."

The old lady began to steam. "That's what's burning me up," she said in an alcoholic tenor. "A bum leaves this here in a room. I pick it up and read it. It's six months old. I'm stuck. They ain't no way I can ever find out how it come out."

"I'd like to tell you about," the Dean said genially. "But I'm in a bit of a hurry. Does Miss Georgia Rountree reside here?"

The old lady wavered. "We don't never put out no information about guests."

"Sorry." The Dean looked sad. "In that case, we'll be going."

"Hold it," she said. "Room 12."

"Thank you." The Dean grew serious. "One good turn obligates another. Now about *Ashes of Heartbreak*. The young doctor comes home from his jungle expedition with the white goddess in time to prevent his innocent wife from marrying the polo playing villain and thus committing bigamy. Valah, the white goddess, marries Bruce, the cattle king, who is rescued ten minutes before his electrocution by the deathbed confession of his wastrel identical twin brother. It is a very happy ending."

Room 12 was back at the end of the hall by the fire escape. The Dean rapped on the panel.

A man opened the door. He was in his vest and shirtsleeves and wasn't too pleased at seeing us. There was a frank, direct, boyish look in his blue eyes and his short-cut, strawcolored hair was rumpled in boyish disorder. Just the spirit of wholesome youth. He looked like what you'd come up with if you'd seen any college campus in the country—but for one thing: there was a little brass-knuckle scar on the tip of his chin. Hardly noticeable—but I'm tenderloin born and raised myself and I know one of the lads when I see one.

"Miss Rountree?" the Dean asked.

The boy stepped back and let us in.

The tiny room was frilled and ribboned like an old-fashioned valentine. There were lace antimacassars and pink satin bows on all the furniture. An imitation Spanish shawl was draped over a wardrobe trunk and a handful of wilted violets floated in a teacup on the dresser.

The brunette sat on the foot of the bed. She was sleek and smooth and vital. She couldn't have been a day over eighteen. She was openly interested in our arrival.

The Dean bowed. "Miss Rountree? I'm sorry to break in on you like this but I have something that I think might intrigue you." He handed her a card. The card said: *Barnstaple Amusements, Inc., Chelsey D. Barnstaple, State Personnel.* Miss Rountree read it carefully.

"We're expanding our chain. Taking over locations here in town. Shake out the deadwood. I have your name on my list as an experienced usher, or usherette, if you prefer, and understand that you are now without work. Could you act as captain and handle a crew of, say, six?"

MISS ROUNTREE bobbed her head. "And how! I could. And do I need the job, mister!"

"Splendid!" The Dean considered. "That fixes everything up." A shadow of hesitancy flickered across his face. "We usually demand references. However, I think we can waive that formality. For the sake of the record, why did you leave your last job?"

Bitterness came into the girl's eyes. "I'll tell you, but if you're from out of town it'll be Greek to you. In the last year there have been in this city three rather terrible deaths.

An old man and his two sons. The newspapers have been stirring up a lot of commotion. They've got it keyed up to a civic scandal." She paused. "It was this scandal that got me fired."

The boy with the scar listened silently. He rolled a cigarette, handed it to her, lit it, and rolled one for himself.

The girl went on: "The deaths, one at a time, showed up an unusual mixup. The old man had a heart attack, it seems, several years back. He thought he was going to die. He made arrangements. He turned his entire wealth over to his sons and lived on his salary as president of the company. The rest of his property—which was a small checking account, he willed directly to the granddaughter of an old boyhood friend. Me." The boy stirred restlessly. "That money was left in trust. I was to get it when I married and settled down."

"Well!" the Dean ejaculated. "Nuptials should prove no difficulty to such a charming—"

"Wait a moment." Georgia Rountree was into her story now, hardly aware of her audience. "It gets worse and worse. The Ambertons had no blood heirs. The two sons left no wills. Their money reverted to their father. With the old man's death I became heir not to a small checking account but to the total fortune. The sole Amberton heir." She pulled down the corners of her mouth and glanced about the room. "I'll take your job. I've never seen a penny of the money and never will. There's a catch in it. The will says that I have to marry but the trustees won't let me. They have the power of rejection."

"I see," the Dean said gravely. "I see." He turned to the lad. "This, perhaps, is the gentleman in prospect?"

The boy looked mean. "That's right, you're staring right at him. They're crooks. They don't like me because of my profession. They say it's a loafer's job."

"And what," the Dean asked, "is your profession?"

"Sentiment writing."

"I beg your pardon?"

The girl eased him out of it. "Hugh writes beautiful poems. Those lines you see on gift cards, poems for birth announcements and mottoes for shut-ins." Miss Rountree's eyes misted. "He has a sweet sensitive soul. They can't keep us apart."

The Dean reached for the doorknob. "Hold a tight bridle and don't do anything rash. This thing will straighten itself out. Good luck. I have to run along and see a man about a sudden demise. You'll hear from me."

Relaxed in the soft cool cushions of a taxicab, I got the old pump handle working. "A funny thing. That Georgia Rountree's a new one on me. I've never heard of her before and I followed the whole thing pretty closely in the newspapers."

"Her name never hit the press. She's been kept in the background." The chief looked at his huge silver watch. "I've known about her for months. Picked up her story from a friend who turns the chopper at the Bijou Theater. She was an usher there and when the sensation broke they dropped her like hotcakes." The boss had his own sources of information: elevator operators, bellhops, bartenders and messenger kids. He'd done many a favor and collected many a valuable tip.

"Gift-card poet!" The Dean sighed. "What next?"

"Who is this Fraley Wilkes?" I asked.

"A designer. One of Amberton's designers."

"What does he design?"

"Mannequins, I surmise."

I stirred this around in my mind. It left me blank. "Tell me," I persisted. "How did you know an artist wrote that note of Gartell's? You didn't even pick it up."

"Didn't need to. It was written in *conté crayon*. An artist's favorite. It's a composition of clay or chalk and makes a much blacker line than an ordinary pencil. Couldn't miss it."

"I don't like this job," I griped. "I didn't like it from the beginning. We're lucky if we get to first base. I despise amateur murder. Amateur killers are half-nutty, if you ask me."

"They certainly are," the Dean agreed heartily. "But this is not amateur crime. It's cold professional slaughter. For profit. Arranged and carried out by veterans. There are experts in this picture—or I shall be greatly surprised."

TEACHER GARTELL had been optimistic when he had described the Elman Building as old-fashioned and ramshackle. It had become so old-fashioned and ramshackle, in fact, that the self-respecting business district had moved away from it with its fingers to its nose. The Elman Building, once in a prosperous commercial neighborhood, was now surrounded by a nest of poolrooms, taverns and pawnshops. The once elegant doorway was pillared on either side by grimy acanthus leaves, stone-carved in deep relief, and the foyer was laid with cracked Italian mosaic. A policeman in the lobby directed us to the third floor. There was no elevator.

The Amberton Company had held down a suite of three rooms: there was the lavatory, the big barnlike office proper and an enclosed alcove with a kidney desk and a broken down daybed where old J. Waldo had relaxed in his pasturage and listened to the sweet music of typewriters banging out orders on the other side of the thin partition.

The assembly was waiting for us in this alcove.

Lieutenant Malloy sat with his knee hitched over the corner of the desk. He was not in a particularly pleasant humor. With him were two men. He introduced them. The most striking—elephantine, square-jawed, with speckled hands and pouchy eyes—was Madison Collins, promoter of crackpot inventions. His companion, a little wiry clothes-tree with a sallow, bloodless face, was Lamar John St. John, exclusive dentist. These two were the chosen trustees of the Amberton estate.

There was a fourth man. He reposed on the daybed in a drunken posture of contorted jubilance. It was Teacher Gartell. The top of his head smashed with a brutal blow, constituted what the medical brethren refer to as a "wet specimen."

"Gad!" I said in the Dean's best tone. "It's the thumbnail Wardlow Rock!" No one paid any attention to me.

Collins seemed to be the wheelhorse of the group. "What's this mean?" he snarled. "We've been waiting for you at the insistence of this officious officer, hah, for an hour and eleven minutes and thirty-one seconds. Why, I couldn't tell you. From your general appearance I should say that you couldn't contribute anything to anything— even information. What's your excuse for holding us up?"

The Dean studied him with interest. "First things first," he answered shortly. "I've been off on a junket." Suddenly, without warning, he turned beetling brows on the dapper dentist. "Did you kill this man?" he demanded.

St. John recoiled with horror. "No! No indeed!"

"Do you have a piece of soap in your pocket?"

"Of all things! Why should I—"

Malloy cut in. "We can do without the monkey business," he declared angrily. "This is no place for a comic. These gentlemen are not here to be insulted. Now here's the lay—let's see you crawfish out of it. These offices have been vacant for some time. The company is moving into more modern quarters uptown. This morning a window washer lets himself in with a pass-key and finds this stiff. I call up Mr. Collins and Mr. St. John. They're directors in the firm and trustees of the estate. I've promised them an early solution."

The Dean listened attentively.

"This corpse is Dorvin Gartell," Malloy announced. "He has a record as long as your underwear. Any policeman that sees him any place at any time takes a second look. Last night Patrolman O'Connor, off duty and taking a short-cut home from a euchre party, passed him in the alley behind your rooming house. Officer O'Connor stood in the shadows and watched him. It looked like he went into the back entrance of your building."

"He did," the Dean admitted promptly. "He wanted to retain me. For what, I never heard. I gave him the bum's rush."

Madison Collins broke out in a bullish roar. "That won't do. You're giving us the run-around. I've heard about you, Rock. Charlatanism and chicanery." He shoved out his jaw. "What's behind all this?"

"Well," the Dean answered thoughtfully. "I'll give it to you as I see it. Absolutely free of fee. First, someone is working a diabolical shuttle. That's the secret to the entire set-up. Second, a safe is about to be robbed—what safe, I can't tell you. Third, there have been four murders so far but the essential murder, the key murder, has yet to take place. Fourth—"

"That's all." Lieutenant Malloy flushed. "You can leave now, the both of you. But stay handy."

THE SIGN over the big arched gate said *Venner Brothers Lumber*. We drove into the yard, left the cab and walked to a long warehouse where a man in gold rimmed glasses was checking a clip-board of yellow sheets.

"Where can I find Mr. Venner?" the Dean asked.

"Which one of us? There are nine." The man's eyes were bright, intelligent.

"It's this way," the Dean explained. "I'm Sectional Directing Adviser of Divisional Unit Three of the Recreational and Vocational Guidance Committee and I have to read a paper." He simpered. "May I take about three minutes of your time?"

"We'll see," Mr. Venner said. "Start off."

The Dean dragged out a ragged envelope and a splintered pencil and prepared to take notes. "Item: what is a shook?"

"Oh, I get you now." Mr. Venner entered into the spirit of the occasion. "You're writing a speech. Well, friend, a shook is a knockdown box. What I mean, it's the pieces of boards sawed up and bundled, ready to assemble: ends, sides and all. They're easier to move that way, take up less space. Shooks are made, in the main, from scrap. They have to be kiln dried or they mold and warp. Fiber is pushing them off the market."

The Dean lifted his eyebrows. "Is that so? You don't sell many then?"

"Not a bundle in months." Venner considered. "Whoa! We did get an order a week or so ago. A nubby little order for twenty-five 2s that wasn't worth fooling with. Customers usually buy them by the carload."

"Now that's interesting!" The Dean made a vague motion with his pencil. "Why such a small—"

Venner spat. "Fellow said he wanted them for bird houses. His hands trembled like a leaf all the time he was talking to me. In my personal opinion—and you can put this in your speech—he was screwier than a bushel of old bedsprings!"

At luncheon over green turtle soup and veal pie, I demanded an invoice. "Boil it down," I suggested. "And what have we got? No client, no prospect of fee, no real crime that actually concerns us. We do a lot of running around at our own expense, ask a lot of questions and get nowhere."

"I wouldn't say that," the Dean objected blandly. "That interview with Venner practically put the thing in the bag."

"You're too much for me!" I tried to bait him. "If you ask me, we're going in circles."

"No, Ben," the Dean protested affably. "No. We're not going in circles. Venner broke the big point. Why did Fraley Wilkes want shooks and not regular boxes? Answer: they're less conspicuous and easier to move." He bared his big teeth. "An ideal way to dispose of a corpse. I wonder it hasn't been done before!"

"You mean cut it up in sections and put in boxes?"

The Dean jerked with distaste. "No. Not that. Much more simple. Easier, cleaner, and no labor at all. Which brings up a visit with Fraley Wilkes, himself—which should prove interesting."

Number 378 Front Street was the worst wing of a dilapidated duplex on a backstreet swarming with children. The clamor from a nearby boiler factory was deafening. Hucksters were calling out their poultry and vegetables, housewives were bawling and gossiping from balconies and windows. It wasn't the atmosphere I'd have chosen for an artist.

The wren that let us in was Vera Madigan.

She gave us each a hard look. She didn't remember me.

I remembered her, though. Vera and I were kids together back in the old slaughterhouse neighborhood. That is, we'd started together—I couldn't keep up the pace. When she was ten she was running with girls who were fourteen, when she was fourteen she was hanging around the depot pointing for Joey Slagle's crap game. She really rushed from then on. Stories came back. Night club entertainer on the South American wheel.

Everybody that knew Vera liked her. She was loyal, generous and honest. She was, however, afflicted with a double curse: simple-minded and too good looking for her own good.

"Do I have the honor of addressing Mrs. Fraley Wilkes?" the Dean asked gallantly.

"That's me." She gave him a million dollar smile. "Come in. Mr. Wilkes isn't in just now but I want to ask your advice."

The Dean bowed. "I've always wanted to see an artist's studio."

She laughed. "The studio's not here. It's down at the Elman Building. In the attic." She led us into the living-room and indicated chairs. We sat down and looked around.

IT WAS the weirdest den this side of the city morgue. Three life-size *papier-mâché* mannequins—one salmon, one gilt and one slate green—undraped and unblessed, stood against one wall. Anyone with half an eye could tell that Vera had been the model. There was a decanter set with a wrenched lock on an end table by the horsehair sofa. Along the mantel ledge, like a row of rotten oranges, were lined eight shrunken Jivaro heads. The bare wooden floor was littered with cigarette stubs and odds and ends of lacy lingerie.

"I'm Wardlow Rock," the Dean began. "And this is my assistant."

"Charmed." She nodded vaguely. She'd lost but little of her beauty with the wear and tear of life. She was still lithe, supple-limbed. She sat poised and erect. From the dainty turquoise heels of her cloth-of-silver pumps to the metallic Grecian curls of her blonde head, she radiated composure and serenity. "You're men," she remarked brightly. "You can help me. I'm trying to make a decision. Shall I have a chime doorbell or a brass knocker or both?"

The Dean was bewildered. "I don't quite get— Oh! I see. You're fixing your home up a bit."

"Not this rat hole," she corrected scornfully. "I'm talking about the other place. The new place. My birthday present."

"I guess I'm not very well posted," the Dean responded. "What about this birthday present?"

"We've lived in this shanty ever since we've been married," the blonde explained. "Now Fraley's got a good job, there's no need for it. I've been coaxing and begging to move in a nicer, cleaner neighborhood. Finally, he's agreed. He's bought me a cute little Cape Cod cottage with green shutters and everything. It's out in the Oak Grove allotment."

"A little lonely out there, isn't it?" The Dean was like a setter at the flush.

"Yes. It's lonely but I'll like it. It'll be a change."

"A change indeed!" The Dean agreed absently. "Where's Mr. Wilkes at the present, by the way?"

"Out there. At the new house. He goes out for a few hours every afternoon. He won't tell me what he's doing. He's getting something ready for me. Some sort of a surprise."

"Think of that!" The Dean arose with a flourish. "It's been quite an experience, this little visit, and I hope to have the pleasure of your company yet again."

On the street his face went stony bleak. "It's pretty terrible, Ben, isn't it? We musn't fumble."

"Where now?" I asked.

"Home. I expect we have a client waiting for our return."

The client was there, all right. Seated in the reception-room on the Dean's rare ante bellum love seat. Big Madison Collins with his speckled hands and cunning pouchy eyes. A few hours had changed him. The bellow had gone out of his lungs, he was harried, eager to please.

The Dean grabbed the advantage. "This is hardly credible. You! I'm busy now. I have no time to banter personal hostilities."

Collins smirked fatuously. "I was a little rough this morning. I apologize. Let's let bygones be bygones. Mr. Rock, you're a crack investigator. I want to hire you." He cocked his head. "I want to know about St. John and that piece of soap."

The Dean guffawed. "You don't trust your fellow director?"

"Just about as much as he trusts me," Collins sneered. "What kind of soap did you have in mind?"

"Any kind." The Dean was annoyed. "As long as it's plastic. Probably ordinary yellow bar soap. And it's no joke. When it makes its appearance there'll be hell to pay. It's the start of the end. After that comes the murder and the looting."

Collins' eyes glowed venomously in their baggy folds of skin. "You should be impounded," he decided. "You rave like a madman." He got to his feet. "I've changed my mind. I can't use you. It'd be dangerous to be associated with you."

The Dean followed him complacently to the door. "I'm sorry you feel that way," he purred, "because you've hired me. We've had a meeting of the minds and that's a contract. Now. Let me give you some advice: Be mighty careful what you do and how you do it. Good afternoon, sir."

CHAPTER THREE
THE SHOOKS

THE DEAN grinned. "We gaffed him, Ben. Our first client. This case needs about three more. The more the better, say I."

He settled back in his broken-down chair and reviewed the situation. "There it is. The whole devilish affair. The complete outline. All the essential facts. It's ghastly, isn't it? There's nothing to do now but to wait. We won't wait long."

"Are you telling me that you can make sense out of—"

"More than sense, Ben. Plan. Well organized, smooth running plan. Look back. One thread holds the entire affair together: *nitroglycerine!*"

"Nitro!" I exclaimed. Light was beginning to dawn.

"That's right. Nobel's blasting oil, incorrectly referred to as nitroglycerine, is actually a trinitric ester of the trivalent alcohol, glycerine, and contains no nitro groups. But that is beside the point. Bart's pistol and Lee's shotgun were simple murder traps. A small charge of nitro, say in an ampule inserted halfway down the barrel, turned the guns into hand grenades. That was the way it was done, you can be sure. The repetition of explosion from pistol to shotgun is too big to swallow as coincidence."

It seemed obvious when you got the idea. "What about the old man and the flashlight?"

"That was the episode that clinched it in my mind. Explosive had proven too successful for the killer. Here he tipped his hand. He overdid it. Let me reconstruct it for you. The killer obtains J. Waldo's flashlight. He removes one of the several cells and puts in its place a neat little package containing a fulminating cap and explosive, connected to the flashlight's circuit. He re-screws the butt of the fiendish instrument and returns it to its familiar place." The chief whitened. "All the old man had to do was to slide the switch. You know now the sort of people we're playing with!"

He paused and studied my face. "You catch about the soap now."

"Yes," I answered, "I do." Locks and tumblers have always been my hobby. For several years they were my profession. I was kind of trouble-shooter for a small safe factory. That's how come I'm with the Dean.

Many's the wrecked safe I've gazed at. Now, there are several methods used by the yegg for blowing a box but, style and opportunity permitting, he favors the soap-and-razor-blade technique. If there's a crack in the door setting, no matter how tiny, he jams a razor blade into it, forces it wider, makes a little trough of soap and pours his soup in the crevice. That's all he needs. Bambo! the safe's open. "Yes. I see what you're getting at," I repeated. "But no one's cracked any safe yet."

"They will, Ben. They have to. They have to lay their hands on a paper. A blackmailing paper. They're after

Georgia Rountree's wealth. Not part of it, not a few paltry dollars—but the total fortune!"

With that, he got out an old alarm clock he was repairing for Mrs. Duffy, our landlady, and shut up like a clam. These gaps between fireworks were the hardest part of a case for him. He had to steel himself to inaction. Finally, with a grunt, he slapped down his forceps and pliers. "Hold down the office," he said. "I'm going out to check on Mrs. Fraley Wilkes' birthday present. I think I'm right but I can't afford to take a chance. A life depends on it."

He'd hardly left before Lieutenant Malloy eeled in.

"Where's the boss?" he asked.

"Have a seat, sir," I said. "If you observed the placard by the entranceway as you entered you know that we offer readings in pedomancy, libanomancy, rhabdomancy—"

Malloy took it with suspiciously good grace. "It's living with Rock that does it," he remarked. "Some day your brain will pull up stakes and hit the road and the white-coated tailors out at Belleview will take your measurement for a sporty canvas jacket. Where's the bigshot?"

"Gone. And don't ask me where."

LIEUTENANT MALLOY thought this over. He got out a stubby pipe, mended with adhesive tape and rubber bands, and chewed the stem. "Ben," he said in a melancholy voice. "I'm going to tell you something I wouldn't tell anyone else. Why am I doing it? I don't know. Maybe because you're sitting there a picture of myself in my youth. Young, happy-go-lucky. They're going to kick me off the force, take away my shield and pension! I'm not thinking about myself, I'm thinking about Martha and the kid."

I was interested in spite of myself. "Why is that?" I asked.

"It's this Amberton case. They want results." He spread the palm of his capable hand, dolefully examined its calluses. "Wardlow Rock's responsible. He's got Captain Kunkle needled up. Give me a tip, Ben. He tells you everything."

"Ha!" I snorted. "He tells me nothing. The last time I heard this story your wife's name was Esther and the time before that it was Molly." I got an inspiration. "I'll make a trade with you." I'd seen the Dean deal with him and something usually came of it. "Here's my tip: this is a professional setup. What I want to know is: do any of the principals in this case have a record down at headquarters?"

"Yes," Malloy said reaching for his hat. "The mannequin model, Vera Wilkes. Shoplifting and shilling, charges dismissed ten years or so ago."

It didn't do me any good. I wanted to know about Georgia Rountree's boy friend, the lad with the brass knuckle scar, the gift-card poet.

The Dean returned smug and self-satisfied from checking his guesses. He'd had a busy and varied two hours. By exercising a little daubery he had managed an interview with the contractor that just completed building the Cape Cod cottage out in Oak Grove. Fraley Wilkes, the contractor said, was a swell guy to work for—didn't hold up the work by changing the plans every day or so. Just one thing. He had them leave the game-room in the basement unfinished; he wanted to surprise his wife. He was an artist and he wanted to do the whole job himself, paint the walls, tint and mix and pour the colored cement for the floor.

The Dean then went out to Oak Grove. The little white cottage with its green shutters nestled at the end of a lane, down in a little hollow. The boss stood on a knoll and scrutinized it. Wilkes' coupe was at the back door so the Dean was careful not to approach too close.

"A Mrs. Tompkins who lives across the pike," the Dean related, "was more than eager to gossip about her new neighbor. A week or so ago Fraley Wilkes drove by her house with a clumsy-covered bundle lashed to his bumpers. Those were the shooks going to the new house. Every afternoon, thereafter, he passed her porch twice. Going, with an empty car, and returning—with a big wooden box beside him on the front seat. Day in and day out, the same thing. Ghoulish, isn't it?"

"Just what's happening?" I asked.

The chief tossed me a quick irritated glance. "You don't know? Preparation for murder. Fraley Wilkes wants to kill someone. He builds the house. Leaves the basement with a dirt floor. He totes in a load of knockdown boxes and starts digging a grave. He does it by stages, every day he works a little and carts off a box of earth. When the tomb is finished, the basement will be clean. Then, when the time comes, he'll make his kill, lay the corpse in the hole, pour his gay colored cement for the game room floor. It's simple and foolproof—or so he thinks."

I felt sick. "How can we stop him?"

The Dean appeared untroubled. "No need to get excited. Nothing will happen until the proper time." He smiled. "Everything's under control."

Here, he drew the line a little too fine. Events were to prove that the case was already breaking under our nose.

ABOUT EIGHT o'clock that evening we snared our second client.

We were sitting in the gray-and-violet twilight, our windows open to the summer swelter, listening to that vespers harmony of a night awakening city which the Dean loved so well, when Georgia Rountree blazed through the doorway. Doctor of dental surgery, John St. John, of all humans, crowded at her elbow.

Miss Rountree stopped dead still and stared at us. She was a snappy little thing rigged out in a saucy Glen Garry bonnet, a fold of gay Scotch tartan looped from her shoulder. I could almost hear her heart beat.

"You're right," she exclaimed softly. "That's the man! Shall I call the police?"

"Sit down, sit down." The Dean pressed them genially. "I gather there's been a misunderstanding. Possibly I can clear it up. That's my craft."

They stood rigidly in the center of the room, ignoring his excessive hospitality.

St. John attracted the limousine trade. You knew why when you listened to him talk. He had a de luxe, gilt-edge lisp with a distinct trace of arrogance. "Calling the police will do us no good," he affirmed. "This man has a pipeline directly into the commissioner's office." He touched his mouth delicately with over manicured fingertips. "We'll have to out-think him. Which should be reasonably easy." He leered icily at the chief. "Sir, this young lady informed me that a man of your description visited her this morning with an absurd proposition of employment. I had no difficulty in visualizing this man as yourself. I charge you with fraudulent intent and demand an explanation. I am trustee to this child's material and spiritual welfare."

The Dean yawned. "That isn't the way I heard it. The last time I talked to Miss Rountree she declared you gentlemen were crooks who hadn't given her a penny of her rightful inheritance and who were preventing her marrying her heart's choice, a lad named Hugh."

The girl flushed. "Why bring that up? That's all over. Mr. St. John and Mr. Collins *want* me to marry Hugh now. They contacted me this afternoon. As a matter of fact, they're rushing me a bit."

"Of course they are," the Dean said agreeably. "They're scared. They're being blackmailed into it. There's a syndicate, a cartel, taking over this business."

The dapper St. John drew himself up haughtily. "You're giving Miss Rountree entirely the wrong—" Suddenly he wilted. "It's the truth!" he admitted. "We are being blackmailed. I can't make any sense out of it. I don't see how anyone can gain anything!"

"I can see," the Dean remarked.

The girl was listening attentively. A hard look came into the corners of her mouth. "All my life I've been kicked around," she announced. "From now on the place is under new management. I'm running my own affairs. I don't know what all this double-talk's about but I'm going to find out." She faced the Dean. "I wouldn't trust you around the corner but somebody's got to step in and clean this up. Will you?"

"I will!"

She was still angry. "Good. If the Amberton estate comes to me I want it without strings, without obligations, to be completely and totally mine! When can you start to work?"

"Now." The Dean got out his Cuban cigar. "Tell me, Doctor, you were present when the Ambertons were buried. Did you actually see J. Waldo lowered into his grave?"

The dentist shook his head. "Of course not! Not him. The other two. You remember Mr. Amberton, Senior, was killed in that cellar blast. He was pretty badly battered. Mr. Collins and myself decided to have him cremated. His ashes are in a crypt down at the crematory. And don't get any ideas in your head about a substitution of corpses. There was none. The body was battered but easily recognizable. It was easily certified by a consultation of Mr. Amberton's physicians."

"There's an error some place," the Dean insisted. "About the grave. I understood—"

"No. You're mistaken." An idea struck him. "It just occurred to me. There is a grave, but of course it's vacant. The Amberton cemetery lot has in its center a larger pyramidal tombstone placed there and lettered many years ago by Mr. Amberton. It was intended as a common headstone for himself and his sons. Each of the three sides bears the name of a member of the family. Lee, Bart and Waldo. Waldo's grave is, as I have explained, unused."

The Dean turned to me. "You see?" he said triumphantly. "I was substantially correct. That explains Captain Kunkle's vampire." To the girl he advised: "Go home and get a good night's sleep. This case will be finished by midnight."

ABOUT FOUR minutes after they left, the telephone rang. I caught it. It was Dr. St. John again. "I'm talking from your corner drug store," he whispered. "Can you hear me. Miss Rountree's just outside the booth and I don't want to raise my voice. There's something important I failed to mention."

I motioned frantically to the Dean; he stepped over and shared the receiver with me.

"I'm afraid I glossed a little in our conversation," St. John continued. "There was no necessity of getting Miss Rountree worried. They blew the safe."

"So I surmised." The Dean's voice boomed into the mouthpiece. "Where is this safe?"

"Hello, Mr. Rock! The family safe out at S-Iron, the old homestead, where Collins and I are quartering *pro tem*."

"Who had access—"

"Collins and I each knew the combination—as trustees. Madison had the key to the inner door, I had the key to the strongbox. They cut the door with a torch and blew the box."

"I won't ask you what they took," the Dean remarked dryly. "Because you wouldn't tell me. I'll look into it. Goodnight."

He hung up carefully and closed his eyes. There was a circlet of perspiration across his forehead.

"Ben," he said, "I'm afraid we've slipped. They've been too quick for us. Get out to Front Street and tell Vera Wilkes to leave town instantly. See that she does. Put her on the bus. Any bus. She can come back tomorrow. Then meet me out at the new Cape Cod cottage. I'm going to Oak Grove!"

"It'll be a pleasure," I said.

The Front Street district isn't a particularly friendly place at night. No folks sitting on doorsteps or standing around lampposts talking and laughing. Just a smoky row of sullen houses on a dimly lighted back street. Mist and damp from the nearby wharf seeped through your clothes, curled about your shoulder as you walked. A blue neon tavern sign offered the sole illumination. The pavement took a dogleg bend and number 378 sat in the crotch—back in the shadows.

The Wilkes' side of the dilapidated duplex was dark—the far side was lighted to a fare-you-well. The old building glared from its recessed gloom like a malignant old bum with a patch over one eye.

I knocked on the door, got no response, circled to the lighted wing and tried again there.

The door flew open. Like it was on a spring. A giant plug-ugly with a gorilla jaw and a beer barrel chest stood smiling at me. He was as high as Ben Franklin's kite. He was dressed in a fluffy Lord Fauntleroy collar; velvet knee breeches clung to his hairy calves. "Come in, brother," he said. "Always room for one more." His big fingers grabbed my lapel, yanked me in, slammed the door behind me.

I looked around me bug-eyed. Two ponies dolled up in rompers were leapfrogging around the room and yelling. A scrawny guy in a baby's sun suit, with a Japanese dragon tattooed on his chest, was playing marbles on the carpet with a fat lady in a middy blouse and bloomers.

My hairy host mounted a tricycle and ding-dinged out to the kitchen. I got the idea. It was a kid party.

The fat lady scrambled to her feet and came over.

"I'm sorry to crash in this way," I apologized. "I just want to inquire about your next-door neighbor—Mrs. Fraley Wilkes. She doesn't seem to be at home. Could you tell me where I might find her?"

"She's here," she said. "In a way."

The fat lady led me over to a corner of the room. A couch had been pulled around facing the wall, out of the hustle and bustle. Vera Wilkes, the Amberton model garbed in a cute little red calico school-dress, lay blissfully asleep. Dead to the world.

"What's wrong with her?" I asked.

"Out. She's passed out."

It didn't sound like Vera Madigan I remembered. "What are you people drinking?" I asked curiously. "Chloral hydrate?"

The fat lady giggled. "It's Preston's party. Preston's in charge of drinks. He's making everybody drink his favorite. Boilermaker-and-his-helper."

Boilermaker-and-his-helper is a long-shoremen's combination: whiskey with a beer chaser. "Alack and welladay," I sighed. "Watch over the child. Don't let her leave this room. Can you keep her here all night? Good."

They didn't want me to leave but I managed to escape.

SO THAT was that. I knew the Dean would raise a rumpus when I told him but I could see nothing else to do. I consider myself a judge of such things and in my unbiased opinion Mrs. Praley Wilkes was belted down until dawn—and the boss himself had said that the case would be over by midnight.

Things were building up to a climax. I got to thinking about Hugh, the gift-card poet with the brassknuckle scar. I stopped in front of the tavern and looked at my watch in the blue light. I was ahead of schedule. Why not take a flier on my own? If I rushed I could make it.

I decided to pay a quick visit to Stable Boy's.

Stable Boy ran a bucket-of-blood card-room behind a delicatessen over on Third. He kept his joint closed tighter than a ten cent clasp knife to the local boys and catered to outside trade, to journeymen with bankrolls. Stable Boy couldn't tell the difference between a Percheron and a rocking horse—he wasn't raised in that kind of a stable— but he knew the migrations of every transient crook that stepped over the county line. He got his moniker from a saucer-sized cauliflower ear.

The Stable Boy was an Artesian well of information if you had an in. I had an in.

I pushed my way through the grimy door, into the little store. The lookout, a paunchy kid in a greasy apron and chef's cap, sat behind the counter practicing card palming. He looked up and batted his eyes.

"Tidings, Fatso," I greeted him. "You know me. Take your foot off the buzzer. And don't let Stable Boy catch you at your manipulating or out you'll go on your mush."

The kid winked insolently. "This Thurston stuff is for my private life. Pass friend. The boss is in the back." He lifted a counter flap.

I stepped past him, edged around a big refrigerator, crossed a back hall and entered a scabby looking door marked *Lavatory*.

The card-room was partitioned from the very bowels of the building. It wasn't large—there were but a dozen or so wire legged tables—but the play and the little bar really paid dividends. The place was a kind of sanctuary and its habitués really forked over for the privilege of hanging around. It was security. It had never had a brawl and was proud of its record. Tonight's business was in a lull, it was a little early for the midnight rush. Stable Boy's patrons were day-sleepers.

Mine host was in a booth in the corner chatting with a couple of customers. I leaned on the bar and waited. He detached himself and came over.

"Well, well." Stable Boy's hideous malformed face broke into a happy grin. "Ben Matthews. How goes the knobs an' dials?"

"I'm out of that racket," I laughed. "I'm a shamus now."

Stable Boy frowned ponderously. "Is that so? Ben, this ain't hardly the place for—"

I cut him off. "Will you help a friend?"

His beefsteak forehead wrinkled in struggling indecision. He nodded.

"First, it's a college-looking boy with a cold blue eye and a scar on the tip of his chin. Do you make him?"

"I ain't never seen him but I make him. You don't want no part of that, Ben. Keep clear," he whispered. "It's poison."

"Second, is there a peterman in town now that uses *both* soup and a torch?"

"Wow!" Stable Boy showed relief. "Why didn't you say so? You want a job did." Before I could prevent him he beckoned to the lads in the booth. They came over suspiciously genial. "Meet a friend, boys." He took a key-ring from his pocket, handed it to me, pointed to a door marked *Private*. "Use my office, gents," he offered. "It's sound-proofed."

THEY LOOKED me over. The smallest, a vicious little parrot-beaked thug in an oversized milk chocolate double-breasted held silent. His buddy, a pimple-cheeked skeleton with marcelled hair and bad front teeth, shrugged. "Why not?" he grated. "What can we lose?"

The "office" was characteristic of its owner. A turkey red carpet, a sway-backed swivel chair, and a battered roll-top desk constituted the entire furnishings. The wall surface, every square inch from baseboard to molding, was thumb-tacked with photos of prize fighters and wrestlers. Every square inch, that is, except for a garish oil painting of a flock of sheep in a snow storm. I gave the chromo a quick gander out of the corner of my eye.

I couldn't help being interested. I had hung it there myself. That's how Stable Boy and I had first met.

The yegg in the baggy suit took the keys from me and locked the door. He gave his pal the go-ahead with his eyebrows. "O.K., Teddy."

"What," demanded Teddy, "was you wanting of us?"

It wasn't getting off to a sociable start. "Boys," I began. "I'm in the safe and lock business, you might say. I want to get into a safe and I can't handle it. Ha!"

The response was frosty.

I fumbled for openers. "What I'm getting at is this— where could I pick me up some helpers?"

The little hood with the baggy suit started to speak but his partner hushed him with a wave of the hand. "And whose box are you fixin' to blow?"

"You're strangers," I answered. "You wouldn't know if I told you. It's out at an old home called S-Iron. Where a family named Amberton used to live."

They looked like someone had suddenly drained off their blood.

"Well, shamus," the little man snarled. "You've gone and done it. You've lifted your top. We place you now. You work for Wardlow Rock."

Terry murmured thoughtfully: "And the man said this room was soundproofed!"

The next thing I knew I was flat on the floor. The boy in the brown suit pulled a *savat* on me. It's a lumberjack's trick. All in all I've done my quota of barroom fighting but this was my first experience with Canuck style. This feet-fighting technique is plenty mean. One instant he was standing there looking me in the eye and the next, something—his heel—smashed into my ankle like an eight pound sledge. It's foolproof—it doesn't telegraph.

By the time I got to my knees, they had out their black-jacks. The next few seconds were pretty bad. They never let my mind clear, my consciousness get set.

Then it came. The split second breathing spell. The room focused itself before my eyes. I was propped in the corner.

They were standing over me—all set to run the string.

I reached out my hand, touched the frame of the garish sheep-in-the-snow painting. I gave the picture a shove, swung it out a couple of inches from the wall.

Just before I slipped into a stupor, I caught the sound of loud excited hammering on the door.

Stable Boy poured peppery brandy down my throat. He had a sashweight under his arm and his monstrous face was twisted in a mixture of sympathy and anger. The thugs had gone. Fatso, the lookout, leaned against the door jamb, an automatic shotgun against his knee.

Stable Boy lifted me gently to my feet. "I leave 'em go," he announced ominously. "With a warning." He straightened my coat. "I make a mistake. Don't hold it against me, Ben. We're still friends, eh? We been friends a long time."

We had been friends a long time. Ever since I had been working for the safe company and I had come out and installed that wall safe for him behind the chromo. Burglar alarm attached: two buzzers, one out front in the delicatessen, one upstairs under Stable Boy's bed.

CHAPTER FOUR
THE FRIGHTENED DUMMY

I CAUGHT up a slice in my cheek with court plaster, washed off a few of the worst abrasions with iodine, and started out to meet the Dean. I didn't anticipate a cordial reception. The Dean had never encouraged independent investigation on my part. When I balanced injuries received against information obtained the result was uncomfortable. I figured I'd have to do some fancy explaining. As things turned out, the boss hadn't even missed me.

I flagged a cab at the corner. The driver took one stare at my battered face and gunned his motor. "Whoa!" I grated. "Or I'll cave in your window. I'm in no mood for a steeplechase. You've got a fare." I opened the door and climbed in. "Oak Grove. I'll say when."

Oak Grove allotment was plenty desolate. I paid off my charioteer, watched his taillights hit hell-for-leather down the road—back to civilization. He'd figured himself in for a stickup. I stumbled around in the brush and located the entrance to the Wilkes' lane.

The cottage lay in a woody depression. It gleamed whitely through the ghostly plumes of shrouding trees. Somewhere in the distance swamp frogs were cutting loose in weird muted minors. I forced my way through a tangle of briars to the front porch.

The Dean emerged from the blackness.

"Well, Ben," he said grimly. "We've slipped. There's been another killing." He fumbled in his coat, got out the butt of a plumber's candle, lit it. "Come in. It's well worth looking at."

Inside there was the smell of drying plaster and new paint. We passed down a narrow hall, through a kitchen gleaming in white porcelain and chromium. The Dean grasped the knob of the basement door. "Down here, Ben. Brace yourself."

The cellar was square and dank. Unfinished walls and a dirt floor. In one corner a stack of cement sacks and a short-handled hoe stood by a mixing trough. A bundle of boards—what was left of Mr. Venner's shooks—was piled neatly in another corner. One of the shooks, assembled into a box, lay in the middle of the room. It was half full of fresh earth.

Two shallow pits had been dug in the dirt floor. The Dean held up his candle. "Here we have the answer to everything. It's not nice." He didn't seem to be downhearted about it.

One pit was empty. In the other was a man. He wore a brown velvet smoking jacket, a cerise sport shirt, and green corduroy slacks. He lay on his back. His beret was placed sprightlily over one eye. The far side of his face was a wreckage of blasted flesh and bone.

"It's Fraley Wilkes, the artist," the Dean explained. "He'll never design another mannequin."

"You seem a little jovial about it."

"I am, Ben, I am. They doublecrossed him and gave him a dose of his own intention. In that shattered brain pan is a small brain that once considered itself a master criminal. Fraley Wilkes was outclassed." He paused.

After a moment, he continued. "Fraley Wilkes laid plans. And plans within plans. And a hatchet sneaked up and got him in spite of it! He now adorns the tomb he dug for his wife."

"For Vera!" I was horrified.

"That's right. Don't tell me you don't grasp it. It's transparent—and has been from the beginning."

"Then Fraley Wilkes knocked off the Ambertons?"

"No. He didn't. He was an opportunist and as the murder sequence unrolled he saw how he could turn it to his advantage. He had blackmailing information. He got that information, by the way, by driving that stake into the grave marked J. Waldo. This was all he needed. The result confirmed his suspicions. He was ready to put on the heat. And he did."

THE DEAN frowned. "You still don't get it? The extra pit here is the giveaway. Now listen: Georgie Rountree, a movie usher, suddenly inherits a tremendous fortune. There is something in the will about marriage. Fraley is naturally a ladies' man. He believes a heavy suit can win Georgia from her gift-card poet. He has this advantage to start: Georgia goes for artists and poets. Wilkes is well established. Hugh isn't. Everything is ready to burgeon." The Dean parted his lips in a silent laugh. "Then the cartel, the syndicate, moved in on him." He gazed down at the body. "And when they did they filled out their own death warrants."

"Who filled out whose death warrant?" There were heavy steps on the stairs and a bull's-eye flash caught us full in the face.

"Lieutenant Malloy!" The Dean greeted him affably. "Alight, sir. You will find this interesting. It's something to write down in your notebook."

Malloy growled as he came forward. He had a companion with him—the nervous cabbie who had driven me out.

"I knowed we'd catch him!" the cabbie shouted. "He said he'd cave in my windows. He was aimin' to heist me but I bluffed him!"

Malloy sighed. He thumbed the cabbie back upstairs. "Go out in the yard and wait for us. It's a false alarm." His face purpled when he noticed the corpse. "What brought you to this catacomb?" he demanded of the Dean. "You're worse than a vulture. How do you find them?"

"Don't question me now," the Dean said. "This business is ready to erupt. I'm going. Meet me at S-Iron in about three hours. I'll have it ready to turn over to you."

Malloy gave him a hard look, set his jaw and nodded "I don't know why I'm doing this but I will. I'll take a chance. Scram." He halted us halfway up the stairs. "Better drop in at your apartment. Mrs. Duffy, your landlady, has been burning the wire to the Missing Persons Department ever since you left the joint. She's off her handle with excitement. She says she has to see you."

On the way back to the apartment, I told the Dean about my trip to Stable Boy's. It was gall in my mouth but the report had to be made. He listened attentively. "It got me nothing but a mauled face," I wound up. "I should have let well enough alone."

"To the contrary. Any information is advancing information." He put it in simple words: "Don't you see what you've done? You've divided the crime into two stages. You've tossed a match into the powder keg. They'll swing into action now. In the open. Quick and mean and deadly. They know we've smoked them out."

"I hope they do," I said. "I'd like to meet that boy again with the musical comedy double-breasted."

"You will," the Dean promised. "You will." He paused, cut his eye at me. "To change the subject slightly, there's a glaring discrepancy in this mess and no one seems to have noticed it. I can't understand how Malloy muffed it. It's this: why did that rural cemetery hire a new sexton? What happened to the old one? Sextons are rarely discharged. It's usually a lifetime job—like a night watchman's."

"Boss," I answered, "no one's said anything to me about new and old sextons. You must have information that I don't have."

"Nonsense!" The Dean broke into his most irritating lecture-room style. "I'll fortify my statement. Kunkle and

Malloy come to us hotter than a forest fire with yarns about vampires. The sexton out at the Amberton cemetery had had the shock of his life: he's discovered a stake driven into J. Waldo's grave. Now J. Waldo is not buried there and as sexton he, of all people, should know it. Ergo: this is a new sexton. He has been hired *since* the death of the last of the Ambertons. I repeat, what became of the other sexton?"

Mrs. Duffy was sitting in her bay window. Watching for us. When Mrs. Duffy was in her crow's nest it meant that things were spouting and sperm at that. She was out in the hall to meet us as we crossed the threshold.

Drenched in lilac perfume and quivering with ribbons and rosettes, she blocked our way. "Say no!" she whispered in tremulous excitement.

The Dean gazed at her fondly. "Say no to what, Seraphina?"

"Say no to the woman on the telephone. She had a loud voice and hiccoughs right in your ear. My female intuition doesn't trust her. She's designing. Say yes to the sweet boy with pretty eyes. He's wholesome."

"I'll try to remember it." The Dean smiled. "What's this all about?"

We finally got the story straight. It seemed that Vera Madigan Wilkes had had an awakening. She'd come to, left the kid party with its boilermakers-and-helpers and was doing the town on a one-woman spree. She was lonesome—she wanted us to join her. She'd called three times: once from a duckpin alley, once from a fire station, and lastly from a cat show at the armory. Her inebriated interests were active and diversified.

"What about the other? The boy with the witching eyes?" the Dean asked.

She pointed dumbly. "In there. In your reception-room waiting for you. I made him wait."

HUGH PEYTON received us blandly. Again I had that fleeting impression that we were confronted with a hotshot gambler. The boy could really put on a dead pan.

The Dean dropped his hat on an ottoman and held up his palm. "Just a minute. Before you say a word. If you address me this is going to cost you money. This consultation is entirely formal and entails the customary proportionate fees. Is that acceptable?"

The young man nodded. "Of course." He pretended to fumble for a beginning. "You didn't deceive me one bit this morning, Mr. Rock," he blurted out. "I knew you were an operator—a professional seer—the moment I laid eyes on you! I'm extremely psychic myself. I didn't know what your game was—and still don't—but I've patronized fortune tellers all my life and I've never found one who wasn't as honest as the day is long!"

The Dean winced. We gave the kid the hawkeye and I swear you couldn't read a thing. He was as gullible as a child—or he was taking us for a glide on the old scenic railway.

"And what is the purpose behind this visit?" the Dean inquired warily.

His answer hung fire. "It's about Georgia. She keeps having the same dream over and over. It must mean something." He whipped a ragged, paper-bound pamphlet from his pocket. The booklet was entitled *La Gitana—Dreams Unveiled*. "Now Georgia dreams about marriage. Let me read you this: 'To dream of marriage is the worst of omens. The vision foretells death.' That sounds pretty bad, doesn't it? Does it mean that Georgia is going to die? Just what is there to this dream magic?"

"You asked for it," the Dean said. "So I'm going to give it to you. Divination is my trade. Oneiroscopy, the study of sleep images and their interpretation, is one of the most ancient of all branches of prophecy. Flammarian the astronomer, Aristides the magnetiser, Plutarch and Cicero, are only a few of its distinguished exponents. The Egyptians considered dreams as communications from the goddess, Isis. Thylbus holds that their predictive value is vastly overrated. He places the ratio of prophetic efficacy at about one in a hundred. I myself would place it even less. The marriage dream-hallucination is actually a variation of the *incubi-succubae* legend. Or such is my personal conviction. The traditional *Oneircritica,* or dream-books, a feeble relic of which you appear to be carrying with you, cannot be summarized in a thimble as you are endeavoring to do. Many intricate influences make up the interpretative quality of dreams: colors, numbers, astral phases, gems. The whole pattern is required." He squinted at his client. "Dreams, I may add, are not admissible as courtroom evidence. They make absurd alibis."

The gift-card poet stiffened. "I'm afraid I don't understand—"

"If you're really interested be at S-Iron, the Amberton mansion, before midnight. I'm throwing a seance."

Hugh Peyton got to his feet. "Thanks. I'll be there." He made a motion towards his billfold. "How much do I owe you?"

The Dean shrugged it off. "Wait until tomorrow. There's no hurry."

For a long moment after he had gone, the Dean stood gazing at his hatband. "That's a suave young man," he mused. "But he's not quite as smooth as he thinks he is. What did you make of the dream hocus pocus, Ben?"

"It sounded to me," I said, "like a guarded threat."

The Dean started. "Absolutely! That's exactly what it was. Remember the empty pit in the cottage basement?"

THE ELMAN BUILDING was stark and deserted in the luminous moonlight. We groped our way into the shadowed cavity of its foyer. The Dean flicked on his pencil flash to get our bearings, shot the beam across the cracked tile floor, around the peeling walls, up to the ornate barrel-arched ceiling. The place was filthy, unsavory. "What we want to see is the attic—Wilkes' studio." The boss was tense in spite of himself. "We'll have to take this mighty carefully."

The building was unlocked, wide open to prowlers. The owners of the Elman Building had a liability on their hands and didn't much care what happened to it.

We climbed three flights of sagging steps, passed the darkened windows of the abandoned Amberton offices, and located a little door at the end of the top hall. "This must be it," the Dean decided. "It's all yours, Benton."

The door was locked. And I mean really locked. I could have picked it but the operation would have taken me ten or fifteen minutes. So I did the simplest and quickest thing. I moved over to the hinge side, slipped out the hinge pins, and lifted the entire door from its frame. "There you are," I said as I set it against the wall. "Burglars have an old adage: locks are only made for honest people."

The Dean was speechless. "Gad!" he whispered. "I didn't intend for you to wreck the place. I hope Malloy doesn't materialize. This would be hard to talk away."

Where a modern building would have had an upper floor, the Elman Building had an attic. It was little more than a roughed-in air space between the top story and the roof. The unpainted flooring stretched without partition or wall from the front of the edifice to the back, and from side to side overhead, the tentlike rafters followed the contours of the roof, hips and eaves and dormers. Down at the far end, in a corner beneath a slanting skylight, was Fraley Wilkes' workshop.

"He chose this place," the Dean explained, "because it gave him a good north light. It's eerie, isn't it?" He switched on a hanging bulb.

Eerie was the word for it. Two long broad tables, set at right angles, formed an L-shaped workbench. A half-dozen *papier-mâché* mannequin heads presumably intended for millinery shops—cluttered one end. The other was littered with sculptor's impedimenta, tools, a hunk of clay. A row of sectional life-casts, torsos, busts, thighs, arms, lined the wall. "Unless I'm greatly mistaken," the Dean remarked, "it was here that Teacher Gartell was murdered."

I was easily convinced. "So Fraley knocked him off?"

The Dean evaded. "One thing we overlooked at the time in Gartell. His profession. He was a forger, a specialist in inks and pencils. Obviously he too reconstructed the author of the note as an artist, recognized the script as being done with *conté crayon*, tracked it to Wilkes. Gartell made the mistake of trying to shake him down."

I found myself inspecting the row of dummy heads. The longer I looked, the funnier I felt. Something wasn't right.

The heads were entirely completed, smoothed, painted and ready to ship. Each was exactly like the others; a *moderne* masklike face, long, narrow eyes, drooping sensuous lips almost Oriental. As my glance shifted up and down the row somehow it always seemed to return to one particular head.

"Listen, chief," I said at last. "You'll have to excuse me for this. I guess I've got nerves. But take a look at that third dummy from the end. It makes me uneasy. It looks like the rest and yet it don't. I can't explain it but there's something about it that looks scared."

The Dean was over it in a flash. "It is different," he agreed promptly. "The left eyebrow has been painted a little broader with a more exaggerated arch. That's what gives it that frightened effect." He took the mannequin in his hand, studied it a moment, wrapped in concentration. Then he did a strange thing: he knocked the ashes from his cigar on the figure's eyebrow, smeared it lightly with the ball of his thumb.

The outline of a jagged scratch appeared beneath the glossy black paint.

"So that's what happened! It was more brutal than I thought." He replaced the mannequin, swept aside the litter of tools and examined the table's edge. A big patch of the surface had been recently scrubbed—clean.

"Fraley Wilkes held him—probably with a wrestler's grip—with his skull on the edge of the bench. An accomplice beat out his brains. Gartell was butchered like an ox and that was the way it was done."

"Look at this," he said tensely. Delicately, he removed a fuzzy yellow hair snagged into a splinter of the table top. "That does it!"

"Low bridge!" I warned. But I was too late.

THEY CAME across the bare floor, Teddy and his beaknosed pal, walking on their toes like ballet dancers.

There was an ugly hunch to their shoulders. I knew it was payoff business. The baby in the baggy doublebreasted was bad medicine. He held his gun plastered to his hip—none of that amateur straight arm stuff—and the gun itself was like a label on a poison bottle: no sight, no trigger guard. Teddy, his rotted front teeth bared in anticipation, waved a .38 with a two inch barrel. I've been around enough to recognize upper bracket triggermen when I see them in action.

"It's the jackpot!" The little hood grinned. "We've got 'em together."

The lad with the marcelled hair was gaping about the studio. "Geeze!" he broke out. "Lookit, Armand! What's them things on the table?"

"Heads," the Dean announced lightly. "Sent over from the hospital. They boil them down for their teeth and bones. Makes very nutritious dog biscuit."

Teddy blanched. "Ain't that awful! There oughta be a law—"

Armand cut him off. "He's ribbing you." He turned to the Dean. "So you're Wardlow Rock!"

"That's right," the Dean agreed pleasantly. "Who are you? I don't recall your faces. You must be beginners."

The beaknosed gunman rose to snap the bait. "That's what you think! We're from out of town."

"Ah." The Dean nodded thoughtfully. "Imported. That explains your rudeness. It explains many other things too.... You see, Ben," he addressed me, "this breaks the case into two stages. The Amberton killings and the safe. These rats were brought in to rob the trustees' safe."

That touched off Teddy. He let loose with a curse and a volley of three at the rapid. One of the slugs ripped the boss's collar, another whacked the floor and the third struck the iron bench vise and went screaming in a ricochet through the glass skylight. The Dean's hand came from beneath his armpit holding his big black Magnum. He moved leisurely and casually, like a three cushion shark chalking up for a run. Actually, it was so fast that the eye couldn't follow it. The heavy pistol blasted once and Teddy's right eye went into vapor. His awkward body whipped to the floor as though it had been jerked with a chain.

I cleared my gun.

Armand was in a quandary. He made the mistake of changing his target. I caught him with two quick ones and my bulldog packs authority.

Gunsmoke and cordite fumes filled the hot room. My ears were ringing with the detonations. The Dean holstered his weapon.

"Corrective shooting!" he exclaimed. "Range finding! I don't see how he lived as long as he did. What did he expect me to do? Send him a trigonometric report of my position? That's the trouble with those hack-sawed barrels. They can put them out fast enough but they can't lay them on the line. I've often said and I repeat—" He reached up and turned off the hanging bulb.

It was then I heard the footsteps on the stairs.

The steps hesitated and then resumed their climb. A high moon, striking through the skylight, laid a shaft of blue across the twisted bodies of the gunmen. It was like the spot in the theater—everything beyond the lip of the luminescence was blinding black. Our visitor reached the top step and started a faltering advance in our direction. I've been raised in a catch-as-catch-can school and have some mighty definite prejudices. I like to see what is going to happen to me. I felt over the Dean's shoulder and snapped on the light.

Vera Madigan Wilkes stood there, weaving and blinking. Her cute little Grecian curls were as immaculate as though she had just left the beauty shop—but outside of that she looked as though she had been grappling with a tornado. Her red calico schooldress was rumpled and mussed and there was a smear of crude oil on her elbow. She snubbed Teddy and Armand and smiled at us. She was twice as pretty as ever and drunk as a sweepstakes winner on the morning after.

"Good grief! What have you been doing?" the Dean demanded.

She made a few vague passes at straightening the pleat in her dress. "I've been working. I've been over on Second Avenue with the night shift taking up street car tracks. That's labor. Sometimes I'm glad I'm just a girl." She peered about the room. "Where's Fraley? I want him to make another statue of me." She got an idea. "Let's get him to make statues of all of us."

The Dean flinched. "Me—a mannequin?" He deliberated. "Fraley, I take pleasure in announcing, will not be here tonight. Now listen, my dear, I have plans for you and you're not going to like them. I'm going to take you home to my landlady. She will give you a hot bath, two cups of black coffee and put you to bed."

VERA WENT along docilely enough. In the cab, the Dean pinned up the front of her dress and tucked her in the corner. "These fun projects are pretty strenuous, aren't they?" he commented. "Tell me this, does Fraley object?"

"I don't think Fraley cares but Madison doesn't like it. He says he's afraid it'll get back to his customers and nobody wants a *papier-mâché* model of an alcoholic."

"Oh. So you know Mr. Collins. Are you by any chance acquainted with the heir?"

"Georgia? Sure. I've met her at Fraley's studio parties. I like her. But I don't like her husband."

The Dean gave me a quick, smug glance. "You mean Hugh? I thought—"

"No one knows about it but me. I heard about it from a friend in Florida. They were married in Miami two years ago. Hugh won't let her make it public. The will says she can't inherit unless her husband has a steady job."

The Dean hacked. "Such a will! And such different versions I've listened to—all of them untenable and intrinsically illegal!" He glowered. "We'll settle this nonsense."

Mrs. Duffy welcomed the model to her bosom like a coast guard cutter bearing down on a castaway. "This, Seraphina," the Dean remarked, "is Vera Wilkes. She needs your warmhearted attention. She's weary. She's been over on Second Avenue taking up street car tracks."

Mrs. Duffy was impressed. "What a cruel way to earn a living! That proves she's honest and innocent." Mrs. Duffy flurried toward the tea kettle "Just leave her to me. I'll fix her up, poor child."

We took a look-see in our apartment while we were there. There was a note under our door. It had been scrawled in great haste and said:

Come out at once. Money no object. You were right. My life's in jeopardy. Don't let me down now.

Madison Collins

"He's trying to salvage," the Dean bit out. "But he's a little late."

Out on the street, I confessed: "I must be dimwitted. There's plenty about this I don't get. Item: Fraley Wilkes certainly knew that J. Waldo was cremated, that he wasn't buried with the boys at the cemetery. Yet, according to you, he drove a stake in the empty plot to see if there was a coffin in it. Also, according to you, he found something that confirmed certain suspicions of his. What were those suspicions and what did he find?"

"He suspected there was a coffin in that grave and that was what he found."

"Good grief!" I ejaculated. "The old sexton. Someone knocked off the old sexton and—"

"Buried him in a casket?" The Dean laughed. "You're macabre-minded. This business is getting you down. No, Ben, it's nothing like that. That coffin, and its occupant, are just where they belong. The cemetery books—or an exhumation for that matter—would prove it."

CHAPTER FIVE
THE SHUTTLE

S-IRON, THE old Amberton mansion, sat back off the road, a lilac windbreak concealing it from public view. We drove straight past its vine-hung gateposts. "The village first," the Dean said. "We'll catch it on our return. First things first. We'll stamp out every spark of this devilish affair."

The hamlet, a clump of thirty or so weatherbeaten cottages was just about extinguished when we reached it. It was a cozy little place with turfed brick walks and the aromatic scent of mossy shingles. We pulled up to the floodlight of the filling station. The proprietor answered our horn reluctantly. "Who," the Dean inquired, "hires and fires the sexton?"

The attendant peeled back the tinfoil from a candy bar. "Squire Keeler. Fourth house on the left." He munched thoughtfully "Ain't no use applyin'. We got us a man."

"Do I look like a sexton?" the Dean shot out angrily. He made a quick recovery. "We're inspectors from the health board. There have been complaints. Sanitation, you know. I'm afraid you people are going to have to transplant your graveyard about a mile down the road. Good evening."

That left him boggled.

Squire Keeler had all his buttons. You could tell that the minute you talked to him. He met us at the door in bifocal glasses and a foolish looking nightgown but the Dean wasn't misled. He knew caliber when he encountered it. "I'm sorry, sir. I didn't know you had retired."

The squire waved us into the living-room. He was a bachelor. There was a hotplate on a priceless rosewood desk. A third of the room was taken up by a huge canopy bed with a pile of empty tin cans under it. Open, annotated books lay everywhere. A bitch setter with a litter of puppies watched us from a silken eiderdown quilt in the corner. "And now, gentlemen, what can I do for you?" Squire Keeler got out a giant calabash pipe.

The Dean produced a card, proffered it to our host. The card read, *Jno. Slack, Tennessee Marble.* The squire took the card politely, twisted it into a tight curl and tossed it on the floor. "Introductions are unnecessary—and they are often unreliable."

The Dean studied him warily. "Why do you have a new sexton?"

Squire Keeler puffed placidly. "We have no new sexton."

"Now that," the Dean said bluntly, "is a baldfaced lie. Facts refute you. You're trifling in a serious affair, sir. Am I to understand that you yourself are involved?"

"It's bad, eh?"

"Very bad indeed."

The squire sighed. "Then I'd better tell the whole story. I'm a miserable liar. So I'll stick to the truth. Dave Reams, our old sexton, and my old friend, is somewhere on this broad continent, on its highways or byways, in a homemade trailer. He's beyond contact and beyond impeachment. What I'm about to say can do him no harm. Dave got his golden opportunity—he cashed in on a little piece of sod. Accepted a big bribe and retired. The lucky devil!"

Great clouds of fragrant smoke ebbed about the squire's angelic cheeks. He went on. "It started some time ago—a week before the first Amberton boy died. One morning old Dave had difficulty in finding his favorite spade. It had been moved from its regular place in the tool-house. A few days later the sod began to die on the Amberton plot. Bart was killed and was buried. For a month Dave fooled around trying to revive that square of sod. He was just getting it green when the spade was stolen again. The sod began to turn yellow. Lee died. The same thing happened all over again and J. Waldo went to meet his maker. Dave began to get scared." The J.P. paused.

"The night after the last death old Dave got to worrying about the thing in bed. He arose, dressed, lit his lantern and went out to the cemetery to look around. He caught a man doing a strange thing. Who the man was and what he was doing, old Dave wouldn't tell me. The man pledged him to silence with a bribe of four thousand dollars. That's the whole truth, so help me, and I hope you can make something out of it."

"I can," the Dean asserted grimly. "Shall I tell you what the man was doing?"

The squire batted his pop eyes. "If you will be so generous, sir, I'll reward you with that lemon spotted pup in the corner. I've been hardly able to sleep—"

The Dean grinned. "We're in a rush. No baggage space for dogs tonight. The man had just finished turning the Amberton headstone when old Dave discovered him. He'd just shifted it a third turn."

WE DISMISSED the taxi at the Amberton gateway and entered the grounds. "Get off that gravelstone drive," the Dean ordered at once, "and walk on the grass. This place is a covey of killers tonight—and set to hair trigger." The matted lilac hedge, seven feet tall at least, walled in the yard from four sides like a wicker barricade. In the center of the lawn, a figment in a hazy nightmare, crouched the great black mansion with its rambling wings and mansard roofs. "We'll just explore around a bit," the Dean suggested. "It saves inconvenience in the long run. There might be an overflow."

A careful search convinced him that the grounds were safe. It was, I might add, as nutty a prowl as I have ever made. The Amberton tribe must have been a select grade of crackpots. The estate was cluttered with birdhouses, big and little, high and low. "Why all the fripperies?" I asked.

The Dean laughed. "The old man's handicraft. He liked to make this stuff and entered it in boys' hobby shows. Probably under a fake juvenile age. He had a set of award ribbons that he cherished like a miser. Believe it or not!" All at once he froze. "So that's it!" he said.

There was a tiny pergola type shed set on piles in the center of a stagnant lily pond. We had noticed it on our first round. Now we returned to it. A rickety rustic bridge arched from the bank to its door. We crossed over. There was a clumsy brass padlock as big as an Oregon apple hanging from the hasp. A blind Chinese could have opened it with a pair of chopsticks. I bent the nib on my fountain pen and had it cracked before the Dean knew what it was all about.

The playhouse in which J. Waldo fled the world and let his second childhood jump the fence was as neat and orderly as an old maid's hope chest. There was a little shelf of books: *Knick-knacks for a Rainy Afternoon, How a Boy Can Help Around the House,* and such stuff.

"It appears," I observed, "that death caught him in production. Hey! What's this? What was he making?"

Three objects were laid out on the bench. A pair of gunsmith's pliers, a glass test tube half filled with an oily liquid and nestling on a pad of cotton batting—and a revolver cartridge. The cartridge was a Magnum .357. The bullet had been removed and the powder emptied into a pile on a square of paper.

Perspiration beaded the Dean's forehead. "So that's what they have planned for me! I'd hate to snap a firing pin on that!"

"How could J. Waldo—"

"Forget J. Waldo. Come on. Let's go inside. I'm in the right mood to present my compliments."

Madison Collins was huddled in the shrubbery at the bank end of the bridge. "Oh! It's you." He produced a pretty poor imitation of surprise. "I saw a light on the water and came out to check up. You were inside? Then you saw that bullet. It's ghastly, isn't it? Someone's preparing some sort of trap. I stumbled on it by accident—that building's never used anymore—and that's why I left you that note to come."

"Of course," the Dean said vaguely. "You're a promoter of inventions, you could grasp its full significance. By the way, just to keep the record straight, who has the key to that pergola?"

"It hangs in the kitchen."

The Dean's teeth showed in a mirthless smile. "It would! Let's go in and sit down. I want to talk to you about a will."

Before we reached the porch, the chief slowed down. "I'd like to get this clear," he said innocently. "Just whom do you suspect—and of what?"

Collins answered with a surge of hate. "I suspect St. John. Of what, I don't know exactly. Of rifling our safe, for one thing."

"Is that so? What was in it?"

"That's the funny part. There was nothing in it but a sealed envelope and that belonged to *him*. He must have wanted to get it out and use it without my knowing it. You see, it takes both of us to get the strongbox open."

The Dean perked up his ears. "An interesting conjecture." He shook his head. "But we'll have to discard it."

WHEN THE two trustees took over the old mansion they did themselves mighty well. As bleak and eccentric as S-Iron was from the outside, you got a surprise when you crossed its threshold. The interior was comfortable and modern and friendly to the eye. The Amberton men had money to spend on solid mellow living and knew how to do it. Huge deep chairs and gleaming wainscotting. A brace of crossed epees above the cavernous fireplace and bullhide rugs on the planked floor.

"Very nice," the Dean commented. "I'd like to have a membership here myself."

Collins stiffened. "Doctor St. John and myself—are simply tenants. We pay our rent, like anyone else, into the estate."

"Certainly. Certainly. I'm familiar with routine. I almost said stratagem." The Dean changed the subject with a wave of the wrist. "Are visitors allowed to sit on these chairs? I have questions to ask."

"Let's go back to the study," Collins suggested. "It's a little more secluded. We won't be disturbed."

That's what he thought.

The study was already in use. We walked in on a conference. Dr. St. John, massaged and powdered and, it seemed to me, rouged a little, lounged behind the desk nibbling the tip of an onyx penholder. A handkerchief had been draped over the table lamp, swathing the room in obscurity. Georgia Rountree sat across from him. You could barely make out her figure in the half-light, her little Scotch cap on her chic round knees. I got the impression that the dentist had just said something funny and that the girl was laughing.

The next instant I knew that I had been mistaken. She was not laughing. She was sobbing.

The Dean lashed out and whipped the handkerchief to the floor. The walls sprang up in a glare of light. "What's taking place here?" he demanded venomously. "No need to answer. I think I know." He turned to the girl. "This man's been blackmailing you, hasn't he?"

St. John was unruffled. "Oh, it's you," he said. "The mountebank." He had a maddening way of slurring his words. "Are you aware that you are invading the privacy of—"

"I am," the Dean snapped out. "And such is my pleasure. I am at this moment awaiting the arrival of the police to make my charges formal. I will, at the proper time, charge you with possessing, or pretending to possess, an incriminating document, or photostatic copy of the same, by means of which you have been exerting criminal pressure upon this child."

Madison Collins looked befuddled. "What in the world is that supposed to mean?" A car pulled into the grounds, braked beneath the *porte-cochere* outside the window. The big man left the room.

He returned with Lieutenant Bill Malloy and Hugh Peyton, the psychic poet. Malloy's shrewd eyes sized up the assembly. He wasn't any too sociable. "This kid a friend of yours?" he asked the Dean. "I picked him up loitering by the gate. He said he was waiting for you. That you were holding a seance!"

"I am," the Dean affirmed. "In fact, I've already begun it. I was saying—"

St. John broke in. "You can't do this, Mr. Rock. It's unethical. You're violating a professional confidence. I'm your client."

"Not so," the Dean denied happily. "You can't trap me there, sir. It was Miss Rountree who desired my services." He turned to Lieutenant Malloy. "Are you ready? Prepare yourself. This is the end." He waited a second for the proper effect. "Doctor St. John is your man."

Malloy was cautious. "Can you make out a case? No tricks."

"Can I? Listen. St. John had grandiose ambitions for wealth. He killed the three Ambertons—in the correct sequence—by using nitroglycerine. The old man's flashlight carried a charge that would lift a freightcar. The sons were slain by a simple device: the insertion, probably with dental plaster, of an ampule of nitro in the barrels of their guns.

Out in the pergola he is working on a similar toy for me. Let me tell you—"

Hugh Peyton made his contribution. "I don't exactly see," he observed, "how you have any evidence. What I mean is, when an explosion is over—blooey! everything is gone. What's left?"

"Plenty," the Dean said. "Most importantly there's always the *source* left. High explosive is like poison. It's a suspicious thing for a layman to have in his possession."

ST. JOHN put on his most arrogant sneer. "Don't be a buffoon. Are you implying that I have nitroglycerine in my possession?"

"Not nitro," the Dean responded pleasantly. "Dynamite. It's not generally known but most criminally obtained nitro is produced from ordinary stick dynamite. The process of derivation is extremely elementary. A matter mainly of solution. The typical composition of ordinary dynamite is sodium nitrate forty-five per cent, wood meal twelve, carbonate and moisture three—and nitroglycerine forty per cent. Professional criminals obtain dynamite usually by looting storerooms of quarries, or other places where blasting is going on." He addressed Malloy. "Any reports of loss?"

Bill Malloy had a camera mind. He never forgot a name, a face or a fact. "Yes," he said thoughtfully. "I place it. One box swiped out at the railroad cut. About a month before the first Amberton murder. Go on. I find myself interested."

The Dean continued. "There's bulk and danger in the possession of dynamite. Where, St. John asks himself with an affected lisp, shall I store it away to be used as I need it? Why not bury it in J. Waldo's cemetery plot?"

The room was deathly silent. Miss Rountree watched him fascinated. Hugh Peyton started to speak, checked himself. Madison Collins listened, fishmouthed. Dr. St. John, of all of them, was at ease. The dentist was really a money-player. The tougher it got the less he seemed to care. This should have been the danger signal but we muffed it.

"Cutting the sod, turning it back to dig, and replacing it caused the grass on the cemetery plot to yellow," the Dean explained. "Old Dave Reams was suspicious. You paid him four thousand dollars to pack up and leave town."

St. John interrupted lazily. "There's no dynamite in J. Waldo's grave—"

"Oh, but there is!" The Dean contradicted him flatly. "The headstone is three-sided—as you yourself told me. You've given it a third turn and rotated the plot order. J. Waldo's name now actually marks Lee's grave. You thought by this means you could lock your secret in forever. Fraley Wilkes investigated. He drove a stake into the fresh earth and discovered Lee's casket. You murdered him for this. You should have slain old Reams. His testimony can hang you."

The next two seconds were amazing. Suddenly, without warning, Madison Collins swung an army automatic into view and blasted his partner out of his chair. Malignant and determined, his shovel jaw thrust out, he stood there pouring the entire clip into his associate. It caught us completely unaware.

"There's a revolver in that desk drawer," Collins explained shortly. "He was reaching for it."

We found the pistol in the drawer all right, but if Collins had seen the dentist move he had better eyes than I had.

"I'll take that gun." The Dean smoldered. He laid the two weapons on the corner of the desk. "This case is only half finished and I intend to complete it without interruption. Will everybody quiet down!"

Confusion blanked out his voice.

Vera Madigan Wilkes, with Mrs. Duffy's boa about her neck and enough mascara on her eyelashes to oil a two-ton truck, wove gaily through the doorway. Still as tight as a bowstring. She advanced straight towards the Dean.

The boss gave her his full attention. "You're supposed to be at home under the covers."

She objected. "Not me. I'm not sleepy. Mrs. Duffy broke out some cold medicine and we killed the bottle. I put her to bed." She blinked about the room. "Hello, people!"

No one answered her.

"It's the brain behind this business," the Dean continued, "that we're after. St. John was just a working partner. Trustee Collins, inform me upon this point: What exactly are the stipulations of J. Waldo's last will and testament?"

COLLINS HEMMED and hawed. "To be frank, the conditions are a little embarrassing to Miss Rountree. You see, while Mr. Amberton felt indebted to her father, he didn't—ahem—have the highest regard for the daughter. If Miss Rountree was single at the death, her money was in trust with St. John and myself. If she was married, it was to pass directly under the guardianship of her husband. Waldo didn't consider her competent to handle her own affairs."

"Mr. Peyton," the Dean announced gently, "you appear to have a fortune in your hands. Does the information come as a surprise?"

Again that poker face. "You talk," Hugh said. "I'll listen."

"That won't do," Malloy broke in. "You claim he has the right to handle the money and yet he's living in poverty."

The Dean nodded. "You've put your finger on the crux. He's a wealthy man and doesn't know it. The true text of the will's been kept from him. It was Miss Rountree's idea. She's the arch criminal in this setup. She connived with St. John. She held back from him—and later from Collins—the fact that she is married. She is an animal of prey and her natural impulse is to act alone. When the will was read she learned that she had acted wisely. St. John was on her side, Collins could be loosened up. Hugh, however, blocked her plan."

Vera moved unsteadily over and put her arm around Georgia's waist. "I don't believe it."

"Well, it's true. Isn't it Mrs. Peyton? You mapped out the whole affair. Foolishly, you put some of it in writing—perhaps in a note of instruction to St. John—which he promptly salted away in the safe. He knew you for what you are—a homicidal she-demon. He used this documentary indiscretion of yours to keep his werewolf on the leash—if you'll excuse a bit of rhetoric. The existence of this paper threatened your plans. You imported Teddy and Armand and got together a little cartel. Your gunmen blew the safe, returned the letter to you. That was the signal for action. You had slipped your leash. You were out to run your own affairs, to rid yourself of the guardianship of a husband.

"You had your own irons in the fire. You had snared Fraley Wilkes in the delusion that you intended to marry him. He prepared two graves—one for his wife and one for Hugh Peyton."

Georgia Rountree's lower lip trembled. "You shouldn't say such mean things. I love my husband. He has a beautiful soul. You make me sound so unpleasant. These things aren't really true, are they? I mean, you really don't have any proof, do you?"

"No," the Dean admitted sadly. "I have no proof."

Malloy hunched his shoulders. "You're talking yourself into a slander suit. This girl's got money now. I'll be getting along—"

The Dean detained him. "Don't leave yet. We're just warming up. Would you be interested in the murder of that third rate crook—Teacher Gartell?" Malloy faltered. The Dean said seriously: "Georgia Rountree Peyton killed him. With her own dainty hands—*and this I can prove.*"

Hugh Peyton, pale as a sheet, listened with a dead pan. Vera and Georgia stood huddled rigidly. Madison Collins sagged.

"Let's hear the evidence," Malloy ordered.

"First, the setup," the Dean said. "Gartell went to Wilkes' studio to pressure him about some shooks. Don't interrupt. Wilkes threw a nelson on him, held his head on the work bench. Georgia clubbed him with a mallet. A wisp of wool from that Highland tartan she's wearing got caught on a splinter. That's interesting in anybody's court. Look for her fingerprints on Gartell's shoes. She helped carry him downstairs. She'd take the lighter end."

That did it. Vera and the brunette went into a scrambling cat fight. At first I thought it was over Fraley Wilkes but then, stupefied, I saw what it was all about. Georgia had St. John's gun from the corner of the desk and was struggling to get it into line. The muzzle floated past me, past Malloy, centered on the Dean.

The model closed in, clinched. There was a muffled report. Georgia slumped to the floor.

Vera touched up her Grecian curls, hiccoughed. "Those things don't scare me," she remarked brightly. "I've seen plenty of them."

The Dean stepped to the body. He parted the plaid at the girl's shoulder. "My best proof. I never got a chance to tell her about it," he said bitterly. I never saw him so griped. "See. She has her tartan pinned with an ordinary spray-pin. She's removed the original brooch with its cairngorm. Because it was bent. As she was scuffling with Gartell in Wilkes' studio the brooch gouged the surface of one of the finished mannequins. It was a telltale scratch. They had no time to destroy the *papier-mâché* head. Wilkes picked up a brush and touched over it in black paint. You see—"

Hugh Peyton stared at the chief, slow comprehension dawning in his expression. "I get it now," he said, "why you wouldn't let me pay you off this afternoon. You're after heavy dough."

The Dean bowed. "Exactly. You are now heir to the Amberton monies. I have worked as your agent. If you'll remember our conversation—when you retained me—we decided fees should be customary and proportionate to service rendered."

He grinned at the mannequin model. "You did a brave thing. I'd like to know you better. Let's go someplace and relax."

"Any place," she agreed, "where I can pick up a boiler-maker."